Mayhem
Goddesses of Delphi Book 2

Gemma Brocato

Copyright

Brocato, Gemma
Mayhem / Gemma Brocato
1. Romance — Fantasy. 2. Romance — Ancient Greek Mythology. 3. Paranormal — Romance — Mythology and Folk Tales. 4. Paranormal — Romance — Magical Realism.

Dedication

For Stephanie Judice

Your wisdom and guidance leaves me forever in your debt.

Acknowledgments

Without help from many quarters, this book might never have happened. My family: Mr. Gemma, and my two children, Erin and Andrew. You support me and cheer me on and remind me of the good that happens when you share a great love.

My editor, Piper Denna, a woman of patience and wit. I can't tell you how great it is to find the funny little notes you string out during the editing cycle.

The KickAss Chicks, The Writing Warriors, and my Sassy sisters, you are all strong, inspiring authors. I am thankful every day for you ladies.

And most especially to my readers. Without you, I'd be out of a job.

Author's Note

I have been intrigued by Greek mythology
since I was quite young. Paintings and depictions
of gods and goddesses have inspired great emotion
and interest in me, making me want to learn more.
So when I decided to write stories shrouded in
mythology, it was natural to pick the Muses.

When I began researching the Muses I was
struck by the myth of Pierus, and how he had nine
daughters, like Zeus. Daughters, named the
Pierides, he believed were superior to the Muses.
So he goaded the Muses into a contest. When they
won, to punish them for their insolence, Zeus
transformed the Pierides into magpies. That legend
became the basis for my stories. Nine muses, nine
mortal men…nine chances at love to save the
world.

The idea that Pierus would enter his offspring
in a battle to take over Olympus evolved naturally.
Every story must have a villain, right? Although, I
frequently want to beat my head on the desk and
wonder why I picked magpies? It's hard to find
nine creative ways to portray the birds. Which is
why I took a little poetic license in the naming of
the birds. Should Pierus and crew ever win a

challenge, all kinds of evil, which already exists in the world, would increase a thousand-fold.

It hasn't hurt that I love history…all kinds of history. So salting bits and pieces of the Muses backstory in through historical events made me smile. I hope you will find these little tidbits as much fun as I did.

I suppose this is where I have to say that any faults or errors in history are mine alone. Hey, if one of my Muses can face a magpie and win, then I guess I can own making mistakes.

Enjoy!

Gemma

CHAPTER 1

The hard metal railing of the platform dug into Nia Thanos's hip when she leaned against it. She shifted to a more comfortable spot and adjusted the focuser on the Helios Institute's long-range telescope. Putting her eye to the eyepiece, she zeroed in on the satellite jetting across the heavens. The sky was clear enough to make out individual stars. A meteor streaked across the top of the field of vision. Through the powerful scope she could make out the Hinomaru emblazoned on the side of the satellite. Japan's circle of the sun.

Checking the time on the digital readout, Nia smiled when she determined the communications spacecraft had lost fifteen seconds on its orbital timetable. She made a time notation on a clipboard attached to the desk-like platform. Her counterpart at the Japanese Space Agency would have to be told one of their thrusters appeared to be failing.

Now, to figure out how to explain to them how

1

she knew exactly what the problem was. It wasn't like she was a rocket scientist. She couldn't even begin to explain to them why an observatory manager would know about the mechanical workings of a foreign piece of space junk orbiting the earth.

They'd think she'd gone off the deep end if she straight out told them she was a Muse.

Older than time. Smarter than the average scientist. Personally acquainted with the mortal known as Galileo. Yeah, the guy known as the father of observational astronomy.

Nia did a quick review of which American Space Agency scientist to share the information with. It would be easy enough to suggest to someone susceptible to her brand of influence that the hurtling sputnik needed an adjustment.

"Nia?"

She turned to see Bradley ambling into the cavernous observatory room. He halted in the rectangle of mid-afternoon sunlight streaming in through the open portal. The ends of his hair winked with golden highlights in the bright light.

She sent him a smile. "What's up?"

"The Campfire Scouts are here. For their tour."

"Oh, fiddle. Is that today?" How had she forgotten another tour?

"I can show them around them if you want." The offer of assistance came with a smile. "I have nothing else on my schedule."

Nia moved across the decking on the platform, her footfalls echoing off the girders supporting the rounded ceiling. "Nah, I've got this. The little nippers usually have interesting questions." She climbed down the steps. "You are certainly welcome to join, if you wish. Always nice to have your creative brand of wit along for these things."

Crossing the room, she made her way to the small table by the door. She took a quick slurp from the drink she'd left there when she'd come into the room. The sugary beverage hit her system with a burst of energy and vigor.

She picked up her smartphone and did a quick check of her email. Still nothing from her sister, Callie, regarding the challenge they faced from Pierus. The presumptive demi-god had surfaced recently and resurrected his daring attempt to free his imprisoned daughters and conquer the world. Starting with her family's corporation, Olympus Enterprises.

Clio, another of her eight sisters had faced the trial last month, and been successful. Now, the first of Pierus's disgusting magpie daughters, Tyranny, was safely locked in the aviary on Olympus. Tension had grown to monumental proportions as they waited to see which of Pierus's daughters would be unleashed next, and which Muse would be chosen to respond.

For now, Nia subscribed to the idea that no news was good news. It was wishful thinking to hope that after his last defeat, Pierus had abandoned his quest to free his daughters from the punishment Zeus had decreed thousands of years ago. Being magpies suited those bitches. In the meantime, all of the Thanos sisters waited and remained vigilant.

Glancing at the bank of world clocks on the far wall, Nia was shocked to discover she'd been in the observatory for three hours. She always lost track of time when gazing at the cosmos.

"Maybe after the tour, you'd agree to go get that drink we've been talking about for the better part of the month." Hope flourished in Bradley's tone.

More like the drink she'd been avoiding for the better part of the month. He was a nice guy, but she wasn't in the least bit attracted to him. And never would be. Head down, she scanned her email messages while mumbling, "You have an appointment you've forgotten about."

Bradley snapped his fingers. "Wait, I forgot I have a session with my personal trainer tonight."

Success! "Oh, guess that drink will have to wait for some other time." Nia didn't know why she didn't just tell him she wasn't interested. Maybe because she hated any form of rejection herself. Had for the entire millennia. In each

4

lifetime, this type of situation had come up. She used to be better at telling people no.

Through the open door, the high pitch squealing of a gaggle of young girls reached the usually quiet confines of the telescope room.

Bradley looked over his shoulder toward the noise filtering in through the open doorway. "We better get going before they shriek the roof down."

Nia silenced the phone and then slipped it into the back pocket of her jeans. As she walked toward the exit, she double-checked she had her nametag on. She did, but it was upside down. A quick flick of her wrist and she righted it. Bradley dogged her heels as she moved toward the steadily increasing sound of little girls shrieking.

A group of girls dressed in identical navy shorts and white blouses waited in the octagonal lobby. All but one had a red kerchief knotted around their necks. The large central room was one of Nia's favorite at Helios. The ceiling was midnight blue with maps of the constellations depicted in phosphorescent paint that glowed at night when the lights had been dimmed. In the center of the room, a recessed area held a mammoth replica of the Earth. The globe rotated in the manner of the real planet, making a full circuit each hour. Strategically placed lights shifted from day to night as the globe spun. It was surrounded by limestone railings. Visitors typically clustered around the observation area and checked the position when they first entered.

The good-sized group of uniformed eight-year-olds stood at the rail, pointing and gesturing as the orb spun slowly on its axis. The group leaders clustered to one side, keeping a watchful eye on their young charges.

Nia made her way to the adults. "Hello, and welcome to Helios."

"I'm Peggy Dartmoor, group leader. Thank you for hosting us today." A woman in yoga pants and a Spandex top extended her hand, offering Nia a limp handshake.

Nia resisted the urge to adjust her hand in the girly grasp and tighten her grip. Instead, she settled for a toothy smile. "We love to have groups of impressionable kids visit. We never know when we might influence someone to be the next Sally Ride." The astronaut was one of Nia's greater triumphs. The first American woman in space had started out wanting to be a professional tennis player.

The vacant look on Peggy's face indicated she might not know whom Nia was talking about. The woman's blond ponytail slapped against her shoulder when she jerked her head to the side. "Bridget, you stop that this instant."

Nia followed the woman's sharp glance to discover a little imp attempting to crawl over the railing onto the globe. Same blond hair, same skinny build. Most likely they were mother and daughter.

Clapping her hands together, Nia raised her voice and began the process of herding cats. "Here now. Why don't we step into the classroom?" She nodded to Bradley, who led the way across the lobby. The troop followed like giggly lemmings.

The little girl not wearing the kerchief attached herself to Nia's side, instead of hanging out with her friends. The cherub, a halo of glittery golden curls surrounding her face, sent her a shy smile. "My name is Hailey. What's yours?"

"I'm Nia."

"It's very nice to meet you, Ms. Nia."

The child's manners and mature demeanor should have charmed the socks right off Nia. But kids and her didn't mix well. Never had. "Pleasure to meet you as well, Hailey. Have you been to the observatory before?"

The kid snuck her small hand into Nia's. "My uncle brought me here last week to see the Per...Per..." she paused and squinted. "Persnickety shower."

Nia grinned. "The Perseid meteor shower?" The spectacular celestial display occurred every August. The observatory always drew a huge crowd for that. Crowds made her tense, but so did children. Nerves tightened along Nia's shoulders. She attempted to disengage her hand from the child's before she broke out in a sweat. Hailey gripped her tighter.

The long blond curls jiggled when the girl nodded her head vehemently. "That's it! Did you see me?"

"There were a lot of people here that night." Nia tossed a frantic glance around for Bradley, spying him already in the classroom ahead. She pointed him out to Hailey as they crossed into the large dimly lit room. "Um, Mr. Bradley can help you find a seat. Why don't you run along and ask him."

The child lifted her eyebrows and made sad eyes at Nia. Sucking her bottom lip between her teeth, she dropped Nia's hand, and tucked hers behind her back. *This is what it feels like to have to reach up to scratch a snake's belly.* Shame flamed around Nia's chest.

She relented. "Listen, Hailey. Maybe you'd like to sit up front while I'm talking?"

"Can I?" Her voice had lost the notes of excitement it had held earlier.

Goddess, she landed in the soup this time. She'd hurt this little girl's feeling simply because young children made her uncomfortable. Stupid phobia. She was a freaking Muse, meant to inspire others toward greatness. Well, who the Hades was going to inspire her to be more comfortable around children? If her gift worked on kids this age, she'd mentally message Hailey to go attach herself to Bradley, or one of the other Campfire Scouts. But, except in rare occurrences, children under a certain age were not susceptible to suggestion.

Too damn bad, as far as Nia was concerned.

"Sure, come on," she told Hailey. "I have rock star seating down in front."

"I have to sit on a rock?" Hailey tipped her head to the side, a quizzical smile on her face.

Note to self—kids take everything literally. Nia touched the child on the shoulder, aiming her toward the front of the small auditorium. Bradley was already passing out the age-appropriate take-home packets they'd designed and prepared for visiting school groups.

Nia left her little shadow in the center seat and walked up the two steps to the raised platform reserved for staff and visiting lecturers. She drew a deep breath and addressed the eager little faces assembled in front of her. "Welcome to the Helios Institute, home of Delphi's world-renowned observatory and planetarium. If you've been here before, please raise your hand."

Ten small hands shot into the air, fingers wiggling. The volume of chatter escalated until Peggy shushed everyone, waving her arms wildly at the girls, a massive scowl on her face.

Nia wasn't bound by age restrictions as far as Peggy was concerned, so she directed a stare at the woman and muttered under her breath, "You look quite tired. You want to sit down." Satisfaction rippled in her ribcage when Peggy yawned and dropped into a seat right next to her mini-me, Bridget.

Nia continued her talk about the facility, gearing the words and tone to the eight-year-olds, not worrying about whether the parents were bored. There was a lot to discover at Helios, regardless of their age.

Clicking the remote that operated the electronics in the room, Nia dimmed the lights and began the laser show that projected various constellations on the ceiling. The professionally narrated show about how the star groupings were named lasted only a few minutes and the audience applauded when it was all done.

Bringing the house lights back up, Nia couldn't help but notice the chagrined look on Hailey's face.

The child waved her hand in the air. "Ms. Nia?"

"Did you have a question, Hailey?"

"Uncle Thomas said the stories are all made up. Those people the constellations were named for never existed."

"We call them myths, but usually, stories like this are handed down from age to age, and might have some basis in true life." Nia knew most of the tales behind the information accompanying the light show were factual accounts. She'd lived through all of them. "But you can choose to believe or not. It's up to you."

"Thomas says not to believe in anything you can't see or touch."

What the heck kind of uncle turns a kid into a jaded skeptic by the third grade? Nia started to argue, but changed her mind. Getting into it with a kid in front of a bunch of other kids would only end in disaster. "Okay, then. Let's continue our tour."

Bradley herded the youngsters out of the small theater. Several of the Campfire Scouts grouped together, alternately whispering behind their hands and pointing back toward Hailey. Nia was certain the cornerstone philosophy of the Scout organization was to be a decent human being. Someone should give the little stinkers the definition of what kindness entailed.

Hailey hung back, crowding next to Nia, as though afraid to catch up with her troop-mates. Nia let her, but kept her own hands in her pockets to make sure Hailey didn't have the opportunity to cling too closely to her.

The girls giggled and the accompanying moms gossiped instead of paying attention to the details of the tour. Resentment simmered in Nia as the entire group grew more distracted. She had many more important things to do than spending time with disrespectful women who should be setting an example for their daughters.

She never liked unleashing her unique brand of persuasion on people who were focused only on the importance of being them. Individuals like that truly couldn't be inspired to think of bigger pictures. Typically they had no interests beyond the tiny universe where they played the sun and everyone else orbited around them. It would be useless to try to nudge the inattentive chaperones to tune in to what the institute was all about. She didn't believe in wasting of her energy.

So rather than send them a mental shut-the-fuck-up command, she cleared her throat quite loudly. It worked in gaining their attention. "We're about to enter the observatory. Each of you will have a chance to look through the telescope to see the stars."

"Ms. Nia?" Hailey spoke up. Her brown eyes were over-large in her face. "It's daytime. How will we see the stars?"

It was something usually asked by the adults. "Excellent question. Even though it is day here, the stars are still out. Because they are a long, long way from Earth, the light from the sun dims their twinkle during our daytime. With my super-duper telescope, we'll be able to see all the way to where they are in space. The stars will look like big points of light in the dark blue sky."

"My mommy and daddy are stars now."

Nia paused as she reached for the handle to pull the heavy steel door open. That sounded like something you'd tell a grieving child. Unsure of how to respond to the girl, she continued opening the door to the observatory.

Her pride and joy — her baby — stood dead center in the massive space. The barrel of the larger refracting scope extended twenty feet from the edge of the viewing platform. A smaller version was piggybacked above it. The entire structure dominated the room and was focused on a section of the sky Nia knew would be visible at this time of day.

Bradley organized the kids in a line at the foot of the viewing platform while Nia hurried up the steps with a wooden box the youngsters could stand on to look through the viewer. She double-checked the sharpness of the image visible in the eyepiece, twisting the focus knob to better define the edges.

She straightened and looked at the line of expectant faces at the foot of the stairs. Pointing to the first child, she said, "Okay, come on up."

One by one, the children all took turns, with the chaperones mixing in. Nia relished the chorus of oohs and aahs as they spied the celestial objects millions of miles away. Once the last person took their turn the tour was officially over. Nia and

Bradley escorted the group back to the main lobby, where parents waited to retrieve their kids. Bradley hustled out of the area without as much as a glance over his shoulder, leaving Nia alone with the dissipating crowd.

The last remaining child was Hailey, who stood forlornly next to Peggy and Bridget Dartmoor. Peggy heaved a deep sigh and checked the time on her phone. "Hailey, your uncle is coming, isn't he? He's late. I have to take Bridget to ballet class."

"He should be here. What if something bad happened to him?"

Now that the tour was officially over, Nia had intended to return to her office. The panic in the child's voice punched her gut like a fist. She might not be the most nurturing woman alive, but she couldn't leave the frightened young girl.

Peggy crossed her arms under her chest, exaggerating her already awesome cleavage. "The only bad thing that's going to happen to him is me yelling at him for being late." She shook her head and muttered, "It'd be easier to get mad if he was ugly as sin."

Nia started to laugh, and quickly hid her reaction behind a cough. Peggy might have thought she was quiet, but Nia had enhanced hearing, part of the territory for being a Muse. Not much escaped her.

And suddenly, she was intrigued by the idea of seeing what Hailey's uncle actually looked like.

The entrance door burst open and a man raced through. He paused just inside, doing a rapid scan of the area. When he caught sight of their little group, his smiling gaze zeroed in on Hailey. Nia felt a sharp pang in her chest. Her breath shortened as the intensity of the man's grin brightened the shadowy lobby. His longish blond hair swept the collar of his cobalt T-shirt. Black jeans rode low on his lean waist. The leather flip-flops on his feet finalized his surfer look. As Hailey hurtled toward him, he stooped low to catch her. The denim of his jeans hugged his powerful thighs in a way that made Nia's mouth water.

Definitely not as ugly as sin.

CHAPTER 2

"Sorry, God, I'm so sorry I'm late."
Dropping to his knees, Thomas Wilde
squeezed Hailey tight.

Her chest heaved against his shoulder and her
relieved breath rushed in his ear. The sharp edge of
her shoulder jammed painfully against his Adam's
apple, but he didn't mind. Never would he
intentionally cause her distress. She'd been through
enough in her short life. She didn't need the
upheaval of thinking he'd left her, too.

Hailey patted his shoulder. "Did you get lost
in work again, Thomas?"

The constriction in his chest eased at the
playful tone in her voice. He shifted away from her
small body and smiled into her eyes. "Yeah. It
seems someone still believes in the Loch Ness
monster. Sent me pictures as 'irrefutable

evidence'."

"Fools." The scoffing laughter pealing out of her mouth was infectious. "Off with their heads."

Thomas groaned. "I should have never introduced you to *Alice in Wonderland*." He pushed to his feet, holding her hand. It still amazed him how quickly the minute pressure of her palm in his managed to stir his heart. When her parents had died at the hands of terrorists, he'd been her only remaining relative. She'd come to live with him two years ago and had burrowed so deeply into his heart he couldn't fathom life without her.

His brain ached as memories best left buried surged up. The loss of his brother and sister-in-law was the most fucked up thing ever. They were great parents, wildly in love with each other and their daughter. They'd been the perfect family unit, representing everything right and magical in the world. Now the image had shattered, along with his niece's heart. Thomas's faith that humans were actually good and decent had exploded just like the bomb that had taken his family's lives.

His world, and Hailey's, had splintered because of asshats who believed their way of life was the only acceptable way. For the past two years Thomas had focused his energy pragmatically debunking myths and legends, in search of something magical to restore his belief in people. So far, his grieving soul had been sorely disappointed.

The dull slap-slap of Peggy Dartmoor's trendy tennis shoes drew his attention. "It's about time you got here, Thomas. You need to be punctual. We have things to do and we simply couldn't imagine leaving Hailey in the care of strangers." She gestured to the woman standing behind her.

There was a myth he could debunk instantly. Peggy would have left Hailey in a heartbeat if she really had pressing matters to attend to. "Sorry, I got caught up with work and then in traffic." He extended his hand to the woman shadowing Peggy and apologized again. "Sorry. Thomas Wilde. I'm Hailey's uncle."

The woman grasped his hand in a firm, no-nonsense grip. Not the namby-pamby type of grip most of the moms in the Campfire Scouts practiced. This woman had a confident, competent grasp. Pleasure shot through him with just the casual touch.

"Good to meet you." Her voice was low and musical, like a bow carefully drawn over a cello.

The sound drew him in and made him pause to inspect the woman. Coppery hair glinted like a nimbus in the light reflected from the gilded ceiling. Her bright blue eyes were sharp, all-seeing. There seemed to be an ancient type of knowledge lingering there. He gave her body what he hoped was a discreet once over and found her curvy in all the right places. The flowing top she wore bared her collarbones and didn't disguise the seductive slope of her breasts. The name badge suspended around her neck proclaimed her Nia Thanos.

When he returned his gaze to her face, the light in her eyes had hardened and her mouth held a closed-lipped smile. Okay, he was clearly not as discreet as he'd hoped.

Hailey tugged on his hand. "Thomas, we saw stars in the middle of the day. I think I saw Mommy and Daddy winking at me."

Despair bloomed in the deepest corner of his heart. He should have never told Hailey they'd become stars. He spent his life disproving legends. But out of desperation, he'd created one of his very own to help soothe his grief-stricken niece when her parents had died.

His brother and sister-in-law would never have made that mistake. "That's nice, munchkin." He lifted his gaze to Nia's to find compassion softening the hard light there.

Hailey spread her arms wide, mirroring the large grin on her face. "We all got to look through Ms. Nia's super-big—"

"So listen," Peggy interjected, her tone edged with saccharine. She laid a possessive hand on Thomas's arm. If only the woman held her vows as sacred as her mani-pedi appointments. "We have to leave. In the future, please be on time to pick up this child." She sneered on the last word.

Peggy's interruption scrubbed the happy from Hailey's face. Anger and shock over the woman's bad manners erupted behind Thomas's eyes. Just one more damning tick on the tally sheet chronicling humans' innate bent toward evil.

Before he could retort, Nia mumbled, "That was rude. You should apologize, you cow." Her words were barely audible to him.

But Peggy paused, eyebrows needled together, as if confused. "I didn't mean that the way it sounded. Hailey is adorable and we don't mind taking the extra time to keep her safe when you're running behind." She smiled brightly at him. "Perhaps next time, you might just give me a call to let me know you'll be a few minutes late."

"Sure, sure," he replied. He flicked a gaze to Nia's face. The woman wore a smirk that intrigued him. Her lips moved and Thomas thought she said something about getting lost.

"We'll be going now." Peggy grasped her daughter's hand and tugged her away. The woman's usual sashaying walk was curiously absent as they left the building.

He turned his attention back to Nia. "I can't believe you just called her a cow."

Nia's eyes widened and her mouth dropped open. She slammed it shut, crossed her arms over her chest, and squinted at him. "I'd never call anyone a name. It would be really bad manners."

"Nope, I heard it. You called her a rude cow." He tipped his head toward Hailey. "Did you hear Ms. Nia say that?"

Hailey's brows crinkled in the middle and she shook her head.

Thomas knew what he heard. He could understand why Nia would say it. Peggy had been a bitch. But why would she deny it when he agreed?

Her plump lips moved again, but this time he heard nothing and couldn't read what she said. It was as if she mumbled in a foreign language, "You're mistaken, Mr. Wilde." Her voice was cool and dismissive.

The frostiness of her tone didn't stop the pinging south of his belt line. If anything, it aroused him more. "Thomas, please."

She gave him an unreadable look before turning her attention to his niece. "Lovely to have met you, Hailey. I hope you'll come back again."

Hailey's curls wobbled as she bobbed her head. "I'd love to. Uncle Thomas can bring me tomorrow. Will you be here then?"

Nia's laugh was significantly warmer than her earlier words. "Tomorrow is Saturday. I won't be here. But I hope you'll come anyway." She nodded at him. "Goodbye."

Without another word, she pivoted and strode

across the lobby. Thomas watched her hips gently swaying as she moved with cat-like grace away from them. Before she disappeared around a corner, she glanced over her shoulder at him, a frown marring the perfection of her brows.

Caught staring after her, Thomas smiled and lifted his hand. Beside him, Hailey did the same, cupping her fingers together in a pageant princess salute.

"I like her," Hailey said, tugging his wrist.

He looked at his niece. "I do, too," he replied.

Too bad he doubted the attraction was mutual.

* * *

As Nia rounded the corner, and knew she was out of sight, she jammed her back against the wall and clutched her throat. Thomas Wilde had heard her nudge. That had *never* happened before. She always set an illusion around her directives. Especially when there was more than one person in the vicinity of the target of her mental pushes.

Thomas was different. He knew exactly what she'd said, even with her efforts to cloak her words. And he'd resisted her silent urging to take his niece and leave. No mortal had ever resisted one of her nudges. Not in this existence or any of her past lives.

Her brain galloped through the reasons it could happen, sizing up an idea, then just as rapidly discarding it.

It made absolutely no sense.

But wait! When Clio had been in the heart of her challenge last month, Zeke Patterson had been revealed as one of Zeus's many minions. Zeke was her sister's partisan. His lifelines mimicked Clio's throughout the ages. When her time on Earth was done, so was his. When she was reborn again as a Muse, he was reincarnated as well. Zeus had recently granted that same power to Clio's lover, Jax.

Was it possible that Thomas was functioning in a similar role? As her partisan? Clio never recognized Zeke from lifetime to lifetime. In fact, the next time she came back, she'd know she had a protector, but she'd never know who was the new Zeke.

And having a man as attractive as Thomas standing by her side throughout the ages wouldn't be a hardship. The man came served with a side of sexy. He also came with a young niece who appeared to be in his charge.

Nia pushed away from the wall and hurried to her office. The instant the door banged shut she snatched the handset from the phone on her desk and dialed her dad's cell phone.

It rang four times before Zeus answered. "Nia, I'm late for a meeting. May I call you back?"

"Oh. Um, sure. That would be fine." She hesitated. Chances were pretty good he wouldn't answer her question anyway. "On second thought, don't worry about it."

"Are you coming for dinner tonight? Gaia is making lamb chops."

"Making or serving?" Her mother was as challenged in the kitchen as the rest of the girls. Meals had always been an adventure to be avoided if possible.

"Serving." The relief in her father's tone rang clear.

Still, it wasn't incentive enough to spend the evening with them. Watching paint dry, or cleaning the lint out of the keyboard on her laptop, would be preferable. Besides, she really hated lamb. "Sorry, Dad. I have other plans.

"A little white lie?"

"Sorry." She'd never been successful at lying to him. Even in the heyday of the space race, when she'd been at her most powerful. He always sniffed out her prevarications.

"I will explain to your mother. But your company will be required for Sunday dinner. It's Mnemosyne's birthday."

Hmm, maybe the goddess of memory would have information about whether a mortal had ever been able to intercept masked nudges. Or Clio. She was the Muse of History. "I'll be there. I look forward to it."

"Good." Nia could visualize her father

bobbing his head in approval. "I love you, daughter." Zeus hung up on the sentiment. Since Clio's run-in with Pierus and his icky offspring, Tyranny, their father had been more vocal about expressing his emotions.

Things in all their lives had changed with the challenge. Anxiety ran high for all of them as they'd waited for Pierus to step forward again and introduce the second of his nine challenges.

If even one of Nia's sisters failed the contest, they'd all lose. And be transformed into magpies for all eternity. Clio had nearly lost when she'd been kidnapped and restrained from helping Jax end a standoff between the Five Nations Block and the much smaller country the greedy bastards had invaded. Thankfully, with the help of the security and communications departments at Olympus, they'd stopped them right in time.

Nia fervently wished the daughter she faced would be Sloth. That bitch had been a very lazy demi-god—she'd be easy to beat. Nia leaned back in her chair and gazed out the window.

The institute perched on the crest of a mountain, with a spectacular view of Delphi. The town sprawled away to the east. As she contemplated the horizon, movement in the bushes caught her attention.

Was that…ah, shit, it *was* a magpie.

The acrid taste of fear rose in her mouth. The

black and white creature hopped from branch to branch, its beak opening then snapping shut. Nia knew if her windows were open, she'd hear its insane chatter.

Directing an enormous amount of mental energy toward the bird, she whispered, "Go. Away." The bird fluttered its wings and hopped to another bush before settling. Its black and yellow eyes were like neon lights as it blinked.

Nia dialed Callie's number. Callie was in the middle of a particularly grueling deadline, so Nia couldn't be sure she'd pick up. "Please answer." She nudged her sister over the phone line, something none of them enjoyed. Each time she'd done it in the past, her head pounded for an hour after. Using electronics in conjunction with her mental capabilities caused a disturbance in Nia's balance and brain waves.

"Good goddess, Nia." Callie's voice dripped sarcasm when she finally answered. "What has your knickers in such a twist you have to punch me to answer?"

Nia didn't think she'd pushed hard enough to make her sister feel like she'd been socked. Fear must have added force to her thoughts. "Have you heard from Pierus?"

"What part of *I'll let you know the second I hear* did you not understand?"

"Callie, please stop being such a bitch." Nia

dug for a calm she was afraid she wouldn't find. "There is a freaking huge magpie sitting in the bushes outside my office. I think this is happening. Do you think it means I'm next?"

"You're kidding."

"Not likely to joke about something like this, am I? Is there one near you?"

There was a moment of silence as Callie must have looked out the window. "Nothing here. Hold on," Callie ordered. The clacking of fingernails moving over a keyboard filled the empty air between them. "Nope, no email from him either. Since it's only—"

Static burst in Nia's ear, cutting off Callie's words. The lights in Nia's office pulsed from light to dim to light again. Nia jumped from her chair, the hair on her arms standing straight up. Pressure built inside her head and her ears popped painfully. What the hell?

"Nia! Are you there?" Concern tinged Callie's voice with an unfamiliar edge.

The line crackled again. "Yeah, I'm here. I'm serious, Callie. I think it's starting again. I'm confident you'll hear from Pierus soon."

She was equally confident it was her turn to take on the maniac.

CHAPTER 3

Someone banged on the door, rattling the frosted glass in the frame. The door swung inward to reveal Bradley. "Nia, you need to see this." He bounced excitedly from one foot to the other.

"Gotta go, Callie. Let me know when he contacts you. And would you mind alerting the rest of the girls? Find out if they've seen a bird." Nia dropped the phone back onto the cradle. When her fingers brushed the surface of the electronic device, a tiny sting of charged current traveled from her hand to her shoulder.

"Damn!" She shook her hand, like the motion would ease the sting. Similar to the electric jolt she'd gotten from shaking Thomas Wilde's hand, but not nearly as pleasurable. "What gives?"

"Just had a coronal burst. It measured off the

charts." His voice squeaked and quaked.

She pushed past him to leave her office. "Have you checked the playback yet?"

The institute had a solar array at the rear of the park-like property. The complex set of dishes and telescopes would have been automatically triggered to record any type of flare or burst on the sun's surface.

Bradley chased after her down the hall. "I left Barry working on it and ran to get you."

Nia broke into a jog. Her sandals slapped against the marble flooring. Normally, she'd enjoy the beauty of the rounded ceilings and celestial maps painted on the walls. But now, the need to get to the observatory trumped every other thought.

Two techs working in the observatory chattered excitedly as they rushed from one workstation to another. Print-outs crinkled between their clutched fingers while they checked data and reports. Noise bounced off the copper dome. The oversized portal in the ceiling clanged, increasing the confused commotion as it slid open. Like a flock of birds they moved to the central control console.

A path cleared for Nia as she joined the cluster around a massive monitor. The computer specialist, Barry, was seated at the com terminal, mumbling incoherently as he pounded on a keyboard. He'd enter a string of data, then backspace over it. His breath came fast and furious, and sweat trickled from his hairline down the side of his face.

"Dammit!" He jabbed the delete key and erased his latest entry, then tried again. "Fuck!"

Huffing out a deep breath, he flexed his fingers and rapidly retyped exactly the same command he'd just deleted. Nia edged around the other techs and laid her hand Barry's arm, funneling calming prods through the point of contact. His shoulders rose, then fell as he took a deep breath. The tension left his arm and he resumed typing, slowly and deliberately. The blank screen over his head suddenly blazed bright cerulean. The spinning wheel appeared, indicating the feedback was loading.

Everyone held their breath as individual sections of the display began to populate with images the solar array had captured. The same image of the sun appeared in six different windows, each one colored differently. The images were captured using their ground-breaking solar dynamics technology. The top dogs at NASA had been so impressed with the technology, they'd paid an obscene amount of money to license it from Helios.

"Get ready for it, folks," Barry cautioned. Glee pushed the normal tenor of his voice at least an octave higher. Nia studied the faces around her, and each person wore a look of anticipation, as though it were Christmas morning.

Biting her lip to contain her smile, Nia recognized the bubbly sensation building in her chest as a kindred eagerness. Even though she'd seen hundreds of solar flares in her lifetimes, this one was the first of the magnitude she suspected they were about to witness.

She trained her gaze back on the monitors as the playback commenced. On the side of the sun's surface, gases churned in a circular pattern, similar to a hurricane, but circling back toward the surface, instead of swirling upward. A sudden, violent burst of energy erupted, ejecting plasma and ionized gas into the atmosphere.

"Jesus, Mary, and Joseph!" Bradley blurted from behind her. "Look at it go."

"Measurement?" Nia demanded.

No one questioned what she wanted to know.

Barry zoomed the controls out on one of the images. "Twenty-five, no, twenty-nine hundred miles above the surface."

Goddess, it had reached record-breaking height. Nia clamped a hand on top of her head. This magnitude of coronal ejection would certainly wreak havoc on Earth. A burst like this would definitely disrupt magnetic fields and electronic devices. "Are you tracking radio waves?"

Barry blew through a few more keystrokes and

a separate monitor flared to life. Rather than the typically gently rolling waves, the tracking lines were jagged, with a large spike about four seconds into the eruption. That would be the jolt that had disrupted her call with Callie.

Nia stared at the onscreen image, struggling for an interpretation that made sense. Something…anything, that was scientific in nature that would negate any supernatural influence and the presence of a magpie outside her window. She came up blank.

"Run that back," Bradley ordered. When Barry compiled, Bradley whistled low. "It's approaching the speed of light, Nia."

"Someone call the National Ocean and Aeronautics Agency. NOAA needs to know they can expect shifts in tides and possible tsunami. Multiple tsunamis," she corrected. A tech scrambled to do as Nia instructed. Sensation in her belly mimicked the radio waves on the screen, like some horrible roller coaster ride. She pressed a hand to her stomach, hoping to control the sickening lurch and roll. "Someone else check the record books. If I'm not mistaken, we've just captured history being made."

Shouts bounced off the dome as everyone cheered her decree.

The celebration was short lived, however. She held up her hands, calming the techs. "That wave will hit within fifteen minutes, give or take. Shut down what you can, but get everything unplugged. We don't want to lose any data or equipment." For a change, Nia was delighted she'd been too busy today to even switch on the elaborate system in her office. Fortunately, she'd insisted on super-charged surge protectors for all the systems. But still, better safe than sorry.

Better alert the media as well. It was convenient to have a sister who was an investigative reporter. Nia pulled her phone from her pocket and swiftly Facetimed Polly.

Her broadly smiling sister answered on the second chime. "What's up, baby sis?"

"Polly, the sun just experienced a coronal mass ejection. I'm talking about history in the making."

"Hold on." The smile disappeared from Polly's mouth, replaced by a grim line as she reached past the screen range. She was back in an instant with a mini voice recorder. Even with access to all the latest electronic gadgets, her sister still clung to more old-school methods. She waggled the machine in front of the screen and depressed one of the side buttons. "I'm recording this. I'm speaking with Nia Thanos of the Helios Institute. Tell me in layman's terms what this news means."

"Basically, the sun just belched out a huge mass of plasma and gases. The ejection reached nearly three thousand miles above the surface."

"How will this affect us on Earth?" Polly propped her phone on something outside the camera frame and grabbed a pen to scribble notes. Nia had a view of the top of Polly's head and ceiling tiles.

"The explosion disrupted the normal rhythm of radio waves that bombard the Earth all day long. The waves, which are moving at the sound of light, will reach our planet in roughly fifteen minutes. Satellite signals will be scrambled, probably in the next three minutes. Phones and data lines will be affected. People need to be warned to unplug whatever electronics are important. Can you get the message out?"

"On it." Polly reached toward her phone as she yelled for her producer.

"Polly, hold on a second." The tendons in Nia's neck stood out as tension mounted. She turned her back to the room and moved off to the side. "Off the record?"

Polly nodded and switched off the recorder. "Shoot."

"It's started." She didn't need to say anything else. Her message was loud and clear.

A grimace tightened the seam of Polly's lips. Her cheeks puffed out as she breathed heavily. "Gotcha. Go take care of alerting everyone who'll be affected by this volley. I'll handle getting the word out to all media outlets. We'll talk later."

Nia disconnected the call and dropped her chin to her chest, summoning the same level of calm she'd nudged Barry with only moments ago.

The buzz of activity reached fever pitch around her. The Institute's techs were busy alerting everyone who needed a heads-up. Nia quickly dialed her NASA contact.

Ken Hillerman answered on the first ring. "Did you capture it?" he asked without preamble.

"We did."

"We'll want playback as soon as you can send it."

"Sure. Ken, the wave is moving fast. It will be on us shortly. Has the NSA been notified?"

"The Deputy Director is on the phone with them now. The Director is on the phone with the president."

Nia hoped the president understood the enormity of the situation. Science hadn't been his strong suit.

Bradley raced to her side and shoved a paper into her hands. Tucking the phone into the nook between her shoulder and ear, she held the printout aloft. "Fuck it all. Ken, we're predicting massive disruptions. The wave will hit Europe first, before moving to Asia, and then to North and South America." A burst of static cranked up in her ear. She waited until it passed before continuing. "Satellites, solar arrays, you name it, functions will be disrupted."

"We concur."

"We're going to switch to the low Earth orbital satellites to maintain a line of communication. I'll be reachable via this route." She spewed out the coordinates and the number of the Institute's LEO sat-phone.

Before hanging up, Ken lowered his voice. "Nia?"

She heard a hesitant note in his tone. "Yeah?"

"You'll need the name of your new liaison. As of tomorrow you'll need to speak to Jenny McGraw."

"Why do I need a new contact?"

"I'm leaving the agency."

"You can't go. We work together so damn well." He'd been her contact for over three years.

"I...uh, I took a new research position in the private sector. But you'll like Jenny. She's easy to work with and smart as a whip."

"You picked a bloody awful time to make your announcement."

"I know. I am sorry. But I'm sure our paths will cross in the future."

"I hope so." She sincerely meant that. She'd enjoyed working with Ken on several projects. Their minds worked in the same manner. Bradley shouted her name, distracting her. Unfortunately, she didn't have the luxury of time to ask the host of questions flitting through her mind. "Ken, I'm sorry, I really have to go. Good luck to you."

"Stay safe, Nia."

"You, too."

The lights flickered in the observatory, but surged back to full strength. All around her, the techs scurried about preparing for Armageddon. Nia prayed to the goddess it wouldn't be as bad as she expected.

CHAPTER 4

By some miracle, the wave dissipated significantly by the time it reached Earth. As if its course had been altered by a large obstacle in its path. From what Nia could glean from the readouts and data collected, whatever the wave had flowed around had acted the way a rock in a stream did, redirecting the flow of water.

There were still disruptions in communication services and feeds from satellites. But somehow, they'd dodged a much larger bullet hurtling toward their little blue planet. It was a head scratcher for sure.

Nia left the observatory, and headed toward her office. As she approached her closed door, the air pressure in the hallway closed in around her, like a giant hug from invisible arms. The disturbance was a good indication that one of her relatives had just materialized directly into her office. Zeus stood framed in the window when she entered.

After a fast peek up and down the hallway to ensure no one else was around, she eased the door shut. "Dad, did you have something to do with the wave missing Earth?"

"I sent Atlas. He managed to slow and redirect most of the impact. Half went harmlessly into space. Unfortunately, the other half of the pulse reached the moon's surface."

"Aw, crap. What's the impact?" Changes in the moon would still affect the tides.

"Atlas apologizes profusely, but apparently, the orbit has been altered."

Nia's world spun drunkenly. "The moon's orbit? That's bad." And wasn't that the understatement of the century. It could be catastrophic. She put her hand on her father's arm. "Take me to the observation deck."

Mist built around them, increasing the pressure on her chest as Zeus moved them through time and space. In the Hollow, everything lost form, including their bodies. Instead, they became auras. Zeus's aura was purple, for the royalty he was, with a vibrant red glow in the center of his chest where a mortal's heart would reside. Nia knew her aura was sky blue, with pinpricks of white light dotting her entire torso. In the ether, she resembled an early morning sky.

The mist thinned as they moved out of the

void to the concrete patio outside. They hovered two inches above the surface momentarily. Before Zeus cleared the misty illusion, he checked the area to be sure they were alone. It wouldn't do to just appear next to unsuspecting mortals.

The coast was clear, so Zeus lowered them to the ground and heaved out a breath, blowing the mist into oblivion. As soon as she was stabilized on solid ground, Nia raced to one of the telescopes they'd installed so the general public could stargaze. She'd have preferred to use her more powerful refracting lens in the observatory, but the room was still crowded with workers. This would have to do.

Without even looking Nia could tell the angle of light reflecting off the moon was wrong. It confirmed Zeus's information: the orb was definitely out of place. A mere mortal might not discern the difference, but she was the Muse of Astronomy. She knew.

The scant difference in the trajectory was going to unleash mayhem on the population.

She swung the telescope in a half-circle until the lens was trained on the moon. Or rather, where it should be. She adjusted the positioning and located her target.

They were in the new moon phase of the lunar cycle, and the sliver of bright light was inches below its normal position in the August sky. And inches, as seen through the telescope, translated to thousands of miles in space.

"This is bad. Really bad," she mumbled. Taking a step back from the viewing scope, she gestured for Zeus to look.

He moved forward and stooped to look through the eyepiece. "When is the next full moon?"

"In three weeks." Nia wove her arms across her body, attempting to control the shivers darting through her. "This is it, isn't it? This is Pierus's challenge. It's my turn."

Zeus straightened and then curled his hand over her shoulder and gave it a squeeze. "Do not jump to conclusions, daughter. It could simply be an act of nature."

"Dad, that ejection was record shattering. We haven't ever experienced anything even close to the magnitude of today's event. This has all the hallmarks of Pierus's sneaky challenge."

"It seems likely," Zeus conceded with a frown. "Have any of your sisters received any communication from him?"

"I've spoken to Callie, but she hadn't heard. Dad, there was a magpie outside my window right before the solar eruption." Dread trailed like a cold, dead hand up her spine. She repressed a shudder.

Zeus closed his eyes. In Nia's mind, his voice boomed, summoning all of his children and Mars,

Olympus's Security Chief, to a meeting at the Athenian the next afternoon. His message came with the not-so-subtle push to be on time.

The directive rattled around her head, pinging loudly. Nia pinched the bridge of her nose. "I'm standing right here, Dad. You could have just told me out loud."

"I was merely following the advice of Virgo. Your sister, Callie, has decreed I'm not very efficient and unleashed the Virgin's unique style of organization on me." Zeus shook his head. "I don't like it very much."

"I know why. A little clutter never hurt anyone."

"Callie insists if you'd lived a less hectic life, you'd have made sure Stonehenge was in the right location."

"I can't apologize anymore for something that happened thousands of years ago."

"It is your fault we have leap years. She isn't likely to ever let you forget that."

"Hey, I don't give her shit about how she messed up with the Dead Sea Scrolls. They'd still be lost if it wasn't for me."

Zeus chucked her under the chin and gave her a toothy grin. "Perhaps, if you did hold her responsible, she'd let your failure go." The king of gods laughed loud and long.

Nia raised her brows, but didn't say anything.

He knew as well as she did that the sun was more likely to rise in the west than Callie was to forget Nia had slipped up. Of course, if Pierus had his way, maybe the sun *would* end up rising on the opposite side of the world.

A booming, pleasant chuckle spilled from Zeus's lips. He wiped tears from his eyes before he spoke. "You girls keep me young."

"Says the gazillion-years old deity." Nia rose on her toes and kissed her father's cheek. Pressure built in her chest cavity as Zeus prepared to leave. She laid a hand on his arm to stop him. "Can you ask Atlas to join us tomorrow? We might need him to rehang the moon."

"Most certainly. I will see you tomorrow at the resort."

With a tiny pop of light, he vanished.

Nia took another look at the moon. The benign orb had ruled the seas and the temperament of mortals since the inception of time. Seeing it even the slightest bit out of place left her out of sorts. Her chest tightened at the idea of the coming challenge. Would she succeed, or would her failure doom her and her sisters to spend an eternity as reviled birds, as foretold by Pierus when he issued his challenge?

Clio had defeated the demi-god and his daughter, Tyranny. Judging by the position of the moon, Nia was pretty certain she'd face Mayhem.

Countless innocent mortals could be maimed or even killed before she got into the heart of her challenge.

Pierus had warned them in the first challenge that there would be one mortal man chosen to help her. But that man would be jaded, and unwilling to suspend disbelief. Perhaps her hardest task was going to be convincing this one person to believe in magic again. To ask *what if?*

Who would be the man destined to stand by her and help achieve victory? Clio had known almost instantly that Jax was the one. Nia searched her mind for which of her male acquaintances could be meant to help save the world.

The only image she could conjure was Thomas Wilde. The startling fact was he'd heard through her illusion when she nudged that awful woman who criticized him and his niece. By itself, that had to be some kind of portent. And she was attracted to the man's casual good looks and innate charm.

There could be worse partners in the quest to defeat one of Pierus's magpie daughters.

CHAPTER 5

Before heading to the meeting at the Athenian, her parents' resort, Nia spent the morning at the Institute. The analysis of the overnight reports would show whether or not the gods had effectively masked the new position of the moon with the web of illusion they'd spun. When she entered the observatory, the weekend techs sat in a corner sipping coffee and shooting the shit. That alone was an indication of success. She held her breath as she typed her way into the report queue on the mainframe.

Phillip, the tech, sauntered over. "You looking for anything special, Nia?"

"No, just had some numbers to run." She nudged him away with a nearly silent mumble. "You should go finish your coffee."

"If you need me, just holler." Phillip patted the

gut overlapping his belt. "Gonna finish my coffee before it gets cold. Maybe have another donut." He returned to the other tech in the corner.

Nia moved her finger down the column of numbers on the monitor, silently studying the report of yesterday's event. She relied on memories of thousands of years to determine that the moon appeared to be sailing in the same spot as it had since the birth of the universe. She breathed a sigh of relief. The secret was safe. For the time being.

The media had scarcely mentioned the news of the coronal burst. Astronomical news typically lost out to reports of terrorist attacks, military build-ups and human interest stories, like dogs or cats finding a family after being lost for months. Normally, the lack of coverage on celestial happenings angered Nia. This time, she experienced only relief that they'd left it alone. In fact, the only inquiry came from a reporter on a radio program called Star Date.

Nia went to the Institute's cafeteria to grab a cup of coffee before heading to her office to return the call. At the condiment station, she added a generous splash of cream and tore open a little yellow sweetener packet. As she sprinkled the contents into the dark brew, she heard her name being called.

"Ms. Nia! You're here. I didn't think you would be." A little hand patted her arm, scattering the powder outside the Styrofoam cup.

Hailey Wilde stood next to her, the little girl's face bright and eager, her green eyes shining with joy. Thomas stood just behind his niece wearing a wide grin. He looked better than yummy in jeans that rode low on his hips and a tight, black T-shirt.

Nia brushed the scattered sugar substitute toward the trash opening in the coffee stand. She smiled at the little girl and leaned her hip on the counter. "Good morning, Hailey."

"You said you didn't work on Saturdays. Uncle Thomas brought me so I could look at the sun. He said it blew up yesterday." Hailey leveled a mature glance at Thomas. "But I think he's wrong. It's still up in the sky."

How did he know? Was he one of Star Date's handful of fans?

"I said it erupted, Hailey," Thomas corrected. He lifted his gaze to Nia's face for a quick glance, and then returned his attention to his niece. "Remind me to get out a dictionary when we get home so I can show you the difference."

The easy relationship between the man and the girl intrigued Nia. She tipped her head and regarded Thomas as he bantered with Hailey. The man's confidence and comfort blasted warmth to Nia's heart. His sun-kissed good looks and his ovary-exploding hard body sent shivers of awareness down her spine. What would he look like in her bed, with no clothes? She bit her tongue to keep it from trailing over her lips like a D-list porn star.

Hailey tugged on Nia's hand. "Can we, Ms. Nia?"

Nia jumped, realizing she was guilty of fantasizing about the uncle rather than focusing on the niece. "I'm sorry?"

A slow, sexy grin spread over Thomas's face, reaching his seaglass-tinted eyes. "Hailey, I'm sure Ms. Nia has other things to do. She doesn't have time to take us to the big telescope."

Charmed that he'd filled her in on what she'd missed while taking a side trip to paradise in her mind, Nia spread her hands. "You know, I don't have to be anywhere until later. I'd be happy to take you to the observatory and let you look at whichever part of the sky you want."

"I want to see the stars we looked at yesterday. Where my mom and dad are."

Nia shot Thomas a helpless look. Had it been a mistake to agree to let the child look through the large scope? A grief-filled shadow flitted over his expression. It made Nia want to kiss the pain away.

Thomas shrugged, apparently as helpless as Nia. "Hailey, I—"

"I know you made that up, Uncle Thomas." Hailey's face was somber as she continued. "But it makes me happy to pretend they're there, looking down on us."

Nia reached for a lid for her coffee. "Pretending is okay, Hailey. The ancients made up a lot of stories to explain all kinds of things. They believed gods lived among the stars. They were called constellations. I happen to know beyond a doubt they made up Sagittarius the archer. But he's visible right now. What do you say we look for him?"

Thomas heaved out a relieved-sounding breath. "Did you know that the Argonauts believe old Sagittarius was placed in the heavens as a guide?"

Hailey shot him a perplexed look, then shrugged. She skipped ahead as they walked toward the observatory.

"Thanks for helping me dig out of that mine field," Thomas remarked quietly as they walked down the ornate hallway. "When she first came to live with me, she cried all the time for her mom and dad. In the day, in the middle of the night, time didn't matter. She was lost and needed her mom and dad."

Nia struggled not to mentally nudge away his sadness. That wasn't what her gift of inspiration was about. "How did she end up believing her folks were stars?"

"I'd read somewhere babies will stop crying when you take them outside. One night, when it was really bad, I dragged a six-year-old into the back yard in the middle of the night. Then I made up a story about her parents being stars and she could talk to them any time she wanted." His face scrunched up in a self-deprecating smile. The diamond stud in his lobe twinkled in the high intensity lights from the arched ceiling as he tucked strands of hair behind his ear. He nudged her shoulder as they strolled after Hailey.

Pleasure zipped through her with the brightness and energy of a hundred fireflies, all lit at once. The intensity of her reaction to him startled her, but she didn't question it. If he heard her nudges, as she was certain he did, then she could accept her attraction to him would be heightened as well.

Knowing the magnetic feelings she had for him might be supernatural in nature didn't stop her from wanting to push him into the small maintenance room they were passing and beg him to strip away her clothing.

A wall of windows flanked the observatory entry, providing a view into the telescope lab. Hailey hopped excitedly in place in front of the secured door to the observatory, motioning them to hurry. No time for a rendezvous in the maintenance closet.

Thomas laid his hand on Hailey's shoulder, stilling her perpetual motion. "Settle down, munchkin. And remember, once we're inside, we keep our grubby mitts to ourselves, right?"

Wide-eyed, the child nodded and thrust her hands behind her back. The kid was definitely a cutie.

Nia waved her name badge over the security reader on the wall by the door. Even though she'd shielded the entry with her own brand of security, the scanner kept the curious at a distance for those times when they didn't want a tremendous number of people just wandering in. That's what the wall of windows was for.

The diode on the security panel flashed green and the lock clicked. Nia pushed the door and held it open for Thomas and Hailey to walk past her. Hailey wriggled her fingers at Phillip as the tech approached.

"Phillip, Hailey would like to see Sagittarius today. Can you make that happen?" Nia asked.

"Sure thing, boss." He held his hand out to Hailey. The child didn't hesitate to slip her hand into his. "Come on, short stuff. I know just where he is hiding." Phillip led her away to the staircase and made a game of them hopping up each step to reach the viewing platform.

"Boss?" Thomas asked.

"I'm the science officer for the Institute."

"Like Spock?"

"You could say that. My job is to explore the

galaxy for new life."

"Ever found any?" Curiosity made his voice climb a little.

"Unfortunately, no." Nia grinned. ""But I remain hopeful."

"Do you really look for little green men?"

No, but she was looking at the most attractive green-eyed man she'd ever seen. "And women. Don't you believe other civilizations could exist?" She tipped her head to the side and studied him.

He frowned. "In all the years we've been able to listen to space, we haven't discovered another species. Therefore, I tend to lean toward a theory of it's only us out there."

"Skeptic."

"If I can see it… " — he ran the tips of his fingers along her arm and leaned toward her— "And touch it, I believe in it. Everything else is simply hocus-pocus. You're a scientist. Do you really believe?"

The smooth glide of his fingers swirled need under her skin, like a ribbon dancing in the wind. "Absolutely. You can't see or touch love, but surely you believe in it?"

He pulled his fingers from her wrist. The brown ring around the outer edge of his green eyes darkened and a ghost of despair flitted across his face. He glanced away toward his niece. When he looked back, his expression was blank. "That emotion is a fallacy. What people think is love is nothing more than a chemical reaction to pheromones, like insects or animals."

"You don't believe that," she accused. And how sad it would be if he did believe it.

He shrugged and moved toward the viewing platform. As he climbed the stairs, the view of his butt almost made her forget he'd just declared that love didn't exist.

Something, or someone, had jaded his view of the world. She studied him as he interacted with his niece. There was love there. She could see it in his affectionate and playful manner as he teased Hailey. She witnessed it from the tactile side of his nature. He was a man who loved to touch. When he'd trailed his fingers over her arm, he'd ignited a fire that still burned in her belly.

The man lied to himself that love didn't exist. And she might be the one to prove to him it did.

When she pinned her gaze on him and poked him with a mental command to look at her, he complied. A grin flickered across his mouth as he needled his brows together.

Barely moving her lips, she mumbled, "Challenge accepted."

CHAPTER 6

Nia lounged against the cushioned back of the glider on the front porch, refusing to allow Callie's resting bitch face bother her. Due to the balmy afternoon temperatures, they were conducting their meeting outside instead of in the boardroom where they typically convened for family meetings.

Next to her, Corie exercised no such restraint. "Callie, we're all busy. I had to call a substitute to teach my intermediate hip-hop class this afternoon. So quit complaining about your deadlines." Despite her harsh words Corie had kept her musical voice soft.

"I hate this damn challenge. It's a bunch of bullshit," Callie said. Gaia tsked her tongue against her teeth and Callie became instantly contrite. "Sorry, Mother. But I need to make my word count today. The story is simply not flowing the way I need."

Aerie's laughter tinkled like wind chimes. Her eyes were alight with humor when she asked, "Do you need a little help from the Muse of Romance?"

"Maybe."

"Wow, Callie!" Nia couldn't hold back her exclamation. "If you'll accept help from one of us, this is one massive writer's block."

"It's like I'm constipated or something. I just can't get the words to come."

"Daughter, do not be indelicate," Gaia chastised. None of them liked when their mother became upset with them. She was less fun than a root canal when she was agitated.

Underneath the massive oak tree in front of the resort's main building, Zeus stood in conference with Mars. Mars shook his head vehemently, but stopped as soon as Zeus raised his hand. Both men were dressed more for a round of golf rather than what amounted to a war council meeting.

Eight Muses, plus Jax, Clio's fiancé, waited on the porch. Polly hadn't arrived as yet. Jax held Clio's hand on his thigh and whispered against the side of her face. His dark curls brushed against the russet hair Clio had tucked behind her ear. Her sister had revealed the truth about being immortal to Jax to convince him to help solve the last challenge. He'd been instrumental in negotiating a truce that circumvented Pierus's machinations to plunge the world toward tyranny.

Aerie's phone buzzed and she picked it up to reply to a text message. Summer was a busy time for a successful wedding planner. She was also making concessions to be here for the family pow-wow.

Terri, Mel and Thalia sat on the loveseat in the small rotunda on the corner of the porch. They were weaving the long stems of white daisies into chains. Nia predicted they'd all be wearing floral crowns before the end of the meeting.

A bright blue Mustang convertible, with the top down, veered into a parking space. Polly had pulled her hair into a casual ponytail for the journey over. The cutoff jean shorts she wore made her legs look longer than usual. Her casual white T-shirt was emblazoned with a fanciful picture of a unicorn. Nia had tried to steal the shirt the first time her sister had shown it to her. A high-spirited unicorn named Amyntas had been Nia's first pet. Thousands of years later, she still missed the old boy.

Polly slipped the strap of her backpack over her shoulder and hurried up the path. She joined Zeus, kissing his cheek, before turning to greet Mars with a hug. The trio proceeded up the steps.

Zeus rubbed his hands together. "Shall we begin?"

"Atlas isn't here yet. Should we wait?" Gaia fretted.

"He has been delayed at HQ. Due to the movement of the moon, there have been some minor adjustments to be made on the star charts. He and his team are all working overtime on it," Nia reported. If the adjustments weren't made, navigational problems would arise. After the encounter with Thomas at the Institute, Nia had checked in at Olympus and helped until she had to leave for the conference. But Atlas already had his instructions and coordinates for the moon's realignment.

Zeus inclined his head her direction. "Nia, would you please brief us on the latest from the eruption on the sun?"

Scooting to the edge of her seat, Nia tapped the menu button on her iPad. She'd already logged in to the corporation's network. Around the porch, her sisters all picked up their devices and opened the meeting app to share her screen.

She cleared her throat as she consulted her notes. "The eruption from the sun's surface would have scrambled all communications on Earth in addition to altering certain physical attributes of our world."

"Like our electronics and computer networks?" Mel asked.

"Yes. Most electronics would have been

rendered temporarily useless. Power plants run on electronics, so basic electrical services would be interrupted. Same goes for governments, corporations and the like. Essentially the world would come to a full stop."

"So why didn't it happen?" Callie asked. Her eyes reflected worry.

Nia typed a command on her tablet, sharing a schematic with everyone else present. "Atlas deflected the radio waves from the solar burst. You can see that half the emissions bounced harmlessly into deep space. No harm, no foul. But the other half slammed into the moon. The impact knocked it out of its normal orbit."

Clio leaned forward. "What effect does that have on Earth?"

"Lunar orbital changes touch all aspects of life. Including behavioral changes in mortals." Nia repressed a shudder. Individuals affected by a full moon were called lunatics for a reason. No one here wanted to see what happened with the moon's trajectory altered. "People will get…a little crazy once the moon hits its zenith, in a little less than three weeks. The new lower orbit will exert more influence on humans."

Zeus appeared deceptively relaxed as he propped his hip on the porch railing. The only indication he wasn't as casual as he appeared was the whiteness of his knuckles as he gripped a can of

Red Bull in his fist. "We believe this is the next of Pierus's challenges."

Callie protested. "But no one has received an email from him."

"A magpie appeared in the bushes outside my office right before the eruption. I'll take that as a sign."

"But, we have no idea what the challenge is. How can we fight whatever it is he has planned if we don't have a clue?" Terri's voice was devoid of her usual lyrical cadence.

"I'm sure we'll find out soon." It worried Nia that she didn't know what the hell she was up against. The tension at the base of her neck gripped painfully. She glanced between Dad and Mars. "Since the flipping bird came to me, and knowing the type of lunacy we can expect from humankind in the next three weeks, I believe my challenger will be Mayhem."

"It fits." Polly's fingers flew over her tablet. "There have been news reports of vicious attacks in public places across Europe. People being stabbed and cut with knives. So far, the violence seems to be restricted to seaports, Marseille, Split, Helsinki. The EU is investigating, but no group has come forward to claim responsibility."

"Then it has begun," Zeus proclaimed.

His words sent chills along Nia's spine and twisted her gut into a vicious knot.

Without knowing what the challenge was to be, she had no way to stop it. Breathing became difficult. "Why hasn't Pierus contacted us?"

Jax clasped his hands over his ear and groaned. "Anyone else noticing the change in air pressure?"

Mars bolted to his feet, knocking his chair against the wall with a rattle. He strode to the edge of the porch just as an inky black mist flowed across the yard in front of the resort. Spreading his feet wide, he crossed his powerful arms over his chest, an imitation of the perfect club bouncer stance. Zeus tossed his can to the side and took up a position on one side of Mars.

The fog swirled and shifted, rising six feet from the surface. Pressure built in Nia's lungs as a shape coalesced within the haze. Overhead, the flapping of wings drew her attention. A large black and white bird dropped from the sky to perch on a low-hanging branch on the oak tree. Beneath the limb, the billowing vapor took the shape of a man. Pierus, in the flesh, so to speak.

The man wore a dark, exquisitely cut navy blue suit. A diamond stud winked in his regimental striped silk tie. His dark hair, peppered with strands of silver, was slicked back from his high forehead. He wore eyeglasses, which Nia knew were only for show. Immortals had perfect vision to go with their perfect health.

"Wow," Jax said. "This guy has more disguises. First a crazy old man, then a poor street musician. Last time I saw him he was dressed in a toga." He joined Mars and Zeus at the top of the steps. "Never really expected to see him in a power suit."

"Pierus is a master of disguise." Clio's tone held equal notes of disdain and defiance. The man had kidnapped her in the midst of a god-created tornado and locked her in a large cage. "But without a costume you can see he's just a piece of shit."

Pierus tsked his disapproval. He jabbed his hands toward each of the immortals present on the porch, as though issuing a mental thrust, ordering them to remain motionless. Breath stalled in Nia's lungs. *What the hell?* He shouldn't have been able to hold the greater gods in thrall this way.

Didn't change the fact that, somehow, he held everyone in place with just a hand gesture. He directed his stare at Nia. Against her will she moved forward past the men clustered at the head of the steps. Her head pounded painfully at the pressure he exerted on her. Her feet barely touched the steps as she was compelled down them.

Digging deep within for resistance, she visualized applying the brakes on her car. She stopped her forward momentum as the picture firmed up in her mind.

Pierus cocked one eyebrow up, yet somehow managed to sneer. He lifted his gaze toward the canopy of the tree. "Mayhem, I believe you will enjoy challenging this obstinate Muse."

The bird cackled insanely. Nia squelched her urge to cringe as Pierus snapped his fingers.

Behind her she heard a massive expulsion of breath as the god released his hold on her family. Mars and Zeus descended the steps to take up positions on either side of Nia; Jax stood directly behind her. Nia knew without looking, her mother and sisters would be arranged in a warrior-like show of solidarity on the steps.

"Pierus, explain this challenge and then be gone. Your very presence is fouling the air I breathe." Zeus's words came out with military precision.

"You really aren't in a position to give me orders. By the time we are done with this hostile takeover, I will own you and all your riches. While that will smell sweet to me, I guarantee you will not find pleasant the stench of the pit into which I cast you and your daughters." His gaze roved over Gaia. "Your lovely wife I will keep shackled to my new executive chair in the Olympus board room."

Zeus growled and lifted his hand, palm out, as though he intended to shove Pierus back to the circle of Hades the man had climbed out of. Pierus extended his hand at the same time, and their wills clashed like lightning in the space between them.

"Enough with the power play antics, Zeus." Pierus straightened his tie, then shot his cuffs, looking every bit the corporate executive he wanted to be. He focused his gaze on Nia as Mayhem descended from the tree to land on his shoulder.

Nia hoped the damned bird would crap on his five-thousand-dollar Hugo Boss suit. Worry crept through her mind like a fat rat. Why had he appeared in person, rather than send an email? She asked, "What do I need to do, Pierus?"

"Originally, your challenge was going to be rather simple. You merely had to convince one man the 'good nature' of human kind does exist. All these puny people hurting and killing each other in the name of religion or cheap gasoline, or politics. Really, they are making it easy for me." Pierus shrugged. He shot a sneer at Zeus. "But, your father complicated your task immeasurably by sending Atlas to save the world from the sun's eruption."

"Who is working with you this time?" Zeus demanded through pinched lips. His fingers flexed near his hips, but he didn't raise his arms. "You haven't the necessary resources to affect the sun in the manner you did."

Pierus waved his hand dismissively. "My partner will remain silent. But thanks to your interference, now Urania—" he pointed toward her. "Uh, Nia will also have to deal with the lunacy caused by the realignment of the moon."

"So, all I need is to convince one person that good still exists in the world?" There had to be something Pierus wasn't telling Nia, some hidden agenda.

"Yes, this one man holds the key. But, in addition to forfeiting your own existence should you fail, the life of an innocent will hang in the balance. In the future, this one individual could lend inspiration to the man working to ease the plight of the very poorest people in the world. You will be responsible for depriving the human race of a great mind when you fail to save the child who would inspire a great scientist." His voice grew louder as he spoke until it boomed in her ears. He jabbed his finger toward her. "When you fail, this person will not create a system for securing healthy living conditions to those who need it most. I believe, for shits and giggles, I'll bind you to a tree so you are forced to watch the suffering and death of the innocent."

The bird on Pierus's shoulder screeched and preened at his proclamation. He lifted a knuckle to the bird's breast and smoothed the ruffled feathers with the back of his finger. The bastard's cool declaration drove a stake of anger straight to her core.

"How long do I have to win?" Nia forced confidence she didn't feel into her voice. Bad enough she and her sisters were at risk. But the loss of an innocent life was too horrible to contemplate. "And are you going to tell me the man's name? Or do I have to guess?"

"So many questions." Pierus shook his head. "Are you not an all-powerful Muse?"

Clio moved around Jax and stepped onto the drive with Nia, jostling Mars to the left to stand shoulder to shoulder with her sister. "We've already proven we're powerful. We defeated Tyranny."

Pierus's eyes flashed with strong emotion. "How is my daughter?"

Clio shot a venomous glare toward the bird perched on his shoulder. "Looking forward to the company of her sister."

"Clio, you aren't helping," Nia muttered. She directed her attention to Pierus. "How long?"

"If you have not accomplished the feat by the first night of the full moon, it will be considered a loss." He shrugged and Mayhem took flight. She became nothing more than a dark blotch on the crystalline blue summer sky.

Mist gathered beneath Pierus's feet as he prepared to leave. Panic flared like July's fireworks in Nia's head. "Wait, you haven't told me the name of the man."

"It could be someone you already know. Perhaps Ken. Possibly, it could be a man you've met recently or one you know from long ago. Or, maybe it's Bradley. You will have to decide. But choose wisely, Muse. The fate of your world, and all its human occupants, is now in your hands." Pierus's body was blanketed in mist, but the sudden fog didn't dissipate his obnoxious laughter as he vanished. The maniacal sound rang off the porch's planked oak ceiling.

Beside Nia, Zeus's shoulders slumped and he hissed out a sigh, then gasped as though he'd been holding his breath the entire time Pierus had stood in front of him.

"Dad, are you okay?" His cheeks had lost their normal ruddy color. Nia grasped his arm and helped him up the steps. Jax took his other arm and together, they led him to the love seat. Gaia slid onto the cushion next to him, fussily smoothing the hair at his temple.

Mars stalked to the spot where Pierus had disappeared. He kneeled and spread his hands over the area, as if seeking some kind of residual supernatural signature.

Nia exchanged a worried glance with Mel. Their father appeared ill, and Nia was certain he wasn't just being dramatic. Mel handed Zeus a glass filled with the nectar he favored over coffee. He waved it off in favor of his Red Bull.

Zeus sipped from the can and then coughed. "I'm fine. Somehow, Pierus managed to hold me in thrall the entire time he was present."

"What the hell?" Callie exclaimed, her eyes wide. "How could he do that?"

"He had help." Mars stomped up the steps. "I pick up indications of two distinct deities. I do not know the identity of the second. The signature is heavily cloaked and it faded rapidly."

"If we don't know who we are up against, it will be harder to win," Mel whined. Concern for their father etched Mel's heart-shaped face and she wrung her hands together.

Nia would have laughed about her sister's over-the-top drama queen pose, but worry strangled the lighter emotion.

"Enough, daughter." Gaia admonished. She stroked her hand down Zeus's arm. "We will not win with negativity. Nia, do you have any idea of the identity of this man you are to convince? We know of Bradley, but not of the other two."

"It most certainly isn't Bradley. For a scientist he totally lacks the skeptical gene. I'm half convinced he believes in the tooth fairy."

"What of the others?" Aerie asked.

"Ken could be my NASA contact, Ken Hillerman."

"It isn't him," Zeus muttered. He knocked Gaia's hand away and pushed upright on his seat.

"Ken is your partisan. Like Zeke is for Clio."

"Really?" Nia would never have guessed Ken. "He's so far away. How can he protect me?"

"Up until now, you didn't need protection. He'll be changing jobs this week and joining the corporation to work for Research and Development. He is relocating to Delphi. Your mother has already prepared one of the cottages by the lake for him. He'll live at the Athenian while we search for corporate housing for him. He arrives tomorrow."

"I spoke to him yesterday. He never mentioned coming here."

Gaia put a hand on Nia's elbow. "We asked him not to mention it to you. But after Clio's run in with Pierus, we thought it best to bring him to Delphi."

Callie tapped her foot. "So that leaves this mystery man. Any idea who that might be, Nia?"

Her sister's impatience was evident in her tone and her incessant fidgeting. Nia banked her frustration with Callie and replied, "I did meet a man yesterday. Right before the solar flare, as a matter of fact. Thomas Wilde."

"*Doubting Thomas?*" Jax's eyebrows shot up.

"What?" Nia drew in a sharp breath. The name seemed familiar.

"It's a television program. This guy, Thomas, chases down myths and urban legends of popular culture and exposes them as frauds. He's a debunker."

That explained his comment at Helios yesterday about the Loch Ness monster. "So he doesn't believe in magic, and goes out of his way to prove it doesn't exist."

Discouragement settled like a wet blanket on her shoulders. She ruthlessly shoved the feeling off. Conceding defeat before her challenge had begun wasn't in her nature. "He could hear my nudges."

Zeus cocked up one brow. "What do you mean, daughter? How did he hear them?"

"When I nudged a rude woman, he heard the command. My voice was inaudible, but somehow he knew I'd called her a cow. Has anyone else ever had a mortal hear a poke this way?"

Her sisters all shook their heads. She looked to Jax, the other mortal who'd helped a Muse with her task. He held his hands up and shrugged. No help there.

Something she'd never seen before, the pale light of unease, trickled in Zeus's eyes. "If this is the man who is destined to stand by you for this challenge, you must be careful. For him to know what we are, gods and goddesses, could spell disaster."

Revealing the existence of deities to a man whose life's work was to disprove magic could be dangerous. Nia smiled. "Or, it could be a stroke of genius."

CHAPTER 7

After dinner, Thomas helped Hailey with a craft project for her summer school then ran a bath for her. While she played in the tub, he tossed in a load of laundry. It was picture day at her childcare center on Monday, and Hailey had insisted she wanted to wear the gauzy, floral top with her white shorts. The shorts had a mud streak on the back and Thomas didn't have the heart to make her change her outfit choice.

He'd come a long way from hanging out with his buddies on weeknights, catching a ball game, or playing pick-up basketball at the gym. Now Hailey was his priority. And she'd come to mean more to him than life itself. He dropped a detergent tab in the washer then shut the lid. By the time water began flowing into the machine, he was on his way to clean up the kitchen. He'd turned into a true domestic god.

As he cleaned up the hot dog and mac and cheese mess, his thoughts turned to Nia Thanos. Nia possessed the classic looks he normally equated with statues of Greek goddesses. Her glorious red hair and startling blue eyes had drawn him in. Less than one percent of the world's population possessed that hair-eye color combination.

Even more rare than that was her challenging Peggy Dartmoor for being rude. Now that he was hanging with the mommy set, he'd noticed Peggy's intentions were as false as her boobs. It had pleased him to see Nia call the witch out the way she had.

Except, had she? Nia's eyes had turned hard and cool before she'd insisted she'd done no such thing. Thomas tugged his earlobe, toying with the small stud he'd worn since his college days. He'd been so certain she'd spoken, especially given that Peggy had actually apologized for her boorish behavior.

Nia had been warm and friendly today when they'd run into her at the Institute again. Her attitude with Hailey had been engaged and kind. The silky feel of her skin when he'd trailed his fingertips down her arm had made him want to bury his hardened dick deep within her warm heat.

The woman was a dichotomy of sweet and sultry.

Had she found him as intriguing? Probably not in his current role of Mr. Mom. Laughing at himself, he wiped a blob of ketchup off the table. He was going to need to work with his niece on her hand-eye coordination.

Hailey called from the bathroom that she was ready to get out of the tub. After he dried her hair, he wove the long curly tresses into her overnight braid.

He pulled the blankets back on the bed, waiting for Hailey to pick a book to read. While she studied the selection, he plumped her pillows just the way she liked them. "Hurry up, munchkin."

Jutting her hip to one side, Hailey shot him an impish grin over her shoulder. "Patience, Unk. I'm deciding between Alice and Arielle."

Please, please, please, no Disney princesses tonight. He didn't think he could handle that. Although Arielle's thick red hair and rocking bod reminded him of Nia. Thomas's palms itched just imagining running his hands over those lush curves. He shook away his thoughts of what he'd like to do with the sexy woman. Right now, he needed to focus on getting Hailey settled for the night so he could research a new debunking project. He'd been using his filming hiatus to look into new myths he could disprove.

Hailey plucked a book from her shelf, handed it to him, then crawled into her bed. *Thank God, no princesses tonight.* He settled next to her, leaning against the pillows.

Before he could begin reading, Hailey laid her small hand on his. "Uncle Thomas?" Her voice was hesitant.

Which was her default tone when she wanted to talk about her parents. He drew a deep breath and responded, "Yes, munchkin?"

"Do you miss my daddy?"

Her question tore his heart as it always did. The sting was swift and razor blade sharp. Doug had been two years older than Thomas, but they'd been best friends. Thomas dropped the book to his lap and wrapped his arm around Hailey's shoulders. He drew his knees up. "I miss him all the time, Hailey. There isn't a single day that I don't think of him and your mom. I tell them how proud they'd be of you, and what a great kid you turned out to be." The sting in his heart relocated to behind his eyes. He blinked. "Except for that one time when you locked us out of the house, you're okay."

She rested her head on his chest. "I talk to them, too. Earlier I told them I thought I'd finally found the right woman to help us."

"What are you talking about? We don't need no stinkin' woman to help us. We're highly capable of helping ourselves."

"But don't you want someone to love, like my

daddy loved my mommy?"

How could he explain he wasn't sure he believed in romantic love? His faith in the emotion died the same day his brother and sister-in-law had. Horribly snatched away by a homemade bomb in a shopping mall. Leaving their precious child in his incapable, inept care. "I kind of have my hands full with you, munchkin. Not sure I'd have time for some other dame."

"I like Ms. Nia. She was really, really nice to me yesterday. When Bridget and her friends were being nasty."

"They were mean to you again?" Anger churned helplessly in his gut. These days it seemed even kids were exempt from basic human kindness.

Hailey had been having difficulty fitting in with the Campfire Scouts. Originally, Thomas had enrolled her in the activity because she'd expressed an interest. In an unmistakably grown-up manner, the kid refused to quit when the other little monsters had teased her about her lack of real parents. He'd spoken to the troop mothers and asked them to keep an eye on the situation, but they didn't. They were probably too busy gossiping about who was having an affair with whom.

"Yeah, but Ms. Nia talked to me and teached me about the telescope."

"Taught you," he corrected as he smoothed his

hand over her head.

"And today she went with us to look at the stars again. Through the big scope instead of one of the smaller ones."

"She did a very nice thing."

"And she's pretty, too. I wish I had red hair like hers. And it's short. Can I get my hair cut like hers?"

"If you want. But, there's nothing wrong with your hair, Hailey. It reminds me of your mom's."

Hailey slid lower in the bed and yawned. "You don't have to read to me tonight. I love you, Uncle Thomas."

"Love you, too, Hailey." He rose from the bed. The sheet was cool when he pulled it up and tucked it behind her shoulders. He bent and pressed a kiss to her forehead. "Light on or off?"

Her gaze flew to the colorful light on the bookshelf across the room. She'd been sleeping with it on since he'd brought her home after the bombing. He knew someday she'd ask him to turn it off…she'd come to grips with the horror of hearing her parents had died. He held his breath as he waited for her answer.

"On."

He eased out a sigh. Today wasn't that day.

Returning the book to the shelf, he toggled the switch on the lamp. Muted rose and purple splotches appeared on the ceiling above the light.

Before he exited the room, he flicked the switch on the wall by the door, turning off the Hello Kitty light on the bedside table. He let his gaze linger on Hailey. The picture of innocence, her dusky eyelashes lay on her cheek. She'd curled one hand under her chin; the other clutched the sheet to her ear. Her narrow chest rose and fell steadily.

Thomas's heart thumped against his breastbone as he watched the little girl fall asleep. As far as he was concerned, the sun rose and set on the child. He eased the door closed, leaving it ajar so he could hear her should she cry out in the night. The nightmares didn't come as often now, but every once in a while, a really bad one popped up like a wicked jack-in-the-box.

On her first night in his home, he'd made a mistake and watched the news reports of the bombing after he'd thought she'd gone to sleep. Hailey's screams had catapulted him from a restless sleep. He'd held her as sobs wracked her tiny body. After that, he'd unplugged the television. And hadn't plugged it in since. He relied solely on his smart phone, tablet and laptop as sources of information about what was going on in the world.

At the moment, none of those devices seemed to be working well. When he tried to place a call to his producer regarding his filming schedule, he got nothing but static. He couldn't connect to the

Internet from either his Mac or his iPad.

Opening the refrigerator, Thomas grabbed a beer, then made his way to the front porch. He dropped down on the top step and sipped the cold brew, holding that first drink on his tongue, before letting the cool liquid slide down his gullet. He gazed at the sky, where stars winked and danced. The moon rode low on the horizon, barely visible over the housetops across the street. He recalled Hailey's words about how she thought she'd seen her parents in the stars. God, he missed Doug and his adorable wife, Cindy. Probably nearly as much as Hailey missed them. A single tear leaked from the corner of his eye, and he wiped it away impatiently.

Pity party, table for none.

Taking a hasty swallow of his beer, he shoved the loneliness aside. There had to be something better to focus on rather than whether he was doing a good job raising a child who'd been robbed of her parents.

He let his thoughts wander back to Nia. His dick jumped to life as he contemplated her sexy smile. Even the ire crackling in her eyes intrigued him when he accused her of calling Peggy a cow. He dragged his thumb over the label on the bottle, wondering if she'd say yes if he asked her on a date.

There was only one way to find out. He'd call

her at work next week. Or, better yet, drop by looking for information that required an expert astronomer.

He had a little time to come up with the perfect question.

CHAPTER 8

Sunday passed in a bit of a blur for Nia. She'd got on her Netflix account and located the *Doubting Thomas* program. The first pot of coffee she brewed lasted through two episodes. Then she ran on her treadmill while viewing the third on her tablet. Having burned off enough calories, she munched her way through a fourth show with a large blue glass bowl filled with popcorn on her lap.

The subject matter of each show was fascinating. The scientific manner in which Thomas went about exposing the myth as, well, myth was entertaining. Nia found herself entranced by the host himself. He resembled a surfer, with his shaggy sun-kissed hair and golden skin. His muscular body didn't appear to have an ounce of extra flesh on it anywhere. She knew in his case the camera hadn't added ten pounds.

In one shot, he'd raised his arms to pull himself onto a ledge on a cliff in Arizona. The T-shirt he wore rose as well, revealing a taut abdomen. Her mouth watered at the sight of deep cuts of muscle on his hips.

She was completely hooked by the fifth episode. In order to debunk the myth of the moment, he'd had to scuba dive in the Sea of Cortez in a skin-tight wetsuit that left little to the imagination. Late in the show, the suit ended up bunched around his waist, exposing a mile-wide expanse of shoulder, ridged abs, and a thatch of red-gold hair on his muscular chest. Tingles burst to life between her legs, roaming down her thighs and up into her belly. Suddenly, it didn't matter that he'd let his eyes roam over her body on the day they met. At the moment, she'd have loved to replace his gaze with his hands.

Mel and Thalia showed up before she could start the next installment. They forced her into the shower and dragged her to a late lunch at their favorite pub, The Rowan Tree. The twins were truly good at distracting her. Mel played straight man to Thalia's clown princess act. They'd made a game of rapid-fire options for getting to know Thomas better. Nia had enjoyed their company, and their quirky suggestions for how to score a date with the man who made a living disproving the existence of myth and magic.

She'd managed to stream eleven of the twenty episodes available before she called it a day. It didn't surprise her to have her dreams filled with images of Thomas.

The magpie she'd already come to despise had been waiting in the bushes for her when she arrived at the Observatory before eight this morning. The bitch cawed insanely, each burst sounding like crazed laughter. Like the bird belonged in an asylum.

She paused by the art deco entryway and glared at the bird. "You'll be seeing your sister, Tyranny, very soon." The bird cackled back at her, as if to say bullshit.

Nia checked with Barry, who had been the overnight tech. Atlas had been a genius at masking the moon's new position. Barry never mentioned a change in orbit. Nia fidgeted as she scanned reports from their world-wide network of labs and observatories. No one else had noticed the shift either. But the illusion of normalcy couldn't last long. And soon, mortals would be affected by change. There'd be no way to hide the reason once the lunacy began.

An email had been waiting for her from the International Space Agency. It didn't surprise her to receive their request for a presentation detailing Friday's eruption. While she worked to create a

PowerPoint slide show with images from the Helios' solar dynamic technology, the door to her office remained open. She'd been working on the display for ninety minutes when a knock on the doorjamb distracted her.

Nia's mouth went dry at the sight of Thomas standing confidently in her doorway. If she thought he looked good on camera, real life was a gazillion times better.

"Good morning." His deep bass voice stroked her senses the same way his gaze stroked her face. Slow. Sexy.

After spending the day watching his TV program, to have him appear in the flesh twisted desire in her belly. Her cheeks heated. "Morning."

His piercing green-eyed stare made her think he knew she'd spent her overnight hours thinking about him. A smile spread across his mouth. He strode three steps into her office.

He extended his hand and when she took it a burst of sensual fire spread from his palm to hers. She had to force herself to release her grip. "Won't you have a seat? How may I help you?"

"I wanted to stop by to thank you again for being so kind to Hailey. You really made an impression." The corners of his mouth tilted up in a quicksilver smile. The kind of grin a woman could happily drown in.

"She's a nice girl. Quite mature for an eight-year-old." Dying to know the girl's story, Nia nudged Thomas to share. She opted for a completely silent command over muttering. She already knew he could hear those thoughts.

He cocked his head to the side. "She is that. I've been raising her since my brother and his wife died a couple of years ago. It's been difficult for her. Kindness like yours makes an impact on a child. And the uncle trying to raise her. Some days, I find myself completely out of my depth."

Relieved, she drew a breath. So far, so good. This time, Nia opted for a verbal request instead of the mental version to encourage him to finish the story. "May I ask what happened? To her parents?" Any history he could share might help her confirm her suspicion that he was the man to help her.

Rubbing a fist over his breastbone, as if the memory pained him, he spoke. "They'd gone Christmas shopping. Just a casual trip, a date really. They'd left Hailey with a sitter, thank God, and had planned to make an afternoon of it. They were in the mall food court when the terrorist's bomb exploded." Thomas blinked away the sorrow in his eyes. "A radical faction that routinely spouts hatred claimed responsibility. Pursuit of unity and brotherhood idiosyncrasies they espouse only served to destroy. It made me lose faith in humans' ability to love one another. Beyond familial love, that is."

Bingo! Thomas *was* the man Pierus had mentioned. Rather than feeling jubilant, Nia felt slightly panicked. How was she supposed to convince this man goodness existed? It wasn't like the challenge came with a road map. And what about the second part of the prediction — that an innocent life hung in the balance. Dear goddess, was that Hailey?

Nia touched her mind to his once again, telling him he wanted to continue the story.

"You're just being nice. You can't possibly want to hear any more of my sad story." The devastating smile was a pale ghost of itself. But it had reappeared.

Had he heard her nudge, or were his words just part of a normal conversation? She had to know before she could continue.

Picturing an arrow, she let her nudge fly silently. *Tell me you honestly still believe in the goodness of man.*

"I can't tell you that."

He'd heard! Nia flattened her hands on the desk.

Thomas shook his head sadly and continued as if she'd spoken aloud. "I disprove myths and legends for a living. And the biggest myth of all is that people are innately good. That trait no longer exists in this world. If it ever did."

"I think you're wrong, Thomas." Leaning

forward, she slid her hands along the desk toward him. "I believe my task is to prove just how wrong you are."

"Hmm. You're certainly welcome to try. Maybe over dinner tonight?" When he laid his hand on top of hers, that frisson of energy sparked between them again. He wove his fingers under hers and lifted their joined hands. He stared deeply into her eyes, waiting for her answer.

She swallowed hard before replying. With his company, saving the world was going to be a pure pleasure. "That's as good a time as any to start."

"See there, I already believe a little." Holding her gaze, he squeezed her fingers, then leaned forward to kiss the tips.

The gentle press of his lips to her knuckles made her stomach jump like water in a hot frying pan. Or maybe it was the connectedness between their gazes. She was drawn to him like iron shavings to a magnet.

"I'll pick you up at half past seven, if that's okay."

He released her hand and she was immediately hit with unexplainable loneliness. It took every shred of will power to not reach out for him again. She jerked a pen from the mug full of them on her desk and pulled a pad of sticky notes from her drawer. While she wrote down her address, Thomas rose from his seat. He slipped his hand into his pocket and waited with his weight propped on one hip. His casual stance accentuated his lean waist and long legs.

Yes, ma'am. Pure pleasure.

* * *

The doorbell chimed promptly at seven-thirty. Nia hurried down the stairs to the mullioned glass in the front door of her turn-of-the-century bungalow. The sun, lowering in the west, splashed a puddle of light across the decorative rug that protected the tiles of her entry hall.

Nia summoned calm with a deep breath as she grasped the knob. Letting him through the front door felt like so much more than just the simple act of allowing someone entry to her home. The minute she opened it, she'd be letting him into her life, and beginning the challenge Pierus had set for them.

Except that Thomas didn't have a clue what he was getting into. It didn't seem fair, but how in the world would she explain to a man whose job included debunking myths, that she was as old as time? In the world's eyes, she was as much a myth as the Kraken.

Shaking her head, she pulled the door open. "Hi." Her words were drowned out by the staccato chattering of a magpie sitting on a limb in a maple tree in her front yard. The bird flapped its wings vigorously and several black and white feathers floated to the ground.

Before greeting her, Thomas turned toward the noise, and then jumped backward as the bird flew straight toward him. Supernatural sound pierced the air as the bird screeched and veered away at the last second. Nia covered her ears and aimed a thought toward the bitching creature to mute her cry. When the bird's cry fell silent and it went into a bit of a tumble before righting herself, Nia knew her jab had scored a direct hit.

"What the hell?" Thomas exclaimed. "Dive-bombing birds? That thing sounded like a banshee."

Nia laughed at the idea of him believing in banshees. Those beings had been made up by smugglers to keep people indoors at night so they could go on with their nefarious ways. Nia had blown away the cloud cover on enough of the bootleggers to make sure they got caught.

"That was weird," she said as she gestured him inside. "I'm almost ready. Just need to grab my purse and set my alarm."

It was an elaborate system Mars had insisted they install after first learning of the challenge from Pierus. If something happened in any of the Muses' homes, the alert sounded at the Olympus home office and a legion of battle ready demi-gods would rush to the rescue. Thalia had accidentally set it off right after hers had been installed. They'd all had a good laugh about that. And Thalia had scored a grown-up sleepover with Xander, the captain of the legion guard.

"Am I dressed okay? You didn't really say where we were having dinner," Nia asked as she glanced over her shoulder at Thomas.

He didn't bother to hide that he totally checked her backside out while he examined her outfit. Which included jeans, a floral blouse and strappy turquoise sandals. An appreciative light deepened his eyes to match her shoes.

"You look great." His husky tone induced fluttering along her spine. "We're going to The Rowan Tree. Do you know the restaurant? It's pretty casual."

"Yeah, it's one of my favorites." Of course, chances were good that she'd run into at least one of her sisters there. It was the Muses' preferred haunt. *Please, don't let it be Callie.* She picked up her purse and turned to face Thomas.

Who'd moved into the space immediately behind her. Caught off guard, she stumbled. Her shoulder brushed against his chest as she pivoted and found herself engulfed in his arms as he steadied her.

"Sorry." She shifted away from his embrace, but he stopped her backward progress.

"I'm not." He searched her face for a moment, and then concentrated his gaze on her mouth. He bent his head and whispered against her lips. "How about we get the horrible, awkwardness of the goodnight kiss out of the way first?"

Cheesy for sure. But she loved it. His breath kissed her mouth an instant before his lips. The brief caress was butterfly soft. She sighed. "Good idea."

His chest rose and fell under her palms, solid and strong. He eased his hands along her arm, leaving a trail of heat in their wake. A broad smile illuminated his face as he wove their fingers together. There was an undeniable link between them. She saw it in his eyes, felt it in his brief kiss.

Thomas Wilde was the man to help her with this challenge. Had to be. Why else would Mayhem have appeared to both of them?

"I'm glad to have that out of the way. Ready to go grab dinner?" Thomas asked.

He still held her hand as he led her through the front door. He scanned the maple tree in the yard, as if looking for more threatening birds, while Nia locked the house.

A big, black BMW sat in her drive. When Thomas turned on the ignition, the theme song from *Frozen* blared from the speakers. He laughed and quickly changed to a rock and roll station. "Somehow, Hailey takes control of the station whenever she's in the car. We listen to Disney a lot. I know all the words to this song. And the dance moves, as well." He mock groaned.

She joined him in laughing. "I'd pay money to see that show."

"No, you really wouldn't. It's unsightly and ungainly."

Nia doubted there was an ugly or awkward thing about him. She'd be willing to bet his dancing would be charming. Catching sight of the pink creeping up his cheeks, she changed the subject. "I have a confession."

Thomas turned on his signal light and slid her a glance as he navigated around the corner. "You're a Disney addict, too?"

"Um...no." His lighthearted banter warmed her insides. "I've been watching your program. It's quite entertaining." He didn't need to know she'd binge watched for an entire day.

"Do you have a favorite episode?"

"The one about the Humboldt squid in the Sea of Cortez was engaging. I caught myself yelling at the TV as you swam toward that nightmare of a sea animal." He also didn't need to know she was yelling that his ass was perfection as the camera operator followed behind him. "What was it you called that thing? Intelligent...opportunistic?"

"Those beasts are considered the big, bad outlaw biker of the marine world. We wanted to capture a group of them communicating and coordinating as they hunt for food."

"Seeing them herding the school of fish was astounding. But things got interesting when the hammerheads showed up. Weren't you a little nervous being surrounded by giant squids and sharks?"

"I live for danger." His laughter was scoffing. "But we were perfectly safe. And the biggest squid we came across was only eight feet. So much for the twenty foot legend."

Only eight feet? Almost two feet taller than Thomas didn't sound like *only* to her. "That episode was recent. Where was Hailey?"

They'd arrived at the restaurant. Thomas guided the car into a parallel parking spot opposite The Rowan as he answered. "We mostly film in the summer, so Hailey goes with me." He checked his mirror, and then shut off the car. The sudden silence wrapped intimately around them. He dropped his hand atop hers on the center console. "She really is the most patient kid. She sat on the boat reading, and coloring, and entertaining the crew. The most interesting moment was when we realized that our underwater camera operator, a former special operations veteran, had learned all the words to all the songs from *The Little Mermaid*. On his breaks, he'd sit with Hailey and color, singing along with her or braiding her hair."

"That's a great story." The heat between their hands blossomed up her arm, swirling languidly like the school of fish had in the Sea of Cortez.

Like a true gentleman, Thomas came around the car to assist Nia out. He dropped his hand to the small of her back as they walked to the crosswalk. The moon was a plump sliver of white against the fading blue evening sky. Although she found its unaccustomed location disconcerting, she knew the power of the gods kept anyone else from noticing.

As they waited for the signal to cross the street, a large, beat-up truck careened around the corner. Tires screeched as the driver steered across two lanes of traffic, headed directly for a group of pedestrians standing near the park entrance across from the restaurant.

A hard, determined expression darkened the driver's face. Horror rose in Nia's throat as she realized the truck was aimed at the innocent people on the opposite corner.

Her scream and Thomas's shout of "look out" filled the air, followed instantly by a sickening thud as the truck slammed into one of the pedestrians. Nia buried her face against Thomas's chest, hoping to erase the image of the body flying through the air like a rag doll.

Summoning her courage, she peeked. The driver exited the truck and stalked around the front end. As he stood over his victim, several other bystanders joined him. After a moment of silence the entire crowd began to disperse. Not a single one of them offered any type of assistance. The driver spat on the downed pedestrian's chest. Without a word, he climbed back into the truck. Revving the motor, he popped the clutch and then lurched away as if nothing had happened.

"God! What the hell is wrong with them?" Thomas grasped her arms and eased her away from his body. "Nia, I have to go help. Call an ambulance." He jogged toward the limp body lying under the bushes by the sidewalk.

Nia dialed emergency services as she chased after Thomas. As soon as the call connected, she hollered, "Someone's been run down by a truck in front of The Rowan Tree." She rattled off the cross streets. "Please send an ambulance."

CHAPTER 9

What the fuck was wrong with these people? Panic and anger crowded Thomas's chest as he raced to help the injured man on the sidewalk. Not only hadn't the bystanders tackled the dipshit who'd driven into the crowd, they'd wandered away from the screaming man as though nothing had happened.

Bile rose in his gullet as he spied the awkward angle of the man's legs—both pointed outward like a broken marionette. The victim continued to scream as Thomas reached him, thrashing his head from side to side. Blood trickling from the corner of the man's mouth splashed the grass with each violent twist.

"Hold still," Thomas commanded in a stern voice. He laid his hand on the man's forehead, hoping to still the motion. "We're calling an ambulance. Do you know the guy in the truck?"

"No," the man bawled. Tears and snot merged with the blood on his face.

Nia joined them, kneeling next to Thomas. "The ambulance and police are on the way. How is he?"

Thomas shook his head. He wasn't a doctor, but even he recognized the man's injuries were severe. Possibly fatal. She laid her hand atop his and pleasant, tingling warmth seeped into his skin. Under their joined hands, the man finally stopped thrashing.

Nia scanned the area, confusion and concern shadowing her face. "Why did everyone walk away? I can't believe none of those people stayed to help."

"I've never seen anything like it. Total lunacy. Jesus, is the moon full?"

Above his head, a bird cackled, the sound harsh and maniacal. Nia drew a sharp breath, her eyes wide as she stared at the black and white animal. He tracked the bird's crazy path from one branch to the next. He looked at Nia in time to see her lips moving.

Although her voice was inaudible, her words reverberated in his head. As if she'd spoken aloud, he clearly heard her tell the magpie to *shove the fuck off*. The bird didn't fly away, just bobbed its head and flapped its wings. The feathers on the ends of the striped wings lifted, like it was flipping Nia off. She squinted hard at the bird, and blew a breath at it. A blast of not-quite pain, more like hard pressure, gripped the base of Thomas's neck. As the man laying before them slipped into unconsciousness, the bird took off. Feathers fluttered to the guy's chest in its wake.

The wail of sirens reached his ears and Thomas breathed easier knowing assistance was coming. He focused his attention back to the injured man. Beside him, Nia gathered the scattered feathers. She stared at them, a frown marring her brow, and then tucked them in her pocket.

An ambulance careened to a halt behind him. One of the paramedics raced to his side, while the others gathered a gurney and equipment from the rear of the truck.

Thomas scooted out of the way to let the EMTs work. He put his arm around Nia's shoulders and held her trembling body close. When she turned her face to his chest, he stroked her hair in a soothing motion.

The cardiac monitor the medic had attached to the guy's chest showed an erratic heartbeat. A loud, solid squeal from the monitor indicated the man's heart had stopped. A more high-pitched whine underscored the other noise as the paramedic applied defibrillator paddles to his chest. The man's body contorted and the heart monitor beeped again. They'd restarted his heart, but Thomas wasn't at all sure the poor schmuck was going to make it.

The police arrived and pulled them to the side, questioning them about what they'd seen.

By the time they were excused from the accident scene, neither of them had much of an appetite. "What would you say to a stroll along the river promenade?" he asked.

Nia chewed her lip as she studied his face. She nodded slowly. "I'd say uh-huh."

He took her hand and they walked in silence toward the waterfront. They passed by the marina before stepping onto the boardwalk leading to the jogging path.

The weather was ideal for this type of evening activity. The mulched walkway was lit at regular intervals with lights designed to look like torches held aloft in the arms of ancient Greeks. The lights had just flickered to life. Even though the sun hadn't gone down yet, there were shadowy areas between the lights.

Nia opened her mouth, then snapped it closed again as shudders wracked her frame. Thomas drew her off the path in a shaded area, and slid his arms around her. The gesture comforted him as much as it seemed to ease her distress.

"Why did they all walk away? All those people. Surely someone was more qualified than us to help that poor man." Nia's voice was muffled against his shoulder. The warmth of her hands oozed into his pecs, triggering a heated response in his groin. Her body snugged tightly to his was about the only thing that seemed right in the world.

"Who knows? Tonight kind of proves my theory that there isn't any good left in the world. People are absorbed in their own lives. They don't care about what is going on around them." He tightened his grip around her waist.

"You can't possibly believe that. What about people volunteering for charities? What about all those random acts of kindness the media likes to report?"

God, he wished he could believe in those things. He rested his hands on the small of her back. "When was the last time you actually read or heard about someone doing anything altruistic? Even the charities you mentioned are only really in it for the money."

She leaned away and gazed into his eyes. "That's an awfully jaded view of the world, Thomas."

"I've seen too much pain and suffering. In my own family and others. Human kindness is as much of a myth as the Loch Ness monster."

"Actually, Nessie isn't myth at all. He's one of Poseidon's offspring condemned to the loch for some infraction eons ago." A shock of her sunny red hair flopped over her brow as she shook her head. A grin spread across her face. "That's it. I'm officially on a mission to enlighten you about the goodness of human nature."

"You're welcome to try." He slanted a kiss across her smiling lips, probed them with his tongue.

She slid her arms around his neck, stretching up on her toes. Her breasts pressed to his chest stirred him. His cock jumped to life. Gathering her closer, he pressed the curve of her buttocks, increasing the contact between her hips and his. He didn't care if she'd become aware of the depth of his attraction to her. Or that the attraction he felt to her happened this fast, or was more powerful than anything he'd ever experienced. Days. They'd known each other only a handful of days, and already, he wanted more with her.

The fact was—he was enthralled by the feel of her body, the press of her lips, the glide of her tongue against his. He let go the residual negativity left by the accident, and the crowd's response. Sinking into the kiss with this gorgeous woman warmed his heart and soul.

He opened his lips on hers and stroked his tongue into the warm cave of her mouth. He backed up until his shoulders contacted the rough bark of a massive, old oak tree. Tightening his grip around her waist, he spun them in a half circle until he had her sandwiched between the tree and his body. The kiss deepened until it bordered on voracious. He was hungry for her in a way he hadn't been hungry for a woman in a long time. There was no denying he wanted this woman. In his arms...in his bed. In his life.

The touch of her fingers on his cheeks incited him. He dragged his lips from hers, then coasted them along her jaw. He buried his face in the hollow of her throat, laving his tongue on the erratically beating pulse he found there. He drew one hand up her ribcage, teasing the underside of her breast before claiming the orb.

Ah, God, it was a perfect fit. The taut nub of her nipple seared the flesh of his palm. He molded the warm mound, flexing his fingers as she moaned quietly in his ear. Working his thigh between her legs, he pressed up into the heat coming from her. What would she feel like surrounding his fingers, or his cock? He rocked against her, encouraging her to ride his thigh as he continued to massage her breast.

Knowing she was moved as physically as he was pushed him closer to an edge he shouldn't plummet over in public. His breath was ragged as he eased away. He leaned his forehead on hers, gazing into her bright eyes.

"I should apologize for getting carried away." Smoothing the strap of her top back into place, he rested his hand on the bare skin of her shoulder. "But I won't."

"I didn't mind." Her husky voice slid across his senses like a good twelve-year-old scotch, heady and filled with heat. To prove her point, she nibbled his lower lip like it was a delicacy.

He threaded his fingers into her hair and spun them again, until his back was against the rough bark, instead of her tender flesh. He spread his legs and she stepped between them, and then laid her head on his chest. His cell phone jiggled in his front pocket.

She started to laugh. "Hmmm, something's buzzing in your jeans. I've never encountered that reaction before." She eased away.

"Now I *am* sorry." He snagged the phone and examined the display. "Nia, I have to take this. It's from Hailey's sitter."

She gestured for him to go ahead, then stepped away to give him some privacy.

She dug in her purse as he answered. "Hi, Marilee."

"I hate to bother you, Thomas, but it's Hailey." Guilt riddled his elderly sitter's voice. "I had the television on and she saw some news reports of a bombing overseas and some other crazy stuff."

There was a reason Thomas had left the boob tube unplugged. Marilee must have really needed to see the news.

This was bad. He'd spent the last two years protecting her from reports of violence. Shoving away from the tree, he paced from one edge of the path to the other and back. It was a short, tight circuit. "How did that happen?"

"I was on the phone with my daughter. Thomas, I swear I thought she was in the kitchen, coloring. Poor little tike must have needed something, so she came to find me. I'm so sorry. She's mighty inconsolable right now."

"Put her on." Anxiety gripped his chest tightly and he sucked in a deep breath to alleviate it as he waited for his niece to come on.

"Uncle Thomas?" Hailey's voice was faint and frightened. "I'm scared. People are awful to each other. Are you okay?"

"I'm fine, munchkin." He moved to Nia's side. "What scared you?"

"The TV man said a bomb blew up somewhere. What if someone else's mommy and daddy got killed?" The kid's sniff told a huge story. She was crying.

Nia tipped her phone toward him, letting him scan the headlines she'd pulled up. She focused her glance on the moon, instead of looking at the phone's display. A frown puckered her brow and her lush lips were pressed together in a tight seam.

In addition to the bombing in Greece, there'd been a riot in London, and a mass murder in

Detroit. Throw in his experience with someone crazy enough to drive a truck into a crowd, and it seemed the world was destined for chaos.

Heart lurching sickeningly, he shoved calm into his voice in an attempt to ease his niece's fright. "Hailey, can you practice the deep breathing I taught you? Ask Marilee to help you. I have to take Nia home. I'll be there in fifteen minutes. Can you hold it together until I get there?"

"Hurry, please," she beseeched him, her sobs audible over the phone.

"I will, munchkin. I'll be there soon, don't you worry. I love you, kiddo. Deep breath in now. Let me talk to Marilee." He grabbed Nia's hand and tugged her along the path as he assured the sitter he was on his way home.

"I'm sorry this turned into such a dud of a date," he said to Nia as they raced from the waterfront. "When Hailey gets like this it's all hands on deck to soothe her."

"It's okay, really. Hailey needs you and she is your priority." Nia was nearly running to keep pace with him. "Thomas, you don't have to take me home. I can get a cab."

They'd reached the street where he'd parked the car. All the ambulances had cleared away, and other than a dark red stain on the pavement, no evidence remained of the accident. Thomas's heart sank further into his stomach. There'd been so much madness in the world today.

"Are you sure?" he asked.

"Go! Hailey needs you." She cupped her hand to his cheek.

Comfortable calm descended with her touch. It was as if he heard her urging him to get a grip for Hailey's sake. Her fingers settled the nervous energy jangling through him.

He pressed his hand over hers. "I really am sorry to end our date this way. I want to call you again, Nia."

"You'd better." Her smile was a thing of beauty in his frantic world. "Will you let me know how she's doing? If I can help in any way, you know I will."

Wrapping her in a tight embrace, he eased out a breath that ruffled her hair. How did she instill such serenity with just a touch? "It might be late before I get her settled."

"Doesn't matter. I'll take the call," she assured him.

Stretching up on her toes, she pressed a tender kiss to his mouth. The soft, swift brush of her lips blew away the last of his jittery, nervous feelings. He knew he wouldn't get to Hailey's side bursting with frustration and anxiety. Thanks to Nia's tranquil magic, he'd be able to deal with Hailey's fright without his own interfering.

He'd do anything he could to keep this woman

close by his side.

CHAPTER 10

As soon as the much calmer Thomas sped away to be with his niece, Nia dialed Polly's number.

Her sister answered on the third ring. "You've seen the news reports?"

"I wish I hadn't. Things are deteriorating more rapidly than I expected." Nia located a vacant bench on the square and moved toward it. "Have you heard about what happened at The Rowan tonight?"

"Yeah. Some crazy guy ran his truck into a bunch of pedestrians. Was that part of the challenge?"

"Probably. It happened right in front of me." Nia repressed a shudder as she sat on the edge of the park bench. Pulling the feathers she'd gathered from her back pocket, she studied them. "Mayhem was there as well. Damn bird is starting to molt. Clio noticed it as well, once she was into her challenge. Like the birds are shedding their avian trappings to become human again."

"We'll stop them."

Nia wished she felt as much confidence as she heard in Polly's voice. "I hope. I do know Thomas is definitely the man I'm supposed to face this challenge with. But his distrust of everything is insurmountable."

"Listen up, sister. Don't get defeated before you've barely begun."

"I won't. But how am I supposed to help him when I don't know where to start? I'm good. I embody the good in mankind, but I can't get him to see past whatever hurt scarred him and his niece. And the current state of events isn't helping."

"It will come to you, Nia. It will come."

After promising to meet Polly for coffee at the Daily Grind the next morning, they hung up. As she stowed the phone in her purse, squawking erupted over her head. Lifting her gaze, she located the source. The magpie cocked her head to the side and cackled. The sound was suspiciously close to laughter.

With a flutter of wings, and a rain of feathers, the bird zoomed from the branch, and flew across the square to light on a statue of Aphrodite that stood in the center of the magnificent fountain.

Jumping from the head of the statue, she landed on the shoulder of the man sitting on the railing. Pierus!

If he was appearing in public this way, he was riding a wave of confidence. He dressed to blend in…a navy sweater vest atop a white T-shirt, and skinny-cut, rust-colored trousers. A fedora sat at a rakish angle on his salt-and-pepper curls. A Greek god dressed like a hipster. What a douche.

His dark brown eyes were piercing as he studied her. Casually, he stood then saluted her. Nia wanted to salute him back, but she only had one finger to give to the effort. A satisfied grin stretched the man's craggy face as he turned. Moving through the gathered crowd, his laughter rang inside her head, right along Mayhem's insane cackling. Fright rose up her spine as she spied the black and white splotch the bird created on the sky.

As Pierus passed two men, a fistfight erupted. Next, he sauntered by two women who began arguing loudly and shoving each other. Mayhem landed on his shoulder again and Pierus's evil laugh echoed aloud this time. The disgusting pair moved past an outdoor café. A waiter dumped a pitcher of water over a patron.

Nia took a deep breath and drew on the spot in her center where her inspiration came from. The only hope for stopping the havoc Pierus and Mayhem left in their wake was to soothe the people in the square with a broadcast nudge. Her midsection heated as she summoned the energy necessary to calm the distress. Scrunching up her shoulders, she blew out a long breath, aiming it at the two fighting dudes. They immediately stopped throwing punches. But the others didn't stop. Something blocked her widespread nudge from being effective. Her head pounded and her heart jackhammered against her ribs with the effort she put into the nudge.

Pierus had found some way to cheat the system, like a dishonest accountant cooking the books.

Nia scurried toward the bickering women, waving her hand in front of them as she approached. Their expressions blanked, then filled with contrition. They immediately apologized and hugged it out. Nia continued after Pierus, making her way toward the restaurant patio. She squinted at the angry waiter and the dripping customer, jabbing them with an instruction to knock it off and make up. The waiter's look of horror told her she'd been successful, but the disgusted patron demanded to see the manager.

Nia opted to ignore the man's continued outburst, knowing some people were just jackholes, completely lacking in proper manners. That kind of person was beyond her ability to inspire to niceness.

She lost sight of Pierus in the crowd, but thankfully, no more violence occurred. He'd made his point. The bastard and his bitchy daughter had volleyed the first shot. But Nia swore she'd get the last one. The challenge was on.

* * *

Hailey hadn't calmed down one iota by the time Thomas arrived home. To make matters worse, Marilee had joined the weeping frenzy. The sight of the kind-hearted woman's red-rimmed eyes and tear stained face pained Thomas. But not nearly as much as the shadow of despair he recognized on his niece's face. It took a huge effort to contain the desire to join them. Crying never brought back the dead.

"I'm so sorry, Thomas. I wouldn't have interrupted your date for anything." Marilee squeezed her hands together, holding them against her ample bosom. She swiped under her eyes, disturbing the wrinkles there. "I just didn't think."

Hailey had launched herself into his arms the instant he walked through the door, and clung like a barnacle to his neck as he attempted to ease Marilee's guilt. "Please don't worry about it. It was bound to happen sometime. I'm only sorry it happened on your watch, and not mine."

Marilee laid a hand on Hailey's head as she prepared to leave. "I pray she'll get past this grief soon. Poor little—"

Hailey sobbed louder, drowning out the rest of the words. Her small body trembled as he held her tight against his chest. He eased his hand up and down her spine. "I'll talk to you tomorrow, Marilee." He stood in the open doorway, watching Marilee hurry across the street. As soon as she shut the door behind her, Thomas hustled through his house. The screen door smacked the wall behind it as he burst into the back yard.

Moving to the center of the lawn, he clutched Hailey to his chest as he plopped down on the grass. She wrapped her thin legs around his waist and held on, pouring out her grief and tears. He rocked back and forth, and softly sang her favorite nursery rhyme into her ear. After several minutes of repeating the refrain, Hailey finally calmed enough to release her strangle hold on his neck.

They both drew a deep breath.

"Better now?" he asked. His cheek and the neck of his shirt were damp.

Hailey hiccupped and nodded, her soft blond curls catching in the late evening stubble on his jaw.

"Okay if I put you down now?"

Her arms relaxed even further.

He patted her back. "We'll just lay out here in the yard for a while and talk to your mom and dad."

She nodded again and crawled off his lap.

Rolling to her back, she rubbed her eyes with her fists. She drew a shuddering breath as Thomas reclined next to her, and stretched out.

Above them, the new moon edged toward a half moon, and stars blinked, as if delivering a message meant just for them. The vastness of the night sky had always been calming. For both of them. Hailey put her hand in his, wrapping all of her fingers around his index finger.

"You want to start or should I?" he asked, turning his face toward her.

They'd developed a mechanism where they took turns talking to Doug and Cindy, telling them what was happening, what scared them, what they'd learned that day. Thomas took as much comfort from it as Hailey. Right now, though, he'd pay money for the instant calm Nia dispensed with just a light touch of her hand.

"I'll go." Hailey looked at him for a long instant, and then turned to look to the heavens. "Tonight I saw a lot of things on the television that upset me. There was a bombing like," her voice hitched, she squeezed his finger harder, but she forged on, "like the one you died in. It was scary. Why are people so hateful and dangerous?"

His gut churned as his niece asked the same question that had plagued him recently. He'd hate if his distrust in man's innate goodness had worn off on this little girl. Hiding his disillusionment from her should have been at the top of his list.

Jamming his other arm under his head he watched Hailey's profile, waiting to see if she'd continue.

Tears twinkled in the corner of her eye, but she rubbed them away with a sigh. "I tried to remember all the good things, like Uncle Thomas taught me. Like how much I like puppies, and ice cream. I didn't do a very good job."

"You did fine, munchkin." Thomas tucked her small body against his, slipping his arm under her until her head rested on his shoulder. Her breathing had slowed as calm blanketed both of them.

"Your turn." Hailey poked his belly.

He considered what he wanted to say to his brother and sister-in-law. He certainly couldn't voice his experience with the crazy accident he'd witnessed. Instead, he opted to share some about his time with Nia. "I had a date with the most amazing woman tonight."

"With Ms. Nia?"

He skimmed over the gory details and went for a redacted version of the truth. "Yep. We took a walk on the waterfront and talked a bunch."

"Did you kiss her?"

"Hey, I'm talking to your mom and dad. You should stop interrupting."

Hailey giggled. "Yeah, but did you?"

He'd lost himself in Nia's arms, in her kiss, in her delicious response to him. "Maybe."

"Will she be your wife? She could help me take care of you."

"Whoa there, Nellie. I said maybe."

"I'm Hailey, not Nellie." She giggled again. If he could keep the conversation light hearted, he might get some sleep tonight. Hailey's elbow dug into his ribs as she rose to look at him. "I wouldn't mind if she came to live with us."

"We barely know her."

"But we like her." Hailey crossed her legs tailor-style, resting her hands on her knees.

"What if she is secretly an alien, or some supernatural being? What if she can make us do things with her mind?" Like soothe his agitated state, or arouse him to painful hardness? He pushed the memory away. He sat up. "Like dance the funky chicken, or tell horrible jokes that make everyone groan."

"Her eyes are too pretty to make you do something silly like that."

The only thing Thomas knew for sure was if Nia had powers like that, and she directed him to take off all her clothes with his teeth, he'd do it in a heartbeat. He gave himself a mental shake. Swiveling until he faced Hailey, he tucked his feet up under his thighs, mimicking Hailey's posture. "She does have pretty eyes. And she is really nice.

Nia wanted to make sure you are okay. We were both really worried about you."

"Can we call her?" Hailey's eyes were hopeful. "We should let her know I'm all better now."

"Are you?"

Hailey chewed her lower lip and concentrated on his chest before answering. "I'm still a little scared. But I don't think I'll have a nightmare. Let's call Ms. Nia."

"You want to?" he asked.

"We should make sure she made it home okay, just like we do with Mrs. Marilee."

"Good point." And a great excuse, Thomas thought, as he dug the phone out of his pocket. His niece's smile was only slightly haunted now. The girl plucked blades of grass as they waited for the call to connect.

"Hello?" Nia's voice came clearly from the speaker.

"Hi. It's Thomas and Hailey. I was just telling Hailey about our walk on the riverfront." Hopefully, Nia would get the message that he hadn't shared the details of the accident they'd witnessed.

"Hi, Ms. Nia." Hailey stopped pulling the grass and stared at the phone he held between them.

"How are you feeling, Hailey?" Concern, shaded by compassion was clear in Nia's tone.

"I'm better. But I'm sorry I made Uncle Thomas come home from your date early."

"I don't mind, Hailey. I'm glad you're okay. I have to say I don't like the news either."

Thomas held his breath, his shoulders drawn up. If she were going to mention the hit and run, she'd do it now.

Thankfully, Hailey didn't give her a chance. The little imp gave him a triumphant smile and rushed on. "Ms. Nia, would you like to come to our house tomorrow for breakfast? Uncle Thomas makes really good French toast. I mean really, really good."

Her laugh was low and musical. "That's generous of you to offer. But—"

"Please say yes. Please." Hailey bent at the waist, extending her hand toward the phone, as if Nia could see her begging. "Uncle Thomas, tell her to come."

"Hang on, Nia," he instructed. He pinned Hailey with a hard stare. "How about you go get ready for bed and let me talk to Ms. Nia alone for a second."

Hailey's smile brightened the dim shadows of the back yard. "Okay! I'll see you tomorrow morning, Ms. Nia." She blew the phone a kiss then popped up. Thomas rocked back on his tailbone and drew up his knees as she skipped across the lawn, and then hopped up the steps to the house.

Once she was safely inside, he leaned his elbow on his knee and lowered his head into his free hand.

He groaned. "I'm so sorry about that."

Nia's laugh jingled from the phone. "I'm not."

Taking the phone off speaker, he pressed it to his ear. "You're not?"

"Not in the least. It was a charming invitation."

"Would you like to have breakfast with us?" Hope floated like a helium balloon.

"I believe I would. What time would you like me to come over for this stupendous French toast?"

"In an hour?"

An instant of silence happened at the other end of the phone. Followed by a short squeaky gasp. "An hour? You mean you'd like me to have breakfast with you in an hour, or sleep over and eat with you in the morning?"

He'd take whatever he could get, but his dick was certainly hoping for the latter. "Is the sleep-over option anything worth considering?"

"Definitely." Her voice was a seductive purr. "But what about Hailey?"

"If we're really quiet, she'll never have to know. She's already expecting to see you in the morning."

"Thomas," she began, but paused. He could almost hear her voice in his mind, telling him to be very certain this is what he wanted.

"Listen, I know we only just met, but we

witnessed some extreme shit tonight in front of The Rowan Tree. And your kiss…Lord, Nia. It spoke to me that we could be good together." Steady breathing was her only response. He rushed on. "I really want you here. We don't even have to…you know. We could just cuddle. Please say you'll come now and stay the night."

"If I come, we both know we won't be only cuddling." The promise in her voice stroked his libido and every fiber of his being stood at attention waiting for her next words. The breath she drew was audible over the phone. "I should probably wait until Hailey is asleep. When will that happen?"

Victory! He struggled to tame the erection pressing into his zipper and to keep jubilation from his voice. "Once I get her settled, she'll fall asleep fairly quickly. Give us ninety minutes just to be sure." He rattled off his address. "I'll leave the front door unlocked."

CHAPTER 11

Nia parked her dark blue Saturn Sky at the curb in front of Thomas's house. Her sisters had laughed at her for buying a car named after the planet. But it was an appropriate car for the Muse of Astronomy. Besides, she loved the sleek lines and powerful engine.

The house was located in an upscale neighborhood filled with stately homes, an abundance of trees and nicely manicured lawns. Small landscape lights illuminated the path from the drive and a post light burned next to the door. She climbed from her vehicle, and gently shut the door. The car alarm beeped softly as she locked it.

The chirp was answered by a horrific squawk. Instinctively ducking, Nia searched the branches of the tree in the neighbor's yard for the source. And, as expected, she found the large black and white bird on a low branch. Mayhem had come to call again.

She swooped off the limb and landed on the sidewalk ten feet from Nia. The bitch hopped forward, rather aggressively. Nia stomped her foot and waved her arms to scare the freaking chatterbox away. When the motion didn't have the desired effect, Nia pictured a lightning bolt in her mind and let it fly toward the bird. With a squawk and a spray of feathers, Mayhem took flight and disappeared into the night sky.

Nia jerked her T-shirt down, and then hiked her overnight bag higher on her shoulder. The moon's temporary position must be affecting her as much as the mortals around her. She must be crazy to be doing what she was about to do. She paused to search her memory for any time—in any of her lives—she'd hopped into a man's bed so rapidly.

But it didn't feel rushed. Just right. There had been time in past incarnations where she'd felt like she'd known someone forever. But it had never been the case of lovers or husbands. And after thousands of years of existence, there'd been plenty of those.

She'd been married thirty, no thirty-one times. And she'd loved each of her husbands. She'd never had children, unlike her sisters. Her head had been too much in the clouds to spare time for kids. But, then, she'd never really wanted any. It would be too difficult to see her children die at the end of their mortal lives. While she'd be reborn in the next generation, her children would be born mortal. Therefore, they wouldn't be reincarnated. Once dead, they'd remain dead.

The one bad thing about her life following the path of a mortal existence was that she was born with detailed memories of each lifetime. She remembered every husband and lover from past lives. She tried to avoid comparing the men, but sometimes, it happened. And right now, not having slept with Thomas, she had a massive sense of anticipation. Much more than in any other age.

The curtain in the large picture window flicked to the side. And Thomas appeared in the scant opening. The drapes floated closed, and ten seconds later, the front door opened, spilling soft yellow light and a shadow across the path. There was a halo around Thomas's torso, accentuating his broad shoulders, lean waist and narrow hips. His golden locks glinted in the reflected porch light, and the stubble on his cheeks winked with red highlights.

He leaned his weight onto one hip, tipping his head to the opposite side. "Are you going to wait for sunrise there, or would you like to come in?"

Her heart raced at the sight of his casual posture and rugged good looks. She started up the path toward him. "I'd love to come in." She paused in front of him and laid her hand on his chest. Beneath her palm, his heart galloped in time with hers.

Lowering his head, he hovered his lips over hers. "Thank you for coming over." The whisper of his breath painted her mouth with promise. He laid his hand over hers.

A halo of golden brown circled the edges of his green eyes. Flecks of gray winked in the depths in his irises. Nia lost herself in the dark blond lashes, gilded by the light reflected on the porch. Lifting her chin, she offered her lips.

Thomas claimed her mouth with a tender, searching kiss. His lips quested over her mouth as he laid his hand on her shoulder blade and drew her closer. Taking a step backward, he moved into the house without releasing her mouth. She followed willingly.

Reaching behind her, Thomas swung the door shut. He flinched when it banged closed, and pulled his lips away.

Resting a hand on her shoulder he pressed the other to her mouth, silencing her question. "Shh. Didn't mean for the door to slam. I'm afraid I might have woken Hailey." His body was tense as he cocked an ear toward the stairwell.

Nothing but silence competed with the rush of blood in Nia's ears. The noise likely hadn't reached the girl's room.

"Whew," he breathed a relieved sigh. Then refocused his attention on her.

The muscles of his chest shifted under her palms as he moved his hands behind her back. Rounding them over the curve of her buttocks, he drew her closer, until the hard ridge of his erection pressed into her belly. The pressure was divine. She wanted to climb him like a tree until she could wrap her legs around his waist.

She slid her arms around his neck, and speared her fingers into the hair curling over the collar of his shirt. Kissing him with eyes wide open, she was warmed by the fire in his gaze. He thrust his tongue deep within her mouth as the kiss turned hungry and searing.

Moving his hands behind her thighs, he lifted her and strode to the stairs. As he climbed, she locked her arms around his neck and her ankles behind his back, opening her center to him. His cock bumped into her with each step he climbed. At the top, he turned left, away from a slightly opened door, and moved stealthily across the landing and down the hallway.

When he entered his room, he pressed her body against the wall. The light switch dug into her back, but she barely noticed, given what was digging into her front. Clutching her hands to his head, she battled his tongue. Her body slipped sideways as Thomas reached for the door and eased it shut with a very quiet snick.

He righted their bodies, and rocked his hips into her. Nia moaned as his erection nudged toward her opening.

She wove her fingers through his hair and tugged. "Thomas, I want you."

He gasped. "Want you, too." Thomas gripped the hem of her shirt and pulled up, skimming his fingers over her ribs as he lifted the fabric.

The lightweight garment floated as he dropped it to the floor. Without taking his gaze from her body, he cupped her breasts and flicked his thumbs across her nipples. Delicious pressure built within her, making it difficult to draw a breath. Nia reached for the buttons on his shirt. Slipping each one from the hole, she spread the fabric wide, revealing thick red-gold hair on his chest. Holding her body in place with his hips, he helped by pulling the tails of the shirt from his jeans. Together, they slipped the fabric over his shoulders until it fell clear of his hands.

Thomas released the front clasp of her bra, exposing her breasts. He claimed one nipple, laving a circle around it before sucking it deeply between his lips. An answering tug built between her legs as a tingle of lust speared from his mouth to her belly. She sighed as he moved to the other breast, giving it equal attention. Jerking her hips forward, she opened more to him.

She wiggled her hand between their bodies and stroked her palm over his erection.

He groaned, grabbed her wrist, and stilled her motion. "You'll undo me." His husky voice wrapped around her senses, an urge she couldn't resist.

Raining kisses along his cheeks and jaw, she begged. "Take me to bed, Thomas."

Lifting her away from the wall, he slid his hands under her butt then strode beyond a small seating area to the king-sized bed, where the covers had already been turned down. When he lowered her to the mattress, it felt like being dropped onto a cloud. Rising up, she shrugged the bra from her shoulders, and then tossed it over the edge.

Thomas licked his lips and watched her, his hard-on straining the front of his jeans. Oh, goddess, she wanted to see what was behind his fly. To egg him on, she braced her feet wide on the bed and let her knees fall to the side, exposing her very core to his gaze. She cupped one of her breasts and lifted, offering herself to him.

"Nia, you are stunning." His smile was slow and wicked as he reached for her waistband. "But I need to see more."

He flicked open the button on her jeans, and lowered the zipper. Before jerking them downward, he spread his hand over her belly, slipped it into the opening and curved his fingers over her mound. Damp heat and zipping shivers rushed between her legs in answer to the fiery brand of his hand. She squirmed as he dragged his fingers over her panties. His brow furrowed as he concentrated on rubbing her clit, then sliding his fingertips along her slit. Light flared behind her eyes with each stroke of his fingers. She arched her head back on the bed and rode the sensation as he massaged her.

"Thomas, please. It's not enough."

He pressed his mouth to her belly and licked into her navel. "No, it isn't," he mumbled against her flesh.

Pulling his hand out of her pants, he wound his fingers into her panties and jeans and tugged down. Nia lifted her hips to help. The bottoms got tangled with the sandals she still wore. He chuckled softly as he worked the first shoe free, then pulled the fabric from her leg. While he struggled with the clasp on the second shoe, Nia ran her naked foot along the bare flesh of his chest. The crisp and springy hair tickled her toes. He finally pulled her other leg free and flung the jeans and shoe to the ground.

Grasping her ankles, he jerked her hips to the edge of the bed. Her legs slid over his shoulders as he dropped to his knees between them. Softly stroking his fingers over her folds, he dipped the tip of one inside her. She angled her hips, begging for more. When she tangled her hands into his hair, he pressed his mouth against her and lapped her with his tongue. Her entire body quivered as he laved and sucked, tenderly nipping her clit. He slipped a finger inside her, setting a rhythm that spoke to her soul. Sensation, hot and erotic, built within her as he added a second finger, then twisted to stroke upward, pushing her toward a precipice with his mouth and hands.

Color burst behind her eyes as a squeak built in her lungs. She bit her lip to keep from crying out as every single neuron in her body fired with pleasure. Thomas continued to lick and nibble, not slowing the motion of his fingers as her muscles squeezed, and tensed. Tears leaked from the corner of her eyes as he finally stilled between her legs. Her inner thighs burned from the stubble on his cheeks, but she didn't care. He kissed away the sting and pulled his fingers from her body. Slipping his hands behind her legs, he gently lifted them, and then placed her feet on the bed. She scooted backward on the mattress, her knees still open and welcoming. He popped the snap on his jeans and carefully lowered the zipper. Hooking his hands under the waistband, he shoved the jeans and boxer-briefs down his legs. His erection bobbed proudly against his body as he freed it. A drop of come beaded atop the broad head, the shaft wide and hard as steel.

She licked her lips, knowing where he was planning to put that.

He stepped free of the pool of material at his feet. Twisting at the waist, he reached toward the bedside table.

"Wait." She stopped him and braced herself on the pillows behind her. "I'm on birth control. And I'm clean. We don't need a condom. Unless you want to."

Heat flared in his eyes, deepening the color to intense turquoise. His chest rose with a raspy indrawn breath. "I'm clean as well. Are you sure?"

"Very sure." She sent him a large grin, and a tiny mental command to join her on the bed.

She needn't have expended that energy. His gaze was eager and incendiary as he climbed onto the bed between her legs. He pressed her back to the mattress and settled, his shaft probing her entryway. Sliding up, the hair on his chest rubbed against her breasts. The skin of his taut belly pressed hotly into hers.

Reaching between their bodies, he guided his tip into her opening. "Nia, you feel so good." He rocked his hips, seating himself further inside her.

His girth filled her as he rode completely home. Their bodies fit together perfectly, his hard to her soft. She arched her back and lowered her hands to his butt, pulling him closer as he moved within her. Setting a slow, easy pace, each go-for-broke stroke took a lifetime but passed in a blink of sensation. Tension built once more, as feeling and light filled her as much as he did. Pulling away, he slid back home again, and again, crooning words into her ears, against her cheeks.

Nia locked her ankles behind his back, and sprinkled kisses along his neck and collarbone. He gasped when her lips closed around his flat nipple. She nipped, then tongued away the sting. His breath shortened along with his stroke, until he pounded ravenously into her. Shoving a hand between them, he pressed a finger against the sensitive nub at the top of her folds, the friction insatiable, undeniable. Pressure climbed until she was so close to the edge. The tension translated to his body. His quiet groans jelled with her moans, until they sang an age-old song of breath and desire together.

"So damn good, baby. So fucking right," he whispered into her ear. "Let go, come with me."

Color flared in her brain as electricity crackled along her spine. An orgasm, as glittery as the heavens, flashed over her. She soared on a sky of sensation as he groaned his own release into her ear. They were so damn right together.

Thomas collapsed on her, his weight warm and welcome. She kept her legs wrapped around his waist and teased the ends of his silky hair with her fingers as they drifted on a sensual sea of feeling. His shaft continued to throb, hot and hard, within her sheath.

He struggled to his elbows, his hips digging into her as he rose slightly above her. She immediately missed the contact between his upper body and hers. She tweaked the hair on his chest, then circled his flat nipple. He groaned and rocked his pelvis in response.

He smiled into her eyes. "I was right." His tone was gloating and filled with humor. He pressed a kiss to the corner of her mouth.

"About what?"

"We're good together." He nibbled the edge of her jaw as he lifted off her. Rolling to his back, he pulled her along with him, until she was tucked against his body, her head on his chest. Thomas's heart beat strongly under her cheek. Sighing, she nestled into his warmth.

Resting one hand on her head, he stroked his fingertips of his other one along her arm. "We didn't move too fast, did we? I'm sorry if you felt rushed."

She lifted her head and gazed into his eyes. "Don't know if you noticed, but I was doing an awful lot of begging. So if any rushing was being done, it was by me. And trust me, this is so far from my usual style, no one I know would recognize me. Well, except maybe Aerie."

"Ari? Who is he?"

"He's a she, and one of my sisters. Out of all of them, she'd be the one to think I'm capable of falling into bed with a man I barely know."

He pressed her head to his chest again, and snugged both arms around her. "How many sisters do you have?"

"Ah, trying to get to know me better, huh?"

Laughter rumbled around his chest. "Better late than never."

"Okay, I'll play." She sat up next to him. Too bad she couldn't tell him her entire story yet. When the time was right, she'd have to reveal herself as a Muse to him. But that time wasn't right this instant.

Her breasts brushed against his groin as she reached over him to snag the sheet and pull it up. His cock jumped to life again. Amusement colored her voice when she mock-scolded him. "Down, boy. We're just talking here." She shifted until her legs lay over his hips.

"Can't help it. Parts of my anatomy have minds of their own."

She dragged the comforter around her shoulders, suddenly shy in his presence. Scooting up against the pillows, Thomas tucked the sheet around his hips, covering his lap. He laid his hand on her knee and fixed a serious look on his face.

She swept a hand down his cheek, pausing to run her thumb over his lips. "To answer your question, I have eight sisters."

His brow jerked up. "Eight? God, bathroom time must have been difficult to schedule while you were growing up. Are you close in age?"

"My oldest sister is thirty-six. The youngest, the twins, are twenty-four."

"And you're…"

"Twenty-seven." More like eight-thousand and twenty-seven. But he'd never understand that.

"Do you get together often?"

"Weekly. We all live in Delphi. It's always been home." In this lifetime. She'd actually lived all over the world. "In fact, I'm meeting Polly, my next oldest sibling, for coffee tomorrow." She glanced at the clock. "Today. After a fabulous breakfast of French toast."

He twisted his head to look at the digital time display. He dragged his hand down his face, the stubble on his chin rasping pleasantly. "I didn't realize how late it was."

"You mean early," she teased.

His teeth flashed white in his smile. "Are all your sisters as good natured as you?"

"Calliope, the oldest, has embraced the bitchy side of her nature. The force is dark within her."

Thomas laughed as he tackled her backward onto the bed, pressing her into the mattress. His hot, hard body covered hers and he slanted a kiss across her lips. "I'm more of a Star Trek kind of guy. I like to think of myself as cool and analytical, like Spock."

"False. You are way more Kirk than Spock. New Kirk, not the old guy."

"You think?" He captured her lower lip between his teeth and tugged. The bed creaked quietly as he worked his thigh between her legs and pressed up. His erection poked into her hip, demonstrating his eagerness.

"Oh, yes," she breathed. She closed her eyes and let sensation flow over her body until it lodged between her legs. Raising one knee, she draped her leg over his, twisting to face him, opening to his desire for her again. "An incurable flirt."

His lips closed over hers and he took them both deeper into the kiss with his demanding tongue. He rolled on top of her and slid home within her body, making her forget all about her sisters, magpies and the challenge she faced in the very near future.

CHAPTER 12

Thomas and Nia rolled out of bed at half past six and grabbed a shower in his spa-like master bath together. Waking with her curled in his arms had been blissful. Being with Nia in the steamy, glass-enclosed space was better than heaven. But when he would have started playing, she'd thrown a washcloth at his head and reminded him she wasn't actually supposed to be here until a little later. Thomas finished the shower in a pouty mood and semi-aroused. Soaping her back without venturing around her front was truly the hardest thing he'd done recently.

As they crept past Hailey's door, he heard the girl's quiet snores. She hadn't woken all night long. Given her state when he'd put her to bed last night, he'd half expected her to wake screaming. But, thankfully, the screams never came.

When they reached the bottom of the steps, Nia patted her overnight bag. "I'm going to put this in my car. I'll ring the bell when I come back," she whispered, glancing back up the stairs toward Hailey's door. "Although that feels sneaky and underhanded."

"I know. I'm sorry. If it's any consolation, you wear sneaky very well." He pressed a kiss to her smiling lips. The idea crossed his mind that he wouldn't mind waking up to her smile every day for the rest of his life.

He released her. The lock on the door clicked when he disengaged it. The door squeaked when he swung it open, and he cast a nervous stare upstairs. Nia scooted through the opening, and Thomas watched the seductive sway of her hips as she hurried toward the car she'd parked on the drive. The cobalt blue vehicle gleamed in the light of the rising sun. The sexy, sleek lines of the car suited Nia.

Thomas's neighborhood was coming to life. The man who lived next door exited his house. As he approached the street, Thomas noted the guy had the bottom of his sweat pants tucked into his socks. Hailey called the guy Mr. Socks, although his name was Johnson.

A jogger he didn't recognize progressed slowly down the street. Birds chirped in the trees and the bushes. The neighbor up the street let his dog out into the yard and the retriever barked loudly. All in all, it was just another day in the 'hood. But knowing Nia was having breakfast with him and his niece, that he'd woken next to her warm body…life just felt different somehow. More hopeful.

Nia used exaggerated caution as she stowed her bag then eased the door closed. She aimed the fob at the car and it chirped prettily. Her grin rivaled the rising sun as she walked back toward the house. An odd look crossed her face as she paused at the end of the path. A large black and white bird cawed at her from the branches of a tree while Nia stood still as a sentinel.

The jogger ran past the end of Thomas's driveway and slowed to a walk, staring at Nia. Even though she stood a good twenty paces from him, Thomas heard her whisper to the man to leave her the hell alone.

Concerned, Thomas moved out to the porch. "Do you know him?"

"No," she stated flatly, glancing briefly over her shoulder at him.

"You sure? I swear you just told him to leave you alone."

Confusion flitted over her beautiful face. "You're clairaudient?"

"If you mean I can hear what you're thinking, that's not likely." Thomas shrugged and watched the man pick up speed as he jogged away. "Are you sure you don't know him?"

"Um...I don't really. I think he's a business acquaintance of my father's." She turned back to track the man's progress down the street.

A shrill whistle pierced the morning quiet. A bird swooped from the tree, diving straight at Nia.

Thomas caught himself ducking on Nia's behalf. She pursed her lips and looked like she blew the bird a kiss. She started when she turned and caught him staring at her from the doorway. The red in her cheeks matched her coppery curls in the early morning sunlight.

He cocked his head and sent her a questioning look. Pitching his voice low, he asked, "Are you okay?"

"Stupid birds. Such disgusting scavengers." She moved up the steps toward him.

"You seem to draw them. That's the second one I've seen with you."

With a grin on her face but shadows in her eyes, she pressed the doorbell, as if she'd just arrived.

"Nice touch." He grabbed her hand and pressed it to his lips, suppressing a smile. He raised his voice and made a production out of greeting her. "Good morning, Nia. Thanks for coming for breakfast. Hailey isn't awake yet but you're right on time." He tugged her across the threshold and wrapped her in a bear hug. Her shoulders shook with laughter.

Releasing her, Thomas stepped back and waved her across the large open space toward the kitchen. He followed, pausing at the foot of the stairs. "Hailey!" he shouted. "Ms. Nia is here. Wake up, sleepy head."

"You want me to run up and wake her?" Nia asked.

He put a foot on the first step. "I'd better do it. You could start the coffee, if you want. Everything you need is on the counter."

"I'll take that deal." Nia continued on to the kitchen.

As Thomas climbed the steps to Hailey's room, he wondered what Nia would make of the pale green walls and dark quartz counters in the spacious kitchen. The room definitely had a manly feel to it, down to the steel gray pans hanging from the pot rack over the stove and the black farmhouse sink. No bowls of lemons, no cute little knick-knacks on the counter. For him, it was just a streamlined room in which he'd learned to cook. Couldn't let his niece starve, so building on the basic bachelor diet of frozen pizza and Chinese take-out had been a necessity.

He pushed open the door to Hailey's room and found her yawning and stretching. He jiggled her toes as he passed the bed. "Morning, munchkin.

Our breakfast guest is here. Time to get up." He snapped off the brightly colored lamp on the bookshelf, then crossed to the window and opened her blinds.

"Ms. Nia is here already?"

"Yep. I let you sleep late this morning." Her yawns were contagious and he barely managed to suppress one of his own. Not that he regretted the reason he'd lost sleep last night. Quite the opposite.

"Can I go down to breakfast in my pajamas?" Her green eyes were round as she looked at him hopefully.

"Better put some clothes on. As soon as breakfast is done, I have to run you to your dance lesson. You'll head from there straight to the Kiddie Campus and I'll go to work."

"You won't *go* to work. You'll come home and work in your office here," Hailey corrected him. The child was as cute as a bug, but took everything literally.

"Fine, I'll come back here to go to work. Happy now?" He bent over and tucked his shoulder into her mid-section, then straightened, lifting her squiggling body in the air.

She squealed a high-pitched laugh as he toted her down the hall to the bathroom. "Put me down! I have to pee."

"As you command." He dropped her to her feet on the plush rug in front of the sink. "Wash up, get dressed, and then come down. I'm going to start the French toast."

Hailey grasped his arm, stopping his departure from the room. "Be sure to use cinnamon. No plain toast, okay?"

He huffed out a breath. "Fine. Fancy French toast for everyone this morning."

Her giggles followed him as he trotted down to the kitchen. The aroma of brewing coffee filled the air as he walked through the doorway. "Good, you found everything."

She turned from looking out the window into the back yard and gave him a slow smile. "Right where you said it would be."

Moving across the room, he rested his hands on the counter on either side of her body. He leaned in and possessed her velvety soft lips with a searing, stolen kiss. He shifted and held her cheeks between his hands and kissed his way over her mouth, and her jaw, and her brow, until he'd kissed every part of her face. She rested her palms on his chest, and stared into his eyes as he pulled back. Her smile was gentle.

Little footsteps pounded down the stairs. Thomas jumped away from Nia. He reached for a pan from the hanging rack as Hailey skittered into the room.

The girl skidded to a stop in front of Nia. "Good morning, Ms. Nia." Good, she'd put on her company manners along with the stretchy leggings and T-shirt. She wore two different colored socks on her feet.

"Good morning, Hailey. Thanks again for inviting me to breakfast."

"Uncle Thomas told me you didn't get to eat dinner last night on account of my being upset. I wanted to make it up to you." Hailey patted Nia's arms, as if to soothe her.

Thomas noted Nia tucking her hands to hidden pockets on her skirt. It bothered him a little that she seemed to shy away from contact with his niece. Based on his own experience, Nia was a tactile person. His body still throbbed with the memory of her hands exploring every inch of him. Upon viewing the engaging grin she offered Hailey, he shrugged the thought away.

Eyes alight with curiosity and a gentle smile on her face, Nia asked, "Are you feeling better this morning?"

Aside from the non-contact thing, Thomas knew Nia had a genuine interest in whether Hailey had recovered from her meltdown the night before.

"Yes, thank you," Hailey replied, putting her hands behind her back and stepping a respectful distance away from Nia. But judging by the expression on her face, it didn't bother Hailey that Nia didn't seem inclined to coddle her.

"Then I don't mind missing dinner with your

uncle at all." Nia shot him a sultry look then rubbed her belly. "But I've been looking forward to breakfast with you."

Hailey opened the dishwasher and pulled out a clean cup, then handed it to Nia. "For your coffee. Do you need cream or sugar?" His little Hailey...the consummate hostess. "Uncle Thomas takes his manly."

Coughing a little, Nia covered her mouth, as if to hide a laugh. "I guess I drink mine manly as well."

Thomas cracked an egg and dumped it into the bowl with a half dozen others. He splashed in milk then whipped the contents with a whisk, the wire clattering against the ceramic bowl. The coffee maker beeped, signaling the brewing was complete.

Hailey plucked a bottle from a slide-out drawer next to the stove and handed it to him. "I told Uncle Thomas to be sure to add cinnamon and vanilla. The toast is yummier that way."

After pouring rich, dark coffee into her mug, Nia grabbed another cup from the open shelf over the machine. She poured Thomas a steaming portion, and then handed it to him. Heat shot up his arms at the brush of her fingers as he accepted the coffee. Her eyes flared wide, signaling him that she'd felt it as well. The pleasant warmth lodged under his solar plexus, heating him in a most erotic way. Willing his dick to calm down, he walked past her to place the griddle on the gas burner. The stove clicked as he ignited a flame of a different sort.

Tipping her head to the side, Nia asked Hailey a question. "Is that his secret recipe?"

"Sillyhead. If I told you it wouldn't be secret anymore. Then you could make your own and you'd never come here again to eat breakfast with us." Hailey opened a drawer, and then retrieved silverware. "This way, Uncle Thomas has to make magic happen in the kitchen for you."

Dull heat flushed into his face. He was pretty sure he'd already done that for Nia. Although the magic they'd made hadn't been in this exact room. But if she were interested he'd be willing to experiment. Fighting to control his body's reaction, he stored the idea in the deepest recesses of his mind.

He caught Hailey's eye. "Munchkin, remember, we've discussed this. There is no such thing as magic. It's all illusion."

"Oh pooh, Unk." Hailey clapped her hands together. "You have to believe in the power of abracadabra."

"Wait a second. Are you telling me Uncle Thomas is a, a…a disbeliever?" Nia's eyebrows rose on her forehead as she teased. "Say it isn't so."

"If you can't see it, or touch it, it isn't real."

Thomas's tone was matter-of-fact flat. He dropped a piece of soaked bread onto the griddle, where it sizzled. "Okay, that sounds over-the-top skeptical. But it would take a ton of effort to convince me something is magical. Like, if you could produce a unicorn, for example." He smiled at Nia then continued. "But you can't, so I declare them totally made up. And, therefore, not in the least bit magical."

"I had a unicorn as a pet once." Nia squinted at him as she lifted plates from a glass-fronted cabinet, her gaze intense. She turned away, mumbling under her breath about showing him, and proceeded to set plates on the counter where they'd eat.

"You did?" Hailey's voice rose.

Suddenly, an image popped into his mind of a graceful horse-like creature with a long mane and a shiny metallic horn protruding from its forehead. A large brown spot that looked like the British Isles appeared on the center of the animal's whitish back.

"Let me guess. This unicorn had a coppery horn and a splotch on its fur in the shape of England." Thomas teased, but as he uttered the words, the image took firmer hold on his imagination.

"Exactly. My pet's name was Amyntas, but I called him Tassie for short." She looked at Hailey as she spoke, and then lifted her eyes to him, as if daring him to dispute what she said. When he remained silent, she continued. "I loved Tassie so much. He was the best pet ever. Never had to clean up after him and," she lowered her voice, "he pooped ice cream."

Hailey giggled, then outright belly-laughed at Nia's silly statement as she laid forks on one side of the massive kitchen island where they'd eat. Thomas couldn't keep the grin from his face at the child's sweet laughter. So very different from last night's desolate tears. When she finished, still giggling, she slid into the fan-back barstool on one end of the oversize island.

Nia joined in the laughter, as though it was a big joke on Thomas. She arranged their cups on the pale yellow placemats, and then dropped onto a chair next to Hailey. But as he scooped a piece of toast from the pan to a plate, another image, one of Nia riding the unicorn in a field of wildflowers, popped into the forefront of his brain. An entrancing picture.

He set a plate loaded with fragrant toast in front of Nia and then sat next to her, shaking his head. "You know, I almost believe you could have had such a pet. I get such a clear picture of you as a child riding a unicorn."

Nia smirked. "Is it possible there *is* magic in your imagination? Maybe you believe in magical inspiration after all."

"Or, I believe you can tell a wonderful made-up story to make me laugh," he countered.

Propping her elbow on the quartz surface in front of her, Nia presented her back to him as she spoke to Hailey. "Young lady, we have our work cut out for us to make him believe."

Thomas trailed his fingers along her spine, from a spot just south of her shoulder blades, to the curve of her waist. All out of sight of Hailey's young eyes. He believed Nia was magic, charming and enchanting both him and Hailey.

"We most certainly do," Hailey said around a mouthful of French toast. She chewed, swallowed and smiled around Nia to him. "But his food is magical."

Nia forked up a bite. Closed her eyes as she chewed. After she swallowed, she pinned him with a simmering glance and moaned quietly, reminding him of their time in his bedroom. "Yes, it certainly is. And so is he."

CHAPTER 13

Nia couldn't believe how much she enjoyed breakfast with Hailey and Thomas. How easily they'd welcomed her into their little family. For the first time in all her lives, she could actually see accepting a child as a daughter.

And that scared the crap out of her.

She'd be a fool to allow an attachment to the girl. A daughter she'd remember and sorely miss in each successive lifetime. And most especially now, when they all faced an uncertain future. If she failed her challenge, all their worlds would be forever changed. And a failure by her would spell doom for all her sisters. The world would devolve into a colorless shell of its current Technicolor state. A tragic, censored existence for mortals…dictated by Pierus and enforced by his daughters. Nine hideous women bent on revenge.

Even after an incredibly bewitching night spent in his arms, Thomas had proven resistant to her inspirations to embrace magic. So far. But she was just getting started. Hinting at her first beloved pet, Tassie, had been divine. But he'd stubbornly refused to accept the idea that unicorns had actually lived at one point. Sure, they'd been rare, and restricted as pets to the gods, but they *had* been real. In his heart, Thomas had accepted the visions of Tassie Nia had sent. He'd described the animal with the exact detail of the image she'd planted.

Unfortunately, his analytical, doubtful mind discounted the possibility. And what was she to do about that?

She took her coffee, and a cup for Polly, to the Muses' favorite table by the window to wait for her sister. The Daily Grind was in the center of one of the blocks comprising Delphi Square. Currently, the regular Wednesday morning farmer's market was happening. Tables and tents of fresh flowers and produce dotted the area around the fountain. Pedestrians meandered across the grassy areas and the cobblestone paths. Something about the scene didn't look right to Nia, but she struggled to determine what was wrong, or missing.

Polly tapped the window by Nia's head, distracting her from the oddity she couldn't define. A gust of warm air caressed Nia's skin as the door opened, then banged shut behind her sibling.

"You ordered for me. You're a good friend, little sister." Polly lifted the cup and slurped down a mouthful. She raised her brows and fanned her hand in front of her mouth. "Hot!"

Nia laughed. "Next time, I'll have them cook it in the sink." It was an old joke from a childhood three lifetimes ago. But it brought a smile to Polly's pretty face.

Polly tucked a strand of her straight, strawberry blond hair behind her ear. Her look turned serious. "Have you been following the news this morning?"

Guilt riddled Nia like holes in Swiss cheese. "I've been busy this morning. Haven't had the news on at all." Tuning into the news of mayhem this morning would have been rude, and probably would have induced more hysteria from Hailey. Especially if the reports were as bad as she suspected, based on Polly's frown. "What have I missed?"

"A not-so-peaceful demonstration in Detroit, a dockside melee in London where the offenders slashed and cut longshoremen on the legs and arms." Polly shuddered. "And my least favorite, a bomb threat at the Eiffel Tower, which created a stampede of tourists from the area. That sent fifty people to local hospitals."

"I saw Pierus this morning. He was jogging

past Thomas's house with Mayhem trailing along. He saw me there as well."

"You've already been over to Thomas's place today? Good on you!"

"Really? You skipped over me seeing Pierus this morning and made the leap to me getting cozy with the man?"

"In the end, when we defeat that asswipe, you and Thomas fooling around is going to be more important. Unless I've misread the situation."

Her sister spoke a truth Nia desperately wanted to believe. She could envision a future with Thomas. If the Fates allowed. "Actually, when I arrived last night Mayhem was already there. Polly, I'm not sure I can inspire him to ask the *what if* question. He's so blasted skeptical."

"Have you told him what you are yet?"

"No. And even if I did, I'm not sure he'd believe me. He hosts a TV program called *Doubting Thomas*. He has a massive broadcast and online following for a reason." Nia toyed with the thick paper jacket on her cup.

"So was it magical in the bedroom?" Polly teased. But she couldn't mask the concern in her voice.

"Oh, that part was magical. But he's stubbornly clinging to his scientific certainty that if he can't see it, or touch it, magic doesn't exist. To top it off, he's clairaudient. He 'hears' my nudges."

"Huh? I've never run across that before. But remember what we learned from Clio's experience. The man we are meant to be with is affected differently by our nudges than other mortals. Maybe Thomas's gift of being privy to your thoughts is because you actually speak them aloud."

"No human ear should be able to hear what I'm saying."

"Girl, I don't know why you can't just silently release your inspiration. The rest of us handle it that way. Shit, I don't even have to look at who I'm inspiring now. You've always had to voice it." Her sister shook her head. They'd had this argument before. "You might have to take your chances and confess to being a Muse to him."

Nia shrugged and trained her gaze on the people on the square. The visual she couldn't quite interpret disturbed her on a visceral level. She gestured to the street scene. "Polly, what's wrong with this picture?"

"Changing the subject won't make the matter go away."

"I know. But really, something I can't pinpoint is wrong in the square. I don't like it."

Polly focused her glance out the window. She straightened in her chair and propped her elbows on the table. "Upon initial visual inspection, I see nothing out of the ordinary." She began inventorying the scene, the way a good investigative reporter catalogs facts. "People milling about. Exchanging currency for product. All very matter of fact. Honestly, Nia, I don't see anything wrong with the scene."

Like the sun slipping behind a cloud, a shroud of impending doom settled around Nia's shoulders. Tension climbed her spine with slithery determination. "Something is definitely off."

Both sisters leaned forward and fell silent as they studied the scene outside the window.

"No one is smiling." Polly exclaimed. "Not one single person."

"And no one is interacting beyond the basic business transactions…no one is talking. Their faces are devoid of expression." She jabbed a finger toward a group of women clustered in the florist tent. There were four women, and not a single one uttered a word. Nia moved to the edge of her chair and laid a hand on Polly's arm. "They should be laughing and talking. But it's like they don't even realize they are part of a group."

"You're right. It's like they are under a spell." Polly's eyes went wide and frantic when she pivoted her head back toward Nia. "Like someone has control of them."

Nia glanced around at the patrons in the coffee shop. Although six other tables were occupied, she and Polly were the only individuals speaking to each other. Everyone else, even the barista behind the counter, appeared frozen. A frisson of oily, dark energy coursed through her body, alerting her to the fact that all hell was about to break loose.

The door to the shop burst open, admitting a harried-looking man with dark blond hair, cut in a military high-and-tight style. The man made nightclub bouncers look scrawny. A white, button-down shirt stretched across his barrel chest. His jeans looked painted on to his legs, which were the size of cannons.

Surveying the room, the newcomer appeared to be looking for someone. When he spied Nia and Polly, he dashed toward them.

He skidded to a stop at their table. "There you are. Things are about to get ugly."

"Who are you?" Nia demanded, cringing away from the guy's outstretched hand.

He flipped his wrist, so it appeared he wanted to shake. "I'm Ken Hillerman. Zeus sent me."

Leaping out of her chair, Nia grabbed her purse from the floor. Wrapping her fingers around Polly's wrist, she dragged her from her chair.

"What the hell, Nia?' Polly jerked her arm, trying to free herself.

"Ken is my partisan. If he says go, we have to." Nia didn't release her grip. "Don't you feel it?" How could she not? Nia felt like she was suffocating under the mantle of repulsive pressure.

"Oh, goddess! It's like something, or someone, has taken control of the atmosphere. Like gravity is all wrong." Polly shuddered in revulsion. The negative energy in the room must have registered on the same visceral level Nia experienced.

The feeling was certainly magnified by the fact the moon was out of place. Even now, while the moon was on the far side of the world and in the middle of the morning. "Dammit. The world is going off kilter faster than I thought. We are barely at the half moon phase."

Around them, people began to rise from their seats. Ken swore in ancient Greek, then switched to English. "Damn! We're going to have to take a stand here."

"What do we do?" Polly asked as she turned toward the interior of the shop.

Every single person in the room stared at the three of them. Malevolence stamped the features of the angry group of patrons.

Ken positioned himself behind the pair, which Nia found odd, since he was meant to be her protector. Shouldn't he be in front?

When he laid a hand on her shoulder, burning energy flared in her ribcage, jolting her energy force, swelling her power. Instinct and the words he projected into her brain told her of his plan. Two men from the table across the room began to advance toward them.

Nia laced her fingers between Polly's. She put her mouth close to her sister's ear and whispered. "There are so many people we'll have to combine our powers to calm them."

Polly nodded and firmed her grip around Nia's hand. "You lead, I'll follow."

Ken flexed his grip on her shoulder and she felt him widening his stance, as though bracing for the attack. Nia sucked in a deep breath and focused her thoughts.

Pale, rose-colored light from Polly's aura filled Nia's vision, mingling with her own sky-colored aura, becoming a light lavender haze within the shop. Cobalt from Ken's aura tinted the edges of the mist. Polly's inspirational force ballooned in Nia's chest. Nia broadened the scope of their mingled power by imagining a funnel with the narrow end situated in the middle of her forehead.

Casting her glance around the room, Nia mumbled a nudge toward the occupants. "You should be drinking your coffee and talking." She released the image of positive force flowing from her forehead and disseminated it over the mortals in the room.

The noise level immediately returned to what she'd expect in a busy coffee house mid-morning. A few individuals remained focused on the trio by the window, and Nia blasted them with direct thoughts to go about their business. Confusion poured over the last few faces, eyes blinking rapidly, and heads swiveling, as if checking to see where they were.

Ken dropped his hands to his hips. "Well done."

When the last of the patrons returned to their seats and their conversations, Nia tugged Polly toward the exit. "We've got to get out there and settle the market crowd before chaos erupts."

They burst through the door into an abnormally still world. The birds sitting atop the statue of Aphrodite didn't emit a single chirp. Even the tree leaves trembling in the summer breeze were eerily silent.

"You want to explain what's going on here?" Ken prodded when he fell into place with the sisters. His dark blond brows were drawn together in a tight line on his forehead. His clever green eyes flashed intensely in the slanting morning sunlight.

"I'm not sure. There's definitely something more than just the failing gravity of the moon at play here. It has to be Pierus." Her words sounded oddly loud, as if she'd uttered them in a vacuum. "I'll get started. Polly, call the other girls and get them here. There's too much area and too many people for just you and I. We'll need reinforcements. Tell them to come in cloaked."

Polly nodded and took a step away to send out a telepathic SOS. Ken laid his hand on Nia's shoulder again, and she felt a surge of energy at the point of contact. Nia waited a second for the sharp, supernatural thump of Polly's alert to quit banging around her brain. The instant the reverberation eased, Nia focused her thoughts on the farmer's market.

Heat flared in her chest as Ken pushed energy through his hand into her. Creating a mental image of a siphon, Nia drew more of Ken's life force into her body, stopping short of draining his strength to empty. Then she aimed their combined vitality at the uneasy crowd before them.

She started at the left, and swept her gaze to the right, diffusing a message of calm to the mortals mingling between the stalls and booths. She felt a curious drain on her own energy as she continued to send the message. Her shoulders slumped forward and she locked her knees to keep from falling.

"Polly! Help me!"

"They'll be here soon." Polly laid her hand at the base of Nia's neck.

The instant Polly's power joined with Nia's, energy billowed within her. Pressure built within her chest as one by one, her other sisters appeared, cloaked in multicolored mists. As each sister arrived, another hand was laid on Nia's body, channeling power through her. Under the conjoined strength of the ten of them together, she straightened. Sweeping her gaze from side to side, Nia trumpeted a message of peace and calm.

The entire effort took less than a minute, but felt like a lifetime to Nia. Once the crowded market returned to normal, Nia crashed to her knees, drained and spent. Her head throbbed again as a message from Zeus arrived. They were all to report to Olympus immediately.

"Someone is going to have to help me." Nia's voice came out shaky and weak. She cleared her throat and dug within for the vigor to journey to the corporate office. "I don't think I can manage the Hollow by myself."

Strong arms wrapped around her shoulders, urging her upright. Ken steadied her on her feet. "I've got you."

The sunlight behind him created a halo in his dark blond curls. Nia gave him a limp smile. "Don't know why, but I pictured you with dark hair. And not quite so muscular."

"Sorry. Partisans only come in shades of blond. Has something to do with our Norse origins."

Summoning words required more energy than she dared expend at the moment. She simply nodded. Around her, the mists of the Muses' presence dissipated, one, by one, until just Ken and Polly were left.

"Ready to go?" Ken narrowed his eyes as he examined her face. "Polly, we might need a little illusion here. I don't think Nia is up to the task of managing a screen and the transport. Can you cloak us?"

Polly stepped closer to place her hand between Nia's shoulders, then touched her other hand to Ken's arm. Warmth and pressure wrapped around Nia as Polly created a mask to keep their sudden disappearance a secret from the pedestrians around them. As Polly projected the illusion of vacant space where they stood, the crowd went about their business, talking, laughing, and bartering.

A vacuum built around the three of them as they moved into the Hollow. Their bodies lost substance and converted to straight light and energy. Vibrant rose glowed in the center of Polly's aura, while orange, a color that complemented Nia's own aura, burned in the center of the bright cobalt glow of Ken's body. The rush of their life forces pumped like blood through arteries—a steady, thumping rhythm.

Nia glanced down at her void form and realized the pinpoints of white light that typically dotted her aura were significantly dulled and pulsed weakly. The battle to calm the crowd in the market had depleted her more than she'd realized.

The Olympus boardroom solidified as they reached their destination in the void. She hovered above the ground for an instant. Her feet crashed to the floor, and her back teeth clacked together painfully as she made a less-than-graceful landing. Except for the heat in her cheeks over the abrupt nature of her arrival, her body frosted, as if she'd spent ten minutes in a meat locker without a coat.

Teeth chattering, she stumbled forward to brace her hands on the gigantic conference table and lowered her forehead to the surface. Ken positioned a chair behind her and urged her into it while Polly rubbed her hands along Nia's arms. The friction and gentle heat from Polly's movement made inroads to the frigidity that had claimed Nia after she'd expended a huge amount of her energy in the market. Pinpricks of power and heat speared her body as each of her sisters infused her with portions of their power.

Across the table from her, Zeus and Mars whispered together. Zeus pinned her with a concerned glance. Summoning her will, Nia lifted a thumb his direction, hoping to convince him all was good. Atlas was on his cellphone in the corner. As her sisters claimed chairs around the table, Gaia materialized, holding a fluffy, sage green blanket between her hands. She hurried to Nia's side and draped the warmed fabric over her shoulders. Shooing Polly away, Gaia claimed the chair to her right, while Ken dropped onto the seat on Nia's left. He scrubbed his hand over his face, wiping away the fatigued expression, then turned his attention to Zeus and Mars.

As soon as this meeting was over, she was going home to take a long nap. When she woke up, she'd concentrate on what it was going to take to save the world.

CHAPTER 14

It irritated Nia to no end when Zeus pulled rank and insisted Ken stay at Nia's house, instead of in a cottage at the Athenian. Of course, Nia hadn't helped matters by refusing to leave the comfort of her home to make a temporary move to the resort. Zeus wanted her protected and nothing would stop him from keeping her safe. At least he hadn't insisted on moving in himself.

Only, having a houseguest, even one as handsome as Ken, was going to cramp her style with Thomas. She'd have to find a way to deal.

The meeting in the Olympus boardroom had been tense. While Nia had regenerated her energy, Polly had recounted the incident in the square with terse precision. During the lengthy session, Gaia had left her hand on Nia's shoulder and gently pulsed energy into Nia's depleted stores. The sensation had swayed her body, as if gliding in a rocking chair. Or moving easily with a lover on a downy soft bed.

Three hours ago, on the return trip to Delphi through the Hollow, Nia was pleased to note her starry aura had revived. Waving off Ken's apologies for her new living arrangements, Nia retreated to the master bedroom and fell into bed.

Shortly before dinner, Nia plodded toward the kitchen, drawn by a rich, savory aroma. She paused in the doorway, amazed to see Ken bustling about, wearing an apron over his white shirt and jeans. He looked downright domestic, and not in the least like a badass protector. Zeke, Clio's partisan, slouched in a chair at the table, his hand wrapped around Nia's favorite coffee mug.

"Ah, you're up." Ken shot her a grin. "Just in time. The beef stew is ready."

"Well, my timing is perfect." She cocked her head to the side as she inspected the messy countertops. "Not a tidy cook, I see."

Dull red flushed into Ken's cheeks. "I'll clean it, I promise."

Yes, you will.

Nia's stomach rumbled as she crossed the room. The meal he'd prepared, including the yeasty dinner rolls still steaming on the plate, smelled delicious. "No worries. I'm just surprised I had the ingredients for this. Are those rolls made from scratch?"

"Yep. And you didn't have everything. I had to send Zeke to the grocery."

"And why aren't you out protecting my sister?" she asked Zeke as she drew a glass from the cupboard.

"Jax has the day off, so he's shadowing her. Zeus requested that I lend Ken a hand and help him get settled here."

Requested? More like ordered, Nia was certain. If she'd thought having one hunky houseguest was going to hinder her growing relationship with Thomas, two would be a nightmare. While Ken filled bowls with stew, Nia twisted the tap to fill her glass with water.

Shaking her head, she edged back to the table and slid onto a seat. "So do I need to make a room ready for you, too?"

"Nah. Ken's a pro. He doesn't need my help."

Setting a pottery bowl on the table in front of her, Ken sought to assure Nia. "You know this is temporary, right? When your challenge is over I'll remain in Delphi, but it won't be necessary for me to live with you. Zeus's insistence that I live here is just his way of being protective." The tight smile Ken sent her did little to assuage her worry. "He said he'd drop by later to check on you."

And that helped even less. The last thing she needed was her dad being overprotective.

Nia stirred her spoon in the chunky stew. "I'm curious. How could you be my protector but live in a different city? How does that work?"

Ken broke a roll open, then grabbed a knife to slather butter on it. "We don't have to be in close proximity to do our job. We have a special link to our charges, so we always know what they are doing. We can be at your side in an instant, if needed."

"You have a window into our lives? Every waking, sleeping, er…not sleeping moment?"

The knife Ken had been using clattered to the plate. Bright red flashed up his neck. "It's not like that. It's not an open window. Shit. It's not even a window. More like a sense. We aren't voyeuristic, if that's what you're worried about."

Indignation swirled around Nia's chest. "Well, wouldn't you be worried? Would you want me peeking over your shoulder all the time?"

Zeke laughed. "Ken, you're really fucking this up. Allow me."

"Go for it, dude." The tips of Ken's ears had gone scarlet.

"Did you ever play operator as a kid, Nia?" Zeke asked.

"That game with two tin cans and a string?"

"Exactly. You're the can on one end and Ken is on the other. The string between you only transmits emotions like fright or pain. We *never* receive flashes of an intimate nature. We only activate when you are in danger or distressed. And we can be at your side in the instant it takes to travel the Hollow."

"Oh." It was a slight comfort to know they didn't know all her secrets.

"Like that time in the seventies, when you were in the car accident. I was the motorist who stopped and helped you until the ambulance arrived." Ken spooned up a bite of stew.

"That was you?" She remembered the accident had been bad. She'd hit a patch ice and slid into a ditch. The front end of her car crumpled and her leg had been trapped under the dashboard. "You look different."

"Our features change in each lifetime. It's a safety measure to keep you Muses from recognizing us."

"So now that Clio and I know you two, can you come back the same in the next life?"

Zeke shook his head. "Probably not. You'll know we're around, but you won't know who we are unless you need us. The difference will be that if you do, you'll recognize us as your partisan when we do show up."

Curiosity got the better of her. "Will that make your job easier?"

"Not necessarily."

Now that her interest had been piqued, the

questions kept coming. "Are you generally employed in the same field as the Muse you watch over?"

"Not always. The Q and A portion of the program is over now, Nia." Ken pressed his lips together, his brows drawn together. "Zeus is already upset that you girls know about our existence. If we spill all our secrets, we can be replaced." His phone pinged and he plucked it off the table. His lips moved as he read the alert.

Contrite, Nia said, "Oops. Sorry. Wouldn't want to cause anyone to lose their jobs."

Zeke grunted. "As long as Pierus is around, no protector is in danger of being unemployed." He swiped his napkin over his lips, then wadded it and tossed it on the table. "So what's your plan to win the challenge, Nia?"

Doubt crushed her chest like a massive boulder. "I don't know."

"You'll need a plan soon." Ken spun his phone so she could see what had distracted him.

A NOAA alert that tides around the world had altered had launched the media into a frenzy. Dismay dragged up her spine with chilled fingers as she read the sensational reports. A meteorologist from the Royal Observatory in Edinburgh had theorized that last week's coronal burst had modified the sun's positioning on its axis. Must be a slow news day elsewhere if weather claimed the front and center spot.

The scientist's theory was solid, but pointed at the wrong orb. Nia rubbed her neck, hoping to ease the sudden tension that came with reading the alert. She wanted to nudge the bastard in Scotland to instruct him to stop sprouting his doom-saying ideas. Too bad her gifts would be greatly diminished by the sheer distance.

"This would be easier if the fix required nothing more than Atlas rehanging the moon in the correct spot," she groused. The whiny, petulant timbre of her voice annoyed even her. She deserved the scowl Ken tossed at her across the table. She sighed and then straightened her spine. "Ken, would you like to take a trip to Helios with me tomorrow?"

"Certainly." His tone mimicked Curly of the Three Stooges. Those bumbling oafs would never have amounted to anything without Thalia's inspiration in the Twenties. Ken stacked their empty bowls. Carrying them to the sink, he glanced over his shoulder. "I'm sure all hell is breaking loose there without you."

She hadn't checked her phone since she'd returned from the board meeting. Glancing toward the little planning desk in the corner of her kitchen, she was startled to discover her purse was not in the normal spot.

Her brows needled together uncomfortably as

she tried to recall the last time she'd seen it. "Damn. I left my stuff in the boardroom," she fretted. "I'll need my ID badge to get into the observatory tomorrow."

Zeke patted her arm. "I'll go grab it while Ken cleans. You still look tired. You should head back to bed."

Smoothing a hand over her wrinkled cotton blouse, Nia protested, "I worked hard this morning."

"The work will just get harder going forward. Rest." Pressure built in the room as he prepared to shift into the Hollow. His features faded as his body became a mass of dark blue light, then blinked out, leaving his chair empty.

Nia muttered to herself as she bustled toward her bathroom. Zeke was right about one thing. She was tired. Every molecule of her screamed in agony with each step, each breath. The places where her sisters and Ken had touched her to bolster her strength stung and burned. Only time would heal those injuries. After a good night's sleep they could go pick up her car and drive to Helios, like normal mortals.

* * *

Sleep had descended as soon as her head hit the pillow, but it hadn't been restful. Her dreams were filled with images of riots, and people being maimed. One particularly haunting image was of hundreds of frightening, partially molted magpies with human eyes spread over telephone wires, fences and playground equipment. It was like a scene from an Alfred Hitchcock movie. Nia had pulled the blankets over her head after that one, calling out for Morpheus to aid her. But still she'd gotten no relief.

Bracing her hands on the vanity the next morning, she peered at herself in the mirror. Goddess, she looked a hot mess. The dark circles ringing her eyes had nothing to do with losing sleep in Thomas's arms the night before. Those she could handle. But her raccoon appearance came from pushing dangerously close to the edge after the night spent with the very sexy man. At least it seemed her reserve energy was back to normal. And most of the aches in her back and shoulders had diminished.

With a grimace, she reached for her comb and gave herself a pep talk. It wouldn't do to show up for work looking as though she'd been through the wringer. Or just crawled out of bed to do the walk of shame.

Standing under a cascade of hot water from her rain head shower, she considered a variety of plans to encourage Thomas to travel back toward the light of magic. She needed to shove her doubts to the background where they belonged. While she didn't doubt magic — she knew it existed, she was living proof—she distrusted her ability to convince a man of the truths behind myths and legends when he made a living disproving them. She'd not been able to convince the druids about placement of the monoliths that told the seasons. The world had been stuck with leap year ever since.

Thomas's belief was the door she needed to open. But dammit! She needed more time with him to locate the lock. Right now, the key was buried so deeply, it might as well be on the moon. Hmmm, maybe she should arrange a trip to the moon for him. She quickly discarded the idea. It was hard enough for her to go. Taking him along was a logistical nightmare. Mortals didn't breathe the way gods did.

When she left the bathroom she heard Ken talking. Either he was on the phone, or Zeke had returned again this morning. She padded down the hall to her bedroom to change her clothes.

Ten minutes later, she ventured back into the kitchen. Ken was alone, and scrolling through the newsfeed on his phone, a cup of coffee cooling on the table in front of him. Her purse was on the floor under the desk, so Zeke had returned at some point.

Ken definitely looked at home. Although she'd rather it was Thomas sitting there. Damn, the man dominated her thoughts. If this was how she reacted after one night with him, imagine what a lifetime might bring. She couldn't afford to let her growing feelings for the man distract her from the challenge.

As soon as she entered, Ken looked up and smiled. "You look better."

"Feel better. Do I have time for breakfast?"

"Yeah. Want me to fix it?"

"Nope. Just going to have an orange."

Ken wagged his finger like a displeased governess. "You need protein for strength right now."

Raising her brow at him, she reached into the refrigerator and grabbed a container of yogurt, and the orange. "Yes, mother. Did you sleep okay in the spare room?" She hadn't had many guests in this house, so she hoped the bed was suitable.

"Not really. You kept muttering in your sleep."

"You heard that?"

"Comes under the heading of distressed, which I'm attuned to, so yeah, I heard."

While she ate, Ken focused on his phone, grunting occasionally, reading the headlines to her. Mayhem must have been tired from causing all the ruckus yesterday. Things seemed pretty quiet around the world. Anxiety soured the taste of yogurt on her tongue. It sucked waiting for the next wave of turmoil Pierus had planned.

When she'd finished off the last section of her orange, Ken stood, pocketing his phone. "Ready?"

"I left my car at the square. We'll have to go there first."

"No worries. Once we are done at Helios, you can drive me to the Athenian. I need to pack a bag if I'm staying here until after the full moon. I'll need my car, too."

"I'm sorry, I should have thought about that before insisting on coming here first."

"Girl, you were hell-bound on getting a nap. Not that I blame you. You're my priority. My shit will always come second to what you need." He grinned as he placed a hand on her shoulder. "You'll do well to remember it."

Her back twinged uncomfortably when she stood. She washed and dried her hands at the sink. She trudged across the room to retrieve her purse. Once it was in hand, Ken moved into place behind her.

Pressure tightened the air around her chest as the real world dissolved into the Hollow. Ken's vibrant cobalt aura flashed into her field of vision. Her own lighter sky-colored aura blended with his as they metaphysically moved from her kitchen to downtown Delphi. The light changed as Ken set them down in an alley around the corner from the square. Brows furrowed, he kept their presence cloaked until they determined the area was clear of mortals. As their bodies solidified again, the cloaking dropped like a blanket falling to the ground. Strolling casually, they exited the dank, narrow alleyway and headed toward her car. Ken's gaze swept the street, while Nia focused on the treetops. She doubted Mayhem would have wandered far away from the scene of their little skirmish yesterday. Relief trickled through her heart when she didn't spy the magpie anywhere near her.

Nia dug in her purse for her keys as they approached her car.

Ken whistled his appreciation. "Sweet ride, Nia. Can I drive?" His tone held a hint of gear-head hope.

"Is chauffeur part of the protector service?"

"Nope. I just always wanted to drive one of these."

She underhand-tossed the keys to him. "I'll navigate."

"I knew I'd won the partisan lottery!" The car chirped as he unlocked it.

"Hang on. You guys switch your charges around for each of our lifetimes?"

"We used to. It added another layer to the secrecy each time. But eventually, we kind of all fell to protecting the same Muse existence after existence." Ken slid into the driver's seat and sighed. The engine growled to life, then purred like a well-fed cat.

Fastening her seat belt, Nia shook her head.

"Have you always been a Ken? Because I'm fighting the urge to say 'Drive on, James.'"

Ken's laugh was swift and infectious. "Our names change in each existence, but I haven't been a James. Not yet anyway. But if the job comes with perks like this car, maybe I will be in my next lifetime."

"Okay, then." Nia chuckled along with him. "Take me to Helios, Ken-James. My presence is needed."

CHAPTER 15

After Nia introduced her new houseguest to Bradley, Barry and the other techs in the observatory, she excused herself, instructing Ken to find her when he was ready.

She left him in Bradley's capable hands and hustled to her office down the hall. The constant ping on her phone was a sure clue her email was exploding with messages from around the world. The Helios Institute was a go-to source of information for astronomical sites as well as some scientific and tabloid journalists. When something as big as tidal shifts occurred, Nia would naturally be the first person many people sought out for the facts.

Ken eventually joined her in her office, placing a paper cup of fragrant, and direly necessary, coffee in front of her. He spun the guest chair around, straddled it, and rested one arm along the back. After frowning at the muddle of papers scattered across the surface of her desk, he pulled a printed lunar chart toward him. Resting his chin on his arm, he studied the complex detail on the page. One good thing about having a partisan who was MIT trained in meteorology was he'd understand every word and line on the chart.

Nia replayed the video from the coronal burst last week as he read. Putting a hand to her neck, she rubbed hard at the knot that had formed while she'd been talking to the director at the Royal Observatory in Scotland. She'd failed to convince him the calculations were wrong and that there was no problem with the sun's axis.

"I wonder how much Mnemosyne would be able to make people forget if she did a broadcast memory wipe?" The goddess of memory was on call for the duration of the challenge. She'd be a good option for removing the most important information. Like the little detail of a celestial body out of place.

"A world-wide broadcast? Has it ever been done?"

"Not to my knowledge. But this Royal scientist's theory is troubling."

"Got a little tension there?" Ken pointed to her shoulders.

She tipped her chin from side-to-side, hoping

for relief. "Yeah. I'm debating how much relief I'd get by travelling to Scotland and gagging this buffoon. He doesn't seem to understand, even though I've sent him doctored data."

"Why would you alter the data?"

The question prickled painfully along her already taut neck. "If we can keep a lid on the moon's new orbit until we fix it, no one will have to know how close the world is to the edge of reason. Better for us gods and goddesses, don't you think?"

Ken shrugged. "Devil's advocate here…the general population discovers you've known but didn't reveal how the world was essentially going to hell. How are they going to take it?"

"Not good." She rolled her shoulders instead of shrugging. "I've got to figure this out. What will make Thomas believe?"

Ken stood. Skirting around her desk, he stopped behind her chair. His hands warmed her tight muscles as soon as he laid them on her shoulders. "Maybe some kind of demonstration. What do you think his biggest hang up is?" He dug his fingers into the knots on her shoulders.

She dropped her head forward, squeezed her eyes closed and moaned. "Goddess, maybe you should give him a massage. Your hands are magic."

Chuckling, Ken swirled his thumbs in circles. "My hands are *infused* with magic. But I doubt that will work for Thomas."

"That's the problem with pairing with a man whose popular television show is called *Doubting Thomas*."

"I can see where that would be an issue." He stilled his hands on her back.

"Hey, keep rubbing. It helps me think."

Ken thumped the heel of his hand down her spine. Sunlight streaming in from her office window flickered over her closed eyelids.

She rounded her back. "Pierus predicted that if I fail, an innocent life would be lost. This person's destiny is to help someone bring aid to the poorest people. What if that person is Thomas's niece, Hailey? She's his world. If anything happened to her he'd never recover."

"We need to figure that out. Maybe the Fates could read Hailey's line. We could ask Lachesis. She spins the length of everyone's life. Makes sense to have her check on Hailey's life span."

"Seems like the challenge would negate all her hard work. Doesn't matter how long the Fates spun Hailey's lifeline. All bets are off if Pierus wins."

"Well, shit! Didn't think about that." Ken sighed. "Another problem we need to address is the identity of Pierus's silent partner."

He shoved his fingers under her hair and massaged her scalp. Tension began to melt faster, in spite of their somber conversation.

Continuing, Ken speculated. "For Clio he enlisted the weather gods to distract her. For you, it's the lunacy unleashed by the alteration in the moon. Can't concentrate on leading Thomas to the big *what if* question when your power is constantly being drained to stamp out these anarchistic fires that keep popping up."

"Could it be Cratus?" She twisted to look over her shoulder at Ken.

He cupped the back of her head and urged it straight again. Keeping his hands moving on her scalp, he mused aloud. "The god of power and strength? Could be. If he is partnered with Pierus that could explain how that dick with ears was able to hold Zeus in thrall when he was present at your meeting at the Athenian. I think I'll ask Mars to do a little digging into that."

She closed her eyes and gave herself over to the pleasure of ease his fingers provided. "I love you, Ken. You're one of the good ones."

His breath tickled her cheek when he bent and whispered into her ear. "Damn straight."

She chuckled, then moaned as he jabbed his thumbs into her neck.

"Oh, good. You're here."

Nia's eyes flashed open when she recognized the voice coming from her doorway.

The smile faded from his face and Thomas narrowed his eyes as he spied Ken. The thin set of his lips spoke volumes about his displeasure in finding Nia with Ken bent over her back, his hands on her head.

A muscle throbbed in his jaw. His brows drew together in a deep, angry vee. "Am I interrupting something?"

CHAPTER 16

Frustration and anger burned through Thomas the instant he entered the office. Why the fuck did some other man have his hands on Nia? The look of pleasure on her face reminded him of their time together the other night. When he'd moved inside her. Emotion blasted through him, a blazing, green-hued monster. It startled him to realize he was jealous.

"Thomas!" Her eyes widened and she sent him a sexy smile. "I wasn't expecting you."

The jackass with his hands on Nia didn't stop massaging her. Teeth grinding together painfully, Thomas curled his hands into fists. "The show is on hiatus for six weeks so I had time. Thought I'd stop by and surprise you." He flicked his glance to the big bruiser behind her, then back to Nia. "Surprise."

Nia knocked the guy's hands away as she stood. Crossing the room, she approached him. She rested a hand on his arm and rose on her toes.

The press of her satiny lips to his in greeting made inroads to the anger and distrust that had claimed him when he first entered the office. He encircled her waist and returned the kiss with a fervor the other man couldn't mistake. He marked Nia as his own and hated himself for feeling like he needed to stake that claim.

When Nia eased away from him, he stopped her backward motion by locking his hands together at the small of her back. "I'm sorry if I'm interrupting important work."

She searched his face, a tiny frown marring the perfection of her brow. "Let me introduce you." Grasping his wrists, she pulled out of his embrace. Holding one hand, she tugged him toward her cluttered desk. A whimsical picture on the wall behind the desk depicted a man hanging stars in the heavens.

"Thomas, I'd like you to meet an old friend and colleague, Ken Hillerman. I know him from NASA, but now he's moving to town to accept a job in research and development." She swept a hand toward the blond hulk. Ken extended his arm in greeting, a gesture that reminded Thomas of gladiators. Nia continued the introduction. "Ken, this is Thomas Wilde."

"Thomas Wilde of *Doubting Thomas*? I knew you looked familiar. Love your show." Ken pumped Thomas's arm vigorously. "Pleasure to meet you."

Nia rolled her eyes at Ken's enthusiasm and gave her head an almost imperceptible shake. Thomas distinctly heard her tell the big dope to cool it, even though her lips hadn't moved. Ken moved a pace backward, hands at his side, palms out, as if conceding something. A snarky grin spread across his face.

Perplexed, Thomas watched the byplay between them. He directed his gaze back to Nia. "I was hoping to get a word with you." He shot a glance toward Ken. "Alone."

"Oh, sure." She smiled brightly at the other man. "Ken, can you give us the room? Bradley should still be in the observatory if you want to check in with him." She jerked her head toward the door.

"Yeah, sure. I was just leaving. It's really an honor to meet you, Thomas. Hope to see you around." Ken strode across the room. The door clicked shut behind him.

In silence, Nia strolled around her desk and took a seat. Thomas followed her, and rested his butt on the edge of the desk. Crossing his arms, he squirmed into a more comfortable position. The tip of his shoe connected with her chair as he swung his leg.

Amusement lit her eyes as he studied her gorgeous face. Too busy the other night losing himself in her body, he hadn't noticed the dark navy ring around the iris of her eyes. The effect was accentuated as a sunbeam leaked in through the blinds.

Cupping her cheek, he leaned forward and pressed his lips to hers. "I didn't get to kiss you good morning today," he whispered into her mouth.

Her lips curved in a smile. She laid her hand on his knee. "No, you didn't. My loss, I think."

Easing away from her, Thomas covered her hand, holding her in place. The heat from her palm scored a direct hit on his groin. Predictably, his dick filled. The heavy, eager weight pressed against the fabric of his jeans. Taking a deep breath, he willed it to cease and desist. "I'm sorry, but I have to ask…who is that guy?"

Confusion flitted over her face. "I told you. He's a co-worker."

"I mean, who is he to you? The pair of you looked pretty chummy when I walked in." His chest tightened uncomfortably. Thomas couldn't remember the last time he'd felt so insecure about a woman's feelings. This thing between them had simply become too freaking important in his life in far too short a span of time. "I'm pretty sure I heard you tell him you love him."

"Thomas, I've known Ken a very long time. But we never have been, nor will we ever be anything more than friends. He's not the man for me." Her eyes sparkled like stars as she gave his knee a reassuring squeeze.

"I don't...I don't know why this was so important to me. But it was. Is." He leaned forward, cupped her cheek and reclaimed her lips.

She opened to him, easing her tongue into his mouth. Tasting of coffee, smelling of lemons and thyme. Wrapping his fingers around her nape, he increased the pressure of his lips and fenced with her tongue, a dominant parry for each of her delicate ripostes. She uncrossed her legs and leaned into him. The skin of her bare knee was cool and satiny beneath his palm. As the kiss deepened, he slid his hand along her thigh, reaching under the hem of her short skirt. He curled his fingers over her inner thigh and squeezed.

Her lips curved against his and she whispered, "Did you lose something?"

Trailing his mouth over her jaw, he nuzzled his way down her neck as he slipped his fingers closer to the apex of her thighs. "I think I've found heaven." He nipped her neck, delighted when she shivered. "Is this okay? In your office I mean."

Nodding, she drew away to look at him. "Probably should lock the door."

Withdrawing his hand from under her skirt, he made sure to stroke his fingertips over her soft flesh on the way. Standing with a stiffy in his pants required a tremendous amount of concentration. The walk to her office door was uncomfortable, but the sound of the lock clicking home made the journey worthwhile. Twisting the cord on the blinds covering the door, he shut the world out.

On the return trip across the room, her gaze followed him, dipping low to his belt buckle then flashing back up. She'd laid her hand on her heart, and he found her pose endearing and seductive.

He spun her chair to the side, and then kneeled in front of her. He gently spread her legs, and as he possessed her mouth once more, he slid his right hand back under her skirt. His shaft jumped as his fingers brushed against the damp silk of her panties. Desire swelled in his chest when she moaned as he pressed the tip of his middle finger against her opening.

She clasped his head and opened her mouth wider, sucking his tongue farther inside. As he pressed closer between her legs, her skirt bunched higher on her thighs. Wiggling his other hand beneath her fine ass, he angled her pelvis, exposing her center.

Hooking his fingers under the lace between her legs, he eased it to the side. The timbre of her sigh was musical as he stroked along her folds. He flicked her clit, delighted to capture her answering moan between his lips. Thrusting his tongue deep in her mouth, he mimicked the movement with his finger. Gasping, she tore her lips from his and arched her neck. Her hips rocked in time with his hand and her juices melted into his palm. She was fucking hot, and passionate...quivering like a leaf in the breeze.

Her breath shortened and his pulse kicked up to match her quiet panting. Twisting his hand, he slipped another finger inside. She shuddered when he touched her in the most sensitive area — her g-spot. As he thumbed the taut nub at the top of her folds, her body tightened and clamped down on his fingers.

Blood sang in his veins, rushed in his ears and pulsed heavily in his shaft. The pressure of his zipper on his dick edged past painful to excruciating. Kneeling on the uncomfortable floor should have distracted him from the plight of his blue balls, but it didn't. It was bliss to watch Nia dance on the rim of rapture, her mouth open on a moan, her eyes squeezed tightly shut, her hands cupping her breasts as he worked his fingers farther inside.

He buried his face in her belly, releasing the groan that had built in his throat as he worked her to a finish. She arched as she reached her orgasm, a quiet cry hissing through her lips.

Thomas turned his head and panted to ease himself away from the precipice, controlling the demand of his body to join her fall into paradise. Her heart thundered under his cheek. She ran her fingers through his hair, toying with the ends as she slumped back into the chair. A long, satisfied sigh slipped between her lips as he wiggled his fingers in her sheath.

Sitting upright, she grasped his bicep and urged his arm back. His fingers slipped from her body, slick and warm from her orgasm. Reaching for the buttons on his jeans, she seemed determine to return the favor.

Her cellphone chimed with an ominous strain of music. It was a selection he recognized from Holst's *The Planets*. Nia paused, her fingers on his waistband, and dropped her head to his shoulder.

"Bloody hell!" She huffed out a breath, and then lifted her face to his. Apology and anger flickered in her gaze. The phone rang again. "I'm so sorry, I need to take this call."

Fighting his grimace, he sat back on his heels and gestured to the phone on her desk. "Go for it."

She mouthed sorry again as she swiped her finger over the screen to answer the call. "Hi, Mar…er, Martin. What can I do for you?"

Unintelligible words flowed from the phone. While Nia listened, her eyes narrowed.

Thomas pushed to his feet. Stepping to the side

to give her as much privacy as possible in the small office, he grabbed a tissue from the desk and handed it to her, before grabbing one for himself. After he wiped his hands, he turned his back and adjusted the raging hard-on aching in his jeans. From the cloud gathering on Nia's face, it didn't look like relief would be forthcoming with her.

"Where?" she asked. The sexed-up color that had risen in her cheeks leeched away as she listened, leaving her ashen. "I'll be there as soon as I can."

Thomas turned around, and balanced his ass on the window ledge. The pressure in his dick had finally lessened enough that the position was only moderately uncomfortable. "Anything I can help with?"

The phone clutched to her chest, and biting her lip, she shook her head. "Not right now." She massaged her temple. "I might ask later, but for now, I have to put out a little fire."

While she talked, Thomas heard her call out for her friend, Ken. How the hell had he heard that? And why the hell was she calling for some other man after what he'd just done to her? Dark jealousy sat in his stomach like a python's most recent meal. He shook his head, brushing the thought away. She hadn't said anything like Ken's name.

"If you want to go…"

She rose from her chair, carefully placing the phone on the desk. With a sultry pout and the sexiest sway in her hips, she moved toward him. "I don't want to go. I *have* to go." She draped her arms around his neck, brushing his chest with her breasts. Her lips were gentle and persuasive as she kissed him.

"Would you be interested in making it up to me later?" He ran his hands down her spine until they rested on the small of her back. He pressed, bringing her hips in contact with his still present erection.

Heat flared in her eyes. "Oh, yes." She bit her lip again. He wanted to soothe the sting with his tongue. She sighed. "But what about Hailey?"

"As luck would have it, the Campfire Scouts are actually camping out tonight. I'm back to baching it."

"Then most assuredly yes." Her quicksilver smile warmed him from head to toe. She stepped out of his arms. "I have to go. I really am sorry we got interrupted. But tonight will be so much better because I'll have time to think of lots of great ways to make it up to you."

She walked him to the door. The window rattled when she tried to open it. With a tiny laugh, she unlocked it, then pressed her mouth to his in a deep, soul-searing kiss. Her lips clung to his for a moment before she pulled away. She swung the door open, and then playfully patted his ass as she scooted him out the door.

The window glass rattled again as she closed it behind him, drowning out his footfalls on the marble floor.

Shoving a hand in his pocket, he strolled down the hall, already looking forward to tonight.

CHAPTER 17

The urgent errand that had called her from Thomas's arms was a need to address a labor dispute in Belarus. Mars had joined her and Ken at the site of a peaceful demonstration that escalated to violence with supernatural speed. They'd all agreed that Pierus or his silent partner had stirred emotions and forced the altercation. Mars still hadn't uncovered which god or goddess might be aiding from the background. Or why.

In the shadow of a dreary industrial backdrop, the rank-and-file had physically engaged management, and the brawl had gotten out of hand. Barely more than a blip on the media radar, but quick intervention was needed to avoid serious injury or loss of life.

With Mars's and Ken's assistance, she'd drawn

power from the sun to temporarily redirect the moon's gravity. Spreading calm over the men and women involved in the melee had been hard work indeed. But with Mars's hand on one shoulder and Ken's on the other, Nia had found the effort less depleting than yesterday's fun and games in the square.

She'd let Ken move them back through the Hollow, conserving her strength. By the time they'd returned to Delphi, Nia had regenerated most of her stores of energy, although a nagging ache lingered behind her eyes. An annoying zing of residual energy plagued her shoulders where the men had anchored her effort.

Ken skirted the front end of her car and headed toward her door. As she alighted from the car, she noted movement at the base of the large maple tree in her front yard. She tensed, expecting to see Pierus or Mayhem in the shadows.

She slumped against the vehicle when Thomas rose off the ground and moved into a ray of moonlight. Idly, she noted the angle of his shadow was oddly elongated across the patch of grass. The moon's orbit was deteriorating even faster than she'd anticipated. In the odd glow, his eyes appeared hard. Like glittering diamonds.

"Oh, bloody hell. I'd forgotten you were coming over tonight," Nia blurted.

Thomas pursed his lips and glared at Ken.

Nia apologized. "Sorry, that didn't come out right."

Without a word, Thomas stalked across the lawn and drew to an abrupt halt in front of her. He crossed his arms over his chest and swung his gaze between Ken and her.

He opened his mouth to speak, but Ken held up a hand and curled it into a fist, cutting off his words. Thomas froze in place. Panic filled his eyes, the only part of his body that could move under the force of Ken's hold.

Rounding on Ken in indignation, Nia hissed at him. "Jesus, Ken! There was no call to spellbind him."

She glanced back at Thomas and laid a hand on his arm, pushing calm through her palm, imagining a soft cottony cloud for him to rest on. His gaze darted toward her and a squeaking breath leaked out between his open lips.

She blinked away angry tears. "I'm so sorry."

"I mean no harm to you, Thomas," Ken explained. Thomas rolled his eyes. Drawing Nia two feet away from Thomas's unnaturally still form, Ken lowered his voice. "You've been looking for a way to convince him about magic. Well, I think I might just have found it. Talk to him. Explain what you are. Don't squander this moment."

"Are you telling me this as my partisan, or my

friend?"

"A little of both?"

"Right now, you aren't being much of a friend to force my hand this way. Maybe in the next life I'll see if you can be sent back as a Doberman."

"Whatever. Just work it out with him. Look at the angle on that shadow." He waved wildly at the splotch of moonlight painting the yard with a silvery glow. "It got wrong entirely too fast. Our calculations were off. We didn't account for the new orbit when determining the cycle. The full moon will happen at least a week early if we don't fix this. We are running out of time faster than we thought possible."

He was dead right. But witnessing the fright and anger in Thomas's eyes didn't bode well for her ability to convince him. Crushing doubt weighed on her shoulders and she slumped.

Swiping a hand over the burgeoning ache behind her eyes, she willed pain and fear away.

Ken squeezed her arm. "You can do this." He stepped away from her and approached Thomas. "It probably won't do me any good to tell you that you'll understand soon. But listen to Nia. Give her a chance to explain. She needs your help, man. The world needs your help."

Thomas's eyes shifted to the side to track Nia's guardian as he turned. Ken's steps thumped on the concrete path as he moved away to enter the house.

"Hey! You need to release Thomas," she yelled at Ken's retreating figure.

The second the door banged behind Ken, the spell broke. Thomas's body jolted and he stumbled. He bent, resting his hands on his knees. When he spoke, his voice came out gravelly and harsh. "What the fuck did he do to me?"

"He put you into a...uh, supernatural timeout." Nia dropped her chin to her chest and prayed for the right words. Lifting her head, she held her hand out to him. "I have to tell you a story. Will you put aside your doubts and listen without judgment?"

Straightening, Thomas crossed his arms over his chest. "I'd say a little explanation is in order."

Based on his posture and the frosty glint in his eyes, Nia was uncertain he'd be open to her explanation. When he didn't reach for her hand, doubt zoomed like a hummingbird straight to her chest. Could she do this? She dropped her arm to her side. Sorrow and suspicion flickered in his gaze—the conflicting emotions confusing her.

"Please make him listen. Let him understand," she muttered to herself as she sent a nudge toward his forehead.

Thomas flicked a gaze toward the closed front door, then to the street before facing her again. "Who are you talking to?"

Of course he'd have heard that even though

she'd barely whispered it. Thomas was clairaudient. The fact he'd heard her thoughts in the past convinced her to believe he was the man to face this challenge with her.

Holding his gaze, she pursed her lips and silently sent him her thoughts. *Nod your head if you hear this.*

Raising his brow to just below a what-the-fuck level, Thomas gave a terse nod of his head.

You can hear me even when I'm not speaking. It's like you have a dog's auditory capacity. Do you hear other people's thoughts?

He squinted his eyes and an intense frown puckered his brow. He waited a moment then huffed out a breath. "No, just your thoughts. But you can't hear mine."

"Was that what you were trying to do just now? Speak to me without vocalizing?"

"Uh-huh." He closed his eyes and leaned toward her.

"If you're trying again, I'm getting nothing."

"I was telling you I'd listen." His glance slid sideways, then back. "I won't guarantee I'll believe. But I'll try."

Gesturing to a bench in the moonlit yard, she invited him to join her there. She moved past him and settled on the decorative seat. The semi-circle of concrete was cool beneath her bare legs. Looking expectantly up at him, she waited until he joined her. The bench was small, and his thigh brushed hers, igniting the familiar slow burn in her belly. Thomas cleared his throat as he scooted to his right, breaking the physical contact.

Yesterday, he'd have pulled her onto his lap. This morning, he would have rolled her onto her back and lifted her skirt above her hips. Now, it was as if he couldn't bear the slightest touch.

Doing her best to ignore the hurtful sting zipping through her chest, she began. "Thomas." She paused as she considered the best way to tell him of her past.

All of her pasts.

Fast and nothing but the facts was the best way to unload on a doubting Thomas. She blurted out, "I am Urania, the Muse of Astronomy, protector of celestial objects and stars." Sharing that secret lightened her heart by half.

A skeptical frown spread over his face, his eyes remained hard. "Nice ice breaker."

Maybe this would be harder than she thought. God, the statement sounded outrageous to her ears—it had to sound freaking insane to a man who doubted for a living.

She twined her fingers tightly together. "Not an ice breaker. Just the start to a story I know you'll find hard to believe. But I'm telling you up front that every word, every detail, is the truth."

He searched her face for a moment and must

have seen sincerity in her expression. His shoulders dipped as he rocked forward and back a few times, deep in thought. His expression made it clear he thought her completely crazy.

Emptying his face of emotion, he asked, "A Muse, like a fictional being who inspired people to create art or music or literature?"

"We all have different spheres of influence. Mine is the heavens."

"All? How many are you?"

"Nine. My sisters are Muses as well."

He pinched the bridge of his nose between his thumb and fingers. "Are you immortal?"

"Yes and no." She dug her nails into her thighs as she sought to explain. "We, my sisters and I, follow the age span of mortals. We share the same life cycle. We're born, we live…we die. But we're reborn with all of our memories intact."

"Like reincarnation?"

"A little different. Reincarnation is something reserved for mortals. Only in rare cases does a mortal come back with memories of previous lives. When they surface, it's what you'd call déjà vu." She shifted in her seat, twisting to face him without closing the distance between them. "When a man dies, he can come back, but it won't necessarily be as a man. Could be a bird, a woman, a horse, a dog…you get the idea."

He nodded. "Is that why you told Ken he'd

come back as a Doberman?"

"I told him that because he was being a jerk. Ken is my partisan. He comes back as a man in each life. His existence mirrors mine. Heck, I didn't even know I had a protector until recently. Zeus has kept them hidden from us throughout the millennium."

"Is Ken immortal as well?"

"Not exactly." She heaved an exasperated sigh. She offered him details he might not need to know. "He's mortal, but with special powers and abilities. He can funnel his energy into another being, or step into the Hollow and travel to a new location in the blink of an eye. He's only around when I need a security force. We've actually just traveled with Mars to Belarus."

"The God of War?"

It didn't occur to him to question that since he'd done delicious things to her body this morning, she'd traveled to a country thousands of miles away and back. Nia understood. Men had long had a fascination with Mars and war. "We've evolved. Now, he's vice-president of security for Olympus."

He laughed. "So Olympus is run like a corporation? Staffed by gods and goddesses."

"And the Titans we've kept on the payroll. There's also one primordial deity, Gaia, and several minor deities on the board. Zeus is the CEO."

"I'm guessing this isn't a publicly held operation."

If he chose to joke about it, maybe he was buying her story. "No, it's held strictly by family. Kind of the Publix Supermarkets of the gods."

That earned her a laugh. "Check on the corporate structure." He looked toward the house again, a frown creasing his forehead. "If Ken is your bodyguard, why is he here now?"

Now they were getting to the meat of the story. "How much Greek mythology do you know? Have you ever tried to bust a myth about the gods?"

He leaned his elbows on his knees, clasped his hands together, and studied them. "I've tried." He twisted his head to look at her. "Honestly, I've never been successful."

"Because we're mythical, but we aren't myths. We've always existed. Gods as a whole are extremely private, though. It's rare for us to reveal our existence to mortals. Hence the ridiculous legends." Nervousness claimed her and Nia jumped up from the bench. She paced in front of him as she explained. "Thousands of years ago, a god named Pierus had nine daughters whom he believed were superior beings to the Muses. Zeus got pissed off and had words with Pierus. Well, they had a lightning sword fight. Pretty spectacular. The battle ended in a draw and that's when Pierus and his skanky daughters first challenged us. When we defeated them, Zeus turned Pierus's kids into magpies forever."

Thomas tracked her path as she moved side-to-side. "That seems harsh."

She stopped in front of him, but agitated energy kept her swaying from foot to foot. "If you'd met his daughters, you wouldn't think so. They represent all the bad things in the world. Tyranny, strife, greed, hunger. My challenger is Mayhem." Nia resumed pacing.

He shot upright on the bench. "Wait a minute. *Is?*"

"Yes, *is*. Pierus re-emerged recently and is up to his old tricks. He's challenged us once again. But this time, he's brought along some new friends. What he's attempting is akin to a hostile takeover of Olympus." She paused in front of the maple tree. The rough bark abraded her arm as she leaned against it. "He's challenging the Muses individually to defeat his daughters. If one of us fails, we all lose. Humans—mortals—will suffer the most."

Rising from the bench, he strode to her. Uncertainty deepened his eyes to the color of the sea where the bottom dropped off. He lifted his hand toward her elbow, but stopped short of touching her.

Instead, he flicked his thumbnail against a knot in the trunk. "What will happen if he wins?"

"My sisters and I forfeit our existence as goddesses and become magpies for the rest of time. I don't want that, because I hated the whole feathers as dresses trend in the twenties. Not a great look on me." Her attempt at levity fell flat. She sighed. "But worse, all of the horrible things Pierus's daughters represent will come to pass. Mortals have stood on the brink of wars and famine before, but this time, they won't be able to step back. Without the Muses around to inspire humans, all light and beauty will fade from the world."

He was silent for a long time. Dread rose with icy tendrils up Nia's spine as she waited for his response. She hadn't been kidding about not looking great in feathers. But that truly was the least of her worries. She'd been watching over and inspiring humans for so long, her biggest fear was the black and white planet they faced without the gifts of the Muses. If Thomas turned away from her now, all would be lost.

He shifted until his back rested against the tree, facing away from her. Looking toward the sky, he folded his arms again. "How exactly am I involved?"

CHAPTER 18

Unbelievable.
Undeniably crazy.

But mostly, it was uncharacteristic for Thomas to want to believe Nia's claim to be a Muse. More outrageous was that he might have some kind of role in saving mankind from a brutal future.

This must be a crazy nightmare, brought on by the events he'd witnessed in the square the other night. Or maybe it was a hallucination. He'd had them before when he'd run a high fever and been severely dehydrated. Those images had seemed ultra-real as well.

Thomas pinched his bicep hard then wracked his brain to try to remember if he'd ever felt pain in a dream before. His logical brain said he must have, but his heart told a different story. As did his muscle, which twinged painfully as he increased the tension between his thumb and forefinger.

"This is insane." He groaned and rolled his head back, looking up through the canopy of the maple's branches, searching for reason. A warm breeze stirred the leaves overhead as his mind trembled and raced. A hint of Nia's citrusy perfume teased his nose.

There was no denying he'd been frozen in place when that dickhead, Ken, had raised his fist. Although Thomas's heart had continued its somewhat escalated beat, he hadn't been able to suck oxygen into his lungs. But the sensation hadn't been suffocating. He didn't lose consciousness, and when Ken had entered the house, he didn't need to gasp, as if surfacing after a long time underwater.

Think, Thomas!

This was what he did. His livelihood was based on poking holes in myths and legends. He exposed charlatans and fraud. As she'd spoken, Nia's tone held only sincerity and truth. The bullshit meter that seemed as much a part of him as his heartbeat hadn't pinged even once as she'd woven her fantastic story.

He wanted to believe her. But he shouldn't. He might as well hop aboard the express train to the asylum.

Groaning again, he bent and braced his hands on his knees. His T-shirt snagged on rough bark as he slid to his haunches. Beside him, Nia pushed away from the tree and paced three feet to the left. Lifting his head, he waited for her answer.

Before she could speak, a large, cackling magpie alighted on the bench where they'd been sitting. From a crouched position, he studied the unusual bird. Something was off—like it didn't have enough feathers to cover its body. The eyes, which should have been dark as ebony, gleamed electric blue in the bird's jet-black head.

"Is that your magpie?"

Nia twisted to look, a scowl marring her smooth brow. "That's Mayhem." She smacked her hands together, a thunderous clap which had no effect. The bird chattered and squawked on, as if scolding them. "You are not welcome here." Nia's guttural voice grated over his senses.

She lifted her arms, palms out and squinted at the bird. As clear as a summer sky, he heard her order the bird away. But her lips never moved. The conversation occurred all in his head.

When the bird didn't fly off, Nia slumped. Thomas hated the defeated set of her shoulders. He spied a long, stout stick two feet from him. The bird's unnerving eyes followed his movement as he reached to retrieve the branch.

He lunged forward and grabbed the limb. Grasping it like a baseball bat, he swung at the foul beast. The creature took to the sky in a screeching, feather-shedding frenzy, and disappeared from view.

Frustrated, Thomas shouted and heaved the stick through the air, following the path the monstrous thing had flown. He rounded on Nia. "Did that fucking thing have human eyes?"

"She's molting. It happened with Tyranny as well. Clio said it freaked the Hades out of her." Nia shuddered. "It's a display of confidence from their side. They fully expect to win this contest."

She turned her back on him and ruffled shaking fingers through her hair. Her posture was straight and rigid, as though she had a rod of steel where her spine should be. Swaying side-to-side, she ignored his presence.

Low, whispery sounds reached his ears, but this time, he didn't understand the words. "Why can't I hear your thoughts right now?"

"What?" She spun around. The lively blue eyes he'd found so intriguing were flat and lifeless.

"I heard you order Mayhem to leave. When you sent your thoughts to me, the words echoed in my mind. But just now, I know you were saying something, but I didn't understand."

"I was talking to myself, not projecting a thought toward a specific target."

She rubbed a hand over her neck, as though in pain. It reminded him of finding her with Ken's hands on her. He trounced down a sudden surge of jealousy. Nia had assured him they were only friends. He took a step toward her. "Is that how it works? You have to target a thought outward?" Oh hell, what was he saying?

"I don't know." She crossed her arms over her belly. "None of us have ever encountered a clairaudient before."

"Clairaudient? Like a clairvoyant?"

Her head bobbed and she shrugged.

He took another step nearer. Wariness filled her eyes, like she thought he was going to restrain her until the men with the white coats arrived. To keep from reaching for her, he tucked his hands in his back pockets.

He drew a breath, released it in a long hiss, and then drew another. "For the sake of argument, let's say I believe you. What do I have to do to help save the world?"

Coppery curls brushed her cheeks as she shook her head. "It will never work. You'll never believe. It isn't in your nature. Figures the man who's supposed to help me is a professional skeptic. It's never going to work."

"Hey, don't discount my nature. What's it going to take?"

"You have to believe in magic." The bare skin of her thighs thwacked dully against the concrete bench as she plopped down.

"I can believe," he said defensively.

Cynical laughter ripped through her tight lips. "Don't you think that's a bit unlikely?"

He sank onto the seat next to her. "I'd like to try."

"There's a Yoda moment in here somewhere." She bounced off the bench as if she didn't want to be near him. She stepped into the patch of moonlight painted across the lawn. "Thomas, we're running out of time. I'm supposed to lead you back to the magic. To make you ask *what if?* And help you accept the answer, regardless of what it is."

"What if what?"

"What if magic does exist?" She paced from one edge of the moonlight to the other, and then back. "But I've heard you tell Hailey more than once magic isn't real. Right now, you've seen things normal mortals never have access to. I've confided my biggest secret to you. I'm magic. I'm a goddamn Muse and you won't accept it."

Leaping from his seat, Thomas scrubbed a hand down his face. "It's a lot to take in." He began to pace alongside her. "You can't unload a bunch of hooey like that and think I'll fall for it hook, line and sinker."

Stopping abruptly she wheeled toward him and squinted. The word *asshat* pierced his mind.

"I heard that."

"You were meant to." Jamming her hands on her hips, she glared at him. "This isn't hooey,

Thomas. This is about the fate of the world. And dammit, that sounded overly dramatic. I—"

Nia splayed her fingers on each side of her head, her mouth open, eyes squeezed shut and her expression pained.

Concern conquered the doubt tainting his imagination. He moved to her side, laying a hand on her arm. Her skin was chilled despite the warmth of the evening. "What's wrong?"

She didn't answer immediately. Her mouth formed words, but he couldn't hear them and he sucked at lip reading, so he had no idea what she might be saying.

"Nia?"

"It's always a bit uncomfortable when Zeus contacts me." Her eyelids bolted open, her eyes flashing an unnatural blue. She chuckled, the sound escalating quickly to a full-on belly laugh. "Thomas, you've been frozen in place, heard my thoughts, and faced down a supernatural magpie, and still, you don't believe." She smoothed a hand over her belly. "But you're about to experience something that will have to convince you of the truth of my story."

Behind her, the front door burst open and Ken rushed through it. "Ready?"

Suspicion flared explosively behind Thomas's eyes. "For what?" He glared at the behemoth of a man as Ken loped to Nia's side. *He'd better not fucking touch her.* The dude's size wouldn't matter…Thomas would find a way to take him down.

Nia laid her hand on his arm, warmth from her palm seeped into him firing all his senses. Her eyes held an apology. "We've been summoned to Olympus."

"You can't just go and leave me here with hundreds of questions. You'll stay to explain if you want my help."

"You've been summoned as well." Nia searched his face, her eyes lingering on his lips.

"The purpose of the trip is to provide you with answers." Ken's shoulder bumped Thomas as the hulky man brushed past. He stopped right behind Thomas.

"Well, then, let's go. How long will it take to drive to the office?" He moved toward Nia's car, but a large hand descended on his shoulder, holding him in place. "What the fuck, man?"

"We don't go by car." Ken offered a smirk then pulled on his ear. "Brace yourself. The first trip is always a bit of a wild ride."

"What?" Worry started roiling in his gut and Thomas spun to face Nia, who'd moved to Ken's side. Pressure built in his ears and around his chest, as if the air had condensed. He swallowed hard to get his ears to pop.

"It helps if you pinch your nose closed and

force air into your sinuses," Ken offered as the pressure escalated.

Nia laid her hand on one of his arms and Ken took the other. The world around him misted and faded into nothingness. Before his eyes, Nia vanished into the mist, leaving a flare of robin's egg blue color in its wake. Pinpricks of silvery light, resembling stars, pierced the space where her torso should have been. In the center, a blob of pale orange pulsed like a heartbeat. *What the hell was happening?*

Thomas's head felt as if it was floating when he turned toward where Ken had been standing. In his place was another splotch of color, this time cobalt blue with a pulse of yellow beating in the center. Alarmed, he peeked down at his body, shocked to see it had turned to silver. At least he retained his human form.

Thomas's heart galloped, his lungs not rising or falling with each breath he struggled to take. The air tightened around his body and he jerked at a loud popping noise in the area surrounding his head. Still shrouded in mist, Nia and Ken's bodies returned to normal.

Glancing down, Thomas realized he floated a good two feet over a worn carpet bathed in lamplight. What happened to the grass? To the moonlight and maple tree in Nia's front yard?

Thomas flailed his arms away from Nia's grasp

and wobbled as the trio eased to the ground. The moment they lost their grip on him, he dropped like a stone the last six inches. His teeth clacked together painfully.

Nia leaped forward to steady him. "I'm sorry for the abruptness of the transport. Are you alright?" She smoothed her fingers over his cheek.

Her eyes were cold, but her gentle touch slowed his frantic heartbeat. "Don't know. That was weird." He laid his hand over hers, savoring the contact and holding her close.

The chilly temperature of her gaze warmed, and her smile was rueful. "If you think that was weird, hold onto your hat. You're about to meet my dad." She grasped his elbow and urged him around.

Yeah, not in Nia's yard anymore. The grass and trees had been replaced by a comfortable sitting room. Portraits of frolicking gods and goddesses adorned the walls. The gleaming hardwood floor was partially obscured by a thick carpet of muted colors.

Directly across from Thomas, a man in black T-shirt and jeans relaxed against the cushions of an antique, horsehair sofa. The bluest eyes Thomas had ever seen softened the secret-agent-man look. Ruddy red colored his cheeks, curly ebony hair was tinged with strands of silver. The overall effect was menacing, approachable, and powerful at the same

215

time. Despite the color in his cheeks, his skin held the pallor most commonly found in hospitals. Pinning Thomas with an assessing look, the man crossed one knee over the other and waited.

The double doors on the other side of the room burst open. A statuesque woman crossed the threshold in a rush. She made a beeline for Nia, and smothered her in a hug, crooning soft, delicate words only Nia could hear. Shutting her eyes, Nia's face transformed from cold and hard into the visage of a woman who knew she was loved. Thomas suffered a pang of emotion at the idea that he wanted to be the man who put that look on her face.

The woman patted Nia's back, and then nudged her away to turn toward him. "You must be Thomas Wilde. I'm Gaia, Nia's mother." Her voice tinkled like delicate wind chimes, and her green eyes danced as she regarded him.

He shot a startled look to Nia before continuing. "Gaia, as in Mother Earth?" Accepting the hand she offered, Thomas felt instantly at ease. "Pleased to meet you."

Gaia beamed while Nia bit her lip. "That's right. You do know your mythology. Allow me to introduce my consort."

Walking across the carpet felt like walking on a cloud, soft and light. Glancing over his shoulder Thomas discovered Nia had remained behind.

Gaia's hand on his arm was firm as she drew him across the room. "This is Zeus, Nia's father."

He had to work to keep his jaw from dropping. Nia's dad was named for the king of gods? Was the entire family delusional? Except...that tiny voice in his skull chided him to look beyond reason. Hell, he was in an entirely different setting than he had been two minutes ago. Zeus extended his hand, and Thomas took it, rubbing his fingers on his temple with the other. He needed to shut down that voice fast. He wasn't going to get sucked into this lunacy.

"Have a seat, son," Zeus invited, patting the cushion next to him.

Thomas sank onto the couch, crowding back into the corner. Nia's posture looked agitated as she paced to the French doors on the far end of the room. She spun and marched back the opposite direction, fists clenched at her sides.

Zeus cleared his throat, claiming Thomas's attention. "I realize this is all hard to take in, but you must trust me, every word Nia spoke is the truth."

"It's a little far-fetched." Seemed like Thomas vied for the title King of the Understatement.

Zeus's laughter filled the room. "Life used to be much simpler. Mortals really believed in our existence. We were not far-fetched in the least in ancient times."

Gaia laughed with him, while Nia tossed him a glare and Ken smirked as he lounged against a sideboard.

Zeus continued. "Son, we need your help."

Tossing his glance between the older man and Nia, Thomas waffled on his stance that the entire episode was a bad dream. "I can't imagine what I can possibly do to save the world. I'm one man."

"But you're the man with the key. Pierus's hostile takeover of my corporation is a sure thing if you won't at least consider the possibility. Mayhem will be unleashed if Nia fails. And she'll be closely followed by the rest of the troubles we've held in check for centuries." Zeus leaned forward and braced his elbows on his knees. The man's intense blue stare bore into Thomas, bruising a path to his soul. "Nia's life would be forfeit. And so might your Hailey's"

"What?" Cold dread gripped the base of Thomas's neck.

"For the love of the gods, Zeus. I hadn't gotten to that part yet," Nia yelled.

"Brutal honesty is called for, daughter. Atlas informed me of his difficulty in rehanging the moon."

Thomas shot off the couch. "Are you threatening my niece?"

"Thomas, no!" Nia exclaimed. "Pierus added an aspect to my challenge. I must persuade you to believe in magic, or not only is my life forfeit, but the life of an innocent hangs in the balance. I believe that innocent might be Hailey. But I don't know. I only know I mustn't fail." Anguish filled her eyes, but Thomas refused to be swayed.

Clenching his hands into fists, Thomas glowered at Nia, then swept the room with his gaze. "Attempting to drag me into your delusion is one thing. But no one better lay a finger on Hailey." He took a menacing step toward Nia to show he meant business.

Ken leaped in front of Nia, cutting Thomas's approach off. Using his broad shoulders, he muscled Nia behind him.

"Thomas, according to Pierus's challenge, it seems Hailey is likely to be a great contributor in alleviating suffering in the poorest nations. We plan to consult Lachesis to find out exactly what her destiny is." Ken crossed his arms over his massive chest.

Ignoring the spark of jealousy generated by Ken's protective behavior, Thomas growled. "Who the fuck is Lachesis?"

"She's the Fate who spins the length of a life," Ken replied as he tightened his arms over his massive chest, popping biceps with enlarged veins running down them.

He snorted. "Of course." Jesus, these people were insane.

Nia shoved Ken from her path and moved toward Thomas, her hand raised, palm out as though entreating him. "We aren't threatening Hailey. We're trying to protect her."

Protect, his ass. The dread in the pit of his stomach reminded him of the day he found out his brother, Doug, had died at the hands of terrorists. This situation felt very similar.

Thomas spread his feet wide and crossed his arms over his chest. She didn't shy away from his combative stance, something he admired even as it pissed him off. The muscles in his jaw jerked with tension as he spat his words out. "You seemed so fucking normal."

"I'm not crazy, Thomas." Her voice was barely a whisper but he heard defeat and defiance in it.

Sweeping a disparaging gaze over the delicate features that masked her insanity, he nearly relented. Despite his anger at the moment, his cock hardened as he took in her curves and her long legs. His physical reaction to her body pointed to how he'd been deceived.

"Was the sex part of your scheme to dupe me this way?"

"No!" Nia jolted backward, clutching a fist to her breastbone. "Please don't think that. I didn't sleep with you because of the challenge. I slept with you because I'm falling for you."

"Right," he scoffed.

"Whether you believe or not, it doesn't change the truth; I'm a Muse. I've existed for thousands of years." She jammed her fists onto her hips. "Here are the facts. One, an ancient deity has challenged my sisters and I. Our lives depend on winning." She lifted her hands and began ticking the fingers of one hand. "Two, the coronal burst on the sun knocked the moon out of orbit. With it out of place, the world is out of balance. Three—"

"What are you talking about? The moon isn't out of orbit." Surely something would have been mentioned in the media.

"Shut up and listen." The command in her tone was undeniable. Something gripped his shoulders, subduing his words. He looked at Ken and found the son of a bitch scowling at him, his arm raised and fist clenched. Bastard had frozen him again. Goddammit, just another facet in this never-ending nightmare.

Nia continued, "Three, to win the challenge I must lead a man, you, Thomas, back to believing in magic. There wasn't anything in the rules about sleeping with said man, or falling in love with him." She stepped back and propped fisted hands on her hips. She nodded to Ken.

The grip on Thomas lessened and he stumbled forward. Nia professed to love him, but he couldn't believe her. Not after so many outrageous statements. Not after the entire surreal experience of this horrible hallucination.

But, God dammit. She professed her love and fuck it all, when he'd heard the words his heart jumped like it was on a freaking trampoline. When the hell had he fallen in love with her?

Eyes filled with entreaty, Nia stood before him. Her voice rang in his head. *Will you help us?*

Buying into her fantasy would only make matters worse. She'd continue to believe she was an ancient being. That her father was the Grand Poobah of all the gods who'd never existed. And it could endanger Hailey's life. His niece was his priority. And would always remain so.

Thomas shook his head. "No." Sharp pain sliced a path through his heart as he uttered the single word. *Why did it ache so much to deny her?*

Nia unfisted her hands and backed a step away from him. And another. Behind Thomas, Gaia gasped and a soft sob filled the air. From the corner of his eye, he noted Ken going to Zeus's side to help him to his feet. The pair moved until they flanked Nia.

She bit her lip and blinked her eyes hard. The single tear trickling from one corner twisted his gut in a wringer. Even though he was in the midst of an awful dream, the anguish in her face crushed him.

He lifted his hand to her arm, but she slid

another pace away, avoiding his touch. "Don't."

"I'm sorry, but I can't buy into this...this altered reality of yours."

Nia edged a step in his direction. "Again, this story is not made up. But, you must believe what you believe." She twisted her head to look at Zeus over her shoulder. "Will you call Mnemosyne? He shouldn't retain the memory of this night. Or of me."

Desolation rode up Thomas's spine at the defeat in Nia's tone. "What are you talking about? You can't toy with my memories. They're mine."

She faced him again, hope in her eyes fading. "You shouldn't have to remember, because any memory you keep of what I've told you will only cause you remorse later on. Guilt can't supplant your need to keep your wits about you. You'll need them to face the dangers and new reality brought about because I've failed at this challenge. Mnemosyne will remove all memory of this night—the trip through the Hollow, the magpies...all of it. She'll also wipe away recollection of the times we shared together." Her voice hitched on her last words. Over her shoulder, she entreated Zeus. "Please make sure he doesn't remember anything except the need to keep Hailey safe."

Zeus nodded, sorrow turning his gaze somber. "We will take care of it."

Another tear traced a slow path down Nia's cheek. "Thank you. I'll be back later to say good bye."

"Nia, no!" Gaia sobbed. "Do not give up. We will figure something out."

"I'm being reasonable, Mother. I suggest everyone else do the same. My fate, and yours," she spared a teary glance at Thomas, "and the fate of all mortals is sealed."

"Daughter…"

Nia held her hand up, stopping Zeus's words. She took a step toward Thomas, and cupped a hand over his cheek. Her eyes darted over his face, as though memorizing the lines and curves of it.

She spoke into his mind. *I swear to you, every word is true. None truer than the words of love I uttered. Please get Hailey out of the city. Keep her safe.* Nia squinted her eyes and he felt her thoughts burning a path to his subconscious. *You will not remember me, or the rest of this night. But you will remember that Hailey's life is in danger. You will take her somewhere safe. Somewhere Pierus cannot find her. Stay safe, my love.*

Rising on her toes, Nia pressed her lips to his. He grasped her shoulders and relished the soft satin of her caress, the first peace he'd felt since she'd found him in the front yard. The air around him tightened, thickened. Sky blue light filled his vision as mist grew in the room.

Nia's softly spoken *I love you* filled his brain as she disappeared from his arms.

CHAPTER 19

Nia escaped into the Hollow after her parting words, her last kiss with Thomas. Her starry aura dimmed by sorrow and pain, and blurred by gathering tears. Misery and bitterness were poor traveling companions.

Thomas didn't believe her. She'd failed her task and it was her fault — and no one else's — the world was about to be plunged into a stark new existence.

As she materialized in her living room, she didn't bother to control her descent. Her feet slammed onto the floor in her living room — one on the lush area rug, the other on the hardwood. The physical pain jolted her hips, causing her to groan.

The instant the mist cleared, she fell to her knees. Bending, she pressed her forehead to the ground. Her throat ached from holding back her sobs while in the void. She gave the anguish her voice. Harsh, wracking sobs claimed her body, shaking and shuddering her form as she cowered on the floor.

When had she fallen in love with Thomas? His denial burned a tormented path through her soul. She'd been optimistic about her chances to save the world with his help. And when she won her challenge, Thomas and Hailey would have been a major factor in the rest of this lifetime. And possibly all of her future lifetimes.

Now, that fantasy was nothing more than ashes on her heart.

The clock ticked loudly from the mantel, marking her remaining moments with rhythmic severity, inexorably counting down the moments. It wouldn't be long before her sisters, and Ken, and her parents reached out to her.

Ken might be first, as he'd have to pick up Thomas's car to return it to him. He'd probably take Thomas to his home first, and tuck him into the king-sized bed. The lovely, plush bed she'd shared with him. And tomorrow, Thomas would fix breakfast in his to-die-for kitchen. No memories would plague him. Not of her sitting at his kitchen island. Not of her laughing conversation with Hailey. Not of the passionate embrace they'd snuck in when the adorable little urchin had left the room to get a book she thought Nia would enjoy. Sharp pain pierced Nia's heart, widening the cracks already there into fissures with no hope of repair.

Gasping to fill her lungs, Nia slammed the door on her memories. At least as she began her life as a magpie, she'd have her last memory of Thomas's kiss to hold close to her new, avian breast.

Not in the right frame of mind to deal with Ken or her parents, Nia roused from her agony and struggled to her feet. To keep any potential visitors at bay, she faced each of the four corners of her house, and sang a song of protection, barring admittance to any and all visitors. The words were rusty and she struggled to remember the correct order. But they'd keep unwelcome guests from intruding on her pity party. Disgust almost made her undo the spell. Hiding was not her style.

She'd only used this unique ability once before. Eons ago when she'd miscalculated and Stonehenge ended up in the wrong spot. Then embarrassment had ridden her hard. She'd cost the world an extra day every four years to correct her mistake. She'd locked herself away from everyone for years then.

Today the world faced a much more dire outcome. She ensured the destruction of mortal comfort. When Pierus rose to power there'd be no more love, nor joy, nor art. His would be a world of black and white. All humans would be forced to toil to bring riches to him and his evil offspring.

After completing her incantations, she trudged to the kitchen to draw a glass of water. Standing on her tiptoes, she reached into the cabinet for a tumbler. Waiting for the water running into the sink to cool, she rubbed her fingers over the rippled glass. A tiny snicker tugged her lips up and she slammed the water off.

In three steps she was at her refrigerator. Jerking the door open, a welcome, cool breeze wafted into her face. An open bottle of Chardonnay sat on the glass shelf, next to a jar of olives. She grasped the neck of the bottle and tugged. She met a tiny resistance, but pulled it free of the stickiness it sat in. The snicker morphed to a smile as she contemplated wiping off the shelf before pouring the wine. A snort escaped her throat as she decided with her world ending soon she didn't need to clean another damn thing.

A chuckle began in her belly as she kicked the door shut. That chuckle became an outright laugh as she splashed the golden liquid into the tumbler, filling it to the top. The laugh morphed into a sob as she recognized the wine's rich color as the exact shade of Thomas's hair with the sun shining on it. Tears scalded behind her eyes, her throat tightened as she fought back the glob of emotion choking her.

"For the love of the gods, you must stop thinking of him. After all, he's never going to think of you again." Her voice was watery as she whispered to herself, dashing the tears from her eyes with the back of her hand. Maybe Mnemosyne could take away her memories as well as Thomas's.

Squaring her shoulders, she took her glass and wandered back to her living room.

Wrapping a soft, woven afghan around her shoulders, she pulled it up until it covered her head but left her face exposed. The blanket draped around her knees as she plopped onto the sofa. Clutching the cream-colored folds of material around her neck, she recited the ancient Greek words that wove a charm of invincibility into the fabric. No one should be able to breach her mind as long as her head remained covered. And goddess knew they'd try.

She reached for the glass she'd set on the table. Tart lemon, smoky oak, and ripe fruit flavors filled her mouth with a warm glow. Rich buttery intensity coated her throat as she swallowed. By the hills of Mt. Olympus, she was going to miss this wine.

Shit, the entire world was going to miss wine.

Quietly savoring the flavor, she slouched against the cushions, in her silent-as-a-tomb house, and awaited destiny. For several minutes she valiantly fought the temptation to watch more of Thomas's shows. But the seduction of seeing his face won the day, and she grabbed the remote.

After navigating through the watch list for *Doubting Thomas* — the name made her choke on his denial — she found the next episode and pressed play.

His rugged, smiling face filled the screen. Sandy blond hair blew in a breeze. Intense green eyes, filled with intelligence, smiled at something a crew member had said. The calm patience with which he explained a myth, then proved irrevocably it was a fallacy. Tears slipped down her cheeks, one plopping in her glass. He couldn't prove she was a fallacy, but he still resisted.

"Water under the fucking bridge, Urania." She dashed the tears away with her fingertips. "You have an eternity as a godforsaken bird to prepare for. Stupid Zeus. Why couldn't he have turned Pierus's daughters into puppies?" She could have lived with that. But a damned dirty bird?

She was unsure of how many episodes she binged on. The incessant tapping against her consciousness, nudges from her parents and sisters, went unanswered. The more wine she consumed, the less vibrant the pokes became. Eventually, her cell phone started ringing. Each time a tone sounded, she identified which sister was calling to talk sense into her. Even the thunderous tones of the ringer she'd set for Mars sounded three times in rapid succession. The number of calls diminished as midnight faded to dawn.

When the final episode ended, her bones creaked as she unfolded her body from the sofa. As she poured a glass of water, through the window over her sink the out-of-place moon, half-shrouded in clouds mocked her. The edges of the gleaming orb blurred, like she had double vision, or was drunk. Or the screen the gods had put into place was faltering, revealing the real position directly below the illusion they'd created.

Spinning to put her back to the window, she gulped the water. Anger she hadn't let climb past the dejection and misery finally surfaced. Lurching back around, she slammed the glass to the counter, shattering it into pieces. Lifting the middle fingers on both hands, she jabbed them toward the window. The first rays of sunlight peeked above the horizon, the promise of a new day coming. The first day of the rest of her life.

Too damn bad that life was numbered in days.

Remorse filled her as she swept up the broken pieces of the tumbler with one hand. She continued to clutch the edges of the afghan over her head, knowing the minute she lowered the fabric, some deity or another would slam their thoughts into her. With cautious steps she made her way to the bath, debating on showering with the blanket.

Facing the mirror, she frowned at her reflection. Dark circles and bleary, reddened eyes scowled back at her. She shook her head. "You've never shied away from a fight before, you stupid cow. Letting Thomas's doubt and denial hold you back from finding an answer is a roadblock you don't need."

Her chest heaved as she drew a lungful of air. She expelled it forcefully. Spreading her feet wide, she braced one hand on the counter, preparing for the onslaught. She uncurled her fingers and the blanket plopped softly to the floor around her feet.

She pressed a hand to her forehead. "Let the shouting begin in three...two..."

Pain and a cacophony of voices blasted into her head. She picked her way through the messages. Some, like those from Thalia, Terri and Corie filled with compassion. Messages of encouragement and *don't let this set-back stop you* from Polly, Mel, and Aerie. Clio's message was a desperate plea for Nia to reach out and contact her and Jax. Callie's words struck home though, and were the first one she gave serious attention.

The pain from the overload of sensory input faded as she considered her eldest sister's harsh shove. *You bitch! This fight isn't over and if you choose defeat, that's on you. Get your sorry ass back in the game. None of us want to spend eternity as goddamned birds.*

Working up a good head of steam, Nia marched to the living room. Her phone rested on the table, right next to the remote. She snatched up the control, aimed it at the television, and ruthlessly shut off the image of Thomas filling the screen. The plastic clunked as she hurled it back to the table and grabbed up her phone.

Her fingers were shaking as she sifted through her favorites list, finding Callie's number at the very bottom. She connected the call before she could change her mind.

Callie didn't bother with a hello. "I knew you'd call me first."

"Gloating becomes you, you scag."

"That's the best you've got?"

"Gaia frowns on me calling anyone the C-word."

Laughter rippled into Nia's ear as she plopped onto the floor.

Callie drew a breath but her voice was still filled with mirth. "Honey, don't you think you have bigger shit to worry about than whether Gaia will wash your mouth out with soap?"

Drawing her knees up, Nia rounded her back and rocked on her tailbone. "Probably. Callie, for the life of me, I don't know what to do."

"I've never seen you so lost and confused."

"Except after that incident with Stonehenge."

"Girl, you have to forget that. Ancient history that not one single mortal cares about."

"Cal, I only care about one mortal. And he doesn't believe me."

Callie's voice was gentle as she replied. "We will work this out. With all of our heads together, we can fix this. How many days do you have left?"

She thought about the failing illusion that the moon remained exactly where it had been for millions of years. She sighed heavily. "By my calculations, about three." The weight of her words sat like a boulder on her chest. Nia rolled to her back and lengthened her arms and legs, hoping to alleviate the suffocating sensation.

"Miracles can be wrought in less time." Callie paused. "Don't you dare give up. You can't. We can't."

They'd loved and guided mortals for so long, giving up would seem criminal. The magnitude of her burden intensified the pressure building between her ribs. She forced it away. Callie was right. They couldn't give up.

Nia sighed. "I'm going to head to Helios, after a brief trip to Olympus to brainstorm with Atlas. Can you let the others know I'm okay? I'll check in with Zeus and Gaia."

"Will do. Proud of you, sis."

Any type of affection was rare coming from Callie. A warm glow suffused Nia's soul. Callie might be a troublesome bitch most days, but she had her moments.

"Hey, Cal? When you take the lazy way and do a broadcast announcement to the girls, please leave me off the distribution list. My head already aches as much as my heart."

"You got it." Callie mumbled something, and a pleasant jab of good will from her sister winged down Nia's spine as she disconnected the call.

A shower first, followed by a trip to the home office, then she'd head to work. She could save the world, with or without Thomas.

CHAPTER 20

Light flickered over his eyelids as Thomas swam toward consciousness. Remnants of odd dreams of traveling through space and oversize birds wisped through his brain, elusive and misty. When he cracked one eye open, searing pain stabbed under his skull. After rumbling in his chest like a rocket ship about to blast off, a massive groan escaped his pursed lips. The hammering in his head almost made him believe he might be hung-over. But his gut didn't churn with the upset that accompanied over-imbibing. He rubbed his fist over his abs and up to the stubble on his chin. The last time he'd gotten rip-roaring drunk was the week after he'd learned of his brother's death.

He didn't remember drinking last night. To be honest, he didn't remember much of anything from yesterday. The entire day echoed of a black hole.

Had he eaten something that made him sick? And where was Hailey? He strained his ears to detect any noise through his open door, hearing nothing but eerie silence. Shit, he'd forgotten. She'd gone with the Campfire Scouts on an overnight trip.

As he rolled to his back a puff of earthy citrus teased his nose. It reminded him of…something. *Damn, why couldn't he pin that memory down?*

Thomas slung his arm over his face and took inventory. The sledge that had been knocking inside his skull receded, leaving a vague ache, minor confusion, and looming emptiness. He breathed shallowly through his mouth and waited for the remaining twinge to vanish. Pushing himself upright on the bed, the sheet puddled around his hips. What the hell? He'd gone to bed in his jeans. Just one more thing he couldn't recall. Bending his knees, he propped his elbows on them and scrubbed his hands over his head and down his face.

Agonizing shards of fire bruised a path from his heel to his already reeling mind once he rose from the bed. He hesitated before taking a second step. Holding his breath, one eye scrunched tight, he moved his right foot in front of his left. *Huh?* He took another cautious step, then another. The pain that had wracked his body a second ago had vanished. *What the fuck is going on?*

He plodded to the master bath and flipped the

shower to the tortuous kneading spray he typically avoided, and then adjusted the temperature to just south of icy. He stood under the harsh torrent of cold water long enough to clear his head and clean his body. With a towel knotted low on his hips and another slung around his neck, he gathered clean clothes from his closet. He tossed the garments on the floor by the vanity and grabbed his brush.

As he raised his hand to comb his hair, he caught sight of a longish strand of coppery red hair snagged between the teeth. He pulled it free and studied it, not comprehending for the life of him whose head it had come from. Brows drawn together in a frown, he stretched the glossy filament between his fingers.

Too long and red to be his. Not curly or blond enough to belong to Hailey. And his housecleaners were all brunettes.

A ghost of an image of bright red hair teased his consciousness. But he couldn't grasp any details or identify the owner. He carefully arranged the strand on the vanity, his gaze returning to it frequently as he dressed. Something about that single thread of hair twanged around the edges of his heart.

Two hours later, with the mystery of the hair unsolved and still niggling, he was seated at the breakfast bar. A neglected cup of coffee sat near his open laptop. A webpage on ancient Greek theories on the tides and cycles of the moon occupied the screen. Being on hiatus allowed him to plan for future episodes of *Doubting Thomas*. On a lark, and needing material for the last of ten episodes, he'd decided this morning to tackle a new myth.

Was it true that individual temperaments could be affected by the phase of the moon? The material he'd reviewed thus far had been entertaining and perplexing. The notebook next to his left hand was filled with hastily scrawled notes and thoughts. He'd printed the word *lunacy* in large block letters at the top and underlined it three times. Beneath it, he'd scribbled *Mayhem*. As he'd written it, he chuckled to himself that the word could apply to his dreams from the night before.

The alarm sensor in his pantry bleated just as the front door crashed open. From where he sat, Thomas watched his niece wave goodbye to someone just before she slammed the door closed.

"Uncle Thomas?" Hailey sang out, looking for him.

"In here, munchkin," he hollered back.

The slap of her footsteps skipped ahead of the silly tune she sang as she headed toward him. "Thomas, we learned a song about pickles. Do you want to hear it?" Not waiting for his answer, she began a catchy little ditty about pickles and motorcycles, spinning in a circle as she sang.

It put a grin on his face. When Hailey crashed

against him, he gathered her up in his arms, settled her on his lap, and hugged her tight. "Your dad and I used to sing that song when we were boys." He joined her in the last verse.

The little cutie dissolved into infectious giggles as he pursed his lips and blew through them to sound like a Harley revving.

She patted his cheeks. "You're a silly." She squirmed on his lap until she faced his computer. She pointed wildly to the laptop. "Hey, it's Ms. Nia!" She jabbed her finger at the screen over a picture in the sidebar. It promoted another page to click on to read more about the Muse of Astronomy.

"Who?"

Twisting she looked at him, a frown pinching her tiny brows together. "Ms. Nia. From Helios."

"Munchkin, I don't know who you're talking about."

As he studied the image an invisible string jerked his heart into his throat. The woman, dressed in a toga, her hair swept up into a sort-of crown on her head, was stunning and familiar. But it was just an artistic rendering of a model. Deep blue eyes blazed below delicately arched brows in the picture. A zing of recognition jangled his brain, but disappeared before he latched onto it.

Hailey reached out and picked up his mug. She sniffed it suspiciously, wrinkling her nose.

"What did you put in your coffee, Uncle T? Ms. Nia had breakfast with us. You made French toast."

Taking the cup from her hands, he set it aside. He lifted her off his lap then stood beside her. "Sorry, kid. Don't remember making a meal for anyone named Nia." An aggravating tap in his chest told him his words didn't quite ring true. "We've talked about you making things up."

"But we did." Hailey stomped her little foot, eyes squinty and lips tightly seamed in a pout. "I'm worried about you, Uncle Thomas."

"Knock it off, munchkin. I'm fine," he reassured her.

"Maybe you need more time on your filming break."

Thomas swept Hailey up under his arm and carried her like a giggly football to the entry hall, where she'd dropped her bag. Lowering her just enough to reach the handles, he waited until she grabbed it before hitching her higher on his side. Holding her like that, he carried his squirming, shrieking burden to her room.

"What do you say we put away your stuff then go grab some lunch? You can tell me what else you did at camp besides riding pickles."

That produced a fresh gale of laughter. "No, silly. We sang songs about pickles. We rode motorsickles."

He mock staggered on the last step. "No!

You're not driving already. You can't even reach the gas pedal." He let out a groaning whine. "I thought I had at least eight more years before I had to worry about you behind the wheel."

When they entered her room, he reached behind her legs and flipped her arse-over-head onto her bed. The backpack flew from her grip and plopped right into a laundry basket in the corner.

Thomas whistled. "Would you look at that?"

"Looks like my stuff is already put away." Hailey bounced off the bed. "Can we go to Helios after lunch to say hi to Ms. Nia?"

"Honey, I don't know her. We have some other errands to run. Some other time, okay?"

"But—"

"Stop, munchkin." He nearly relented at the dawning disappointment in her eyes. But he held firm. "We'll try to find her when they have the Founder's Day celebration on Saturday."

"But that's two days away." She stuck out her lower lip and crossed her little arms over her chest.

Thomas held back his laughter at her pouty display. "You'll live. It's on the grounds at the Institute. If there is a Ms. Nia, she's bound to be there, don't you think?"

"Yeah!" Hailey bounced enthusiastically around him. "The Scouts are having a place there to 'cruit new members. They're giving away chocolate bars and popcorn."

"We'll add them to our list of things to see before we check out the carnival rides." Although, riding the kiddie coaster with Hailey *after* she'd eaten chocolate and popcorn might not be the optimal order.

Hailey grabbed his hand and tugged him toward the door, interrupting his mental rearranging of their activity list. Her excited chatter lasted all the way down the stairs, and then out the door to the car.

CHAPTER 21

Two days had disappeared with no progress made toward a solution. No other man burst forward to suddenly embrace magic and defeat Pierus. Nia dug deep through all of her previous lifetimes and memories, searching for the answer. *Morose* best described her mood.

Atlas had materialized in her office three times with updates on his efforts to rehang the moon in the correct spot. They were closer, but he and his employees were struggling with the effort to move mountains, so to speak. He didn't take kindly to her suggestion of using a giant supernatural fulcrum and a little Gorilla Glue to stick it back in place.

Mars had summoned her to the security department meeting at Olympus in the middle of last night. She'd lurched from a dream about

Thomas with tears streaming down her face. But she'd trounced on the memories with both feet and moved through the Hollow to the corporate boardroom with renewed resolve.

The news from Mars was that they'd uncovered Cratus's complicity in Pierus's scheme. The god of strength and power had conspired to incapacitate Zeus to keep him from aiding his daughters in future challenges. Apparently it had pissed Pierus off that Zeus had interfered with Clio's round. A bit of a double-edged sword, since Pierus himself was aiding his daughters. Cratus had been sequestered in a shielded cell in the deepest recesses of Hades.

Zeus had been at the meeting as well. Concern blasted against Nia's skull as she took in his pallor and the exhaustion lurking in his smile. When she questioned him about his health, he'd dismissed her worry with a negligent wave of his hand. By the end of the meeting, his color had been restored and the smooth authority in his voice had returned. But after he'd dismissed everyone, he slouched back in his executive chair and rubbed his temples.

Ken had remained at the headquarters to consult with Mars and help Atlas figure out if repositioning the moon was possible. Nia had given all the observatory techs the night off, so she'd been alone when Clio and Jax had popped in to keep her company. She was at work monitoring

Atlas's efforts to restore the heavens to order.

After greeting her with a brotherly hug, Jax cleared his throat, his dark brows drawn together. "Stupid mortal question here. What's holding the Earth in place while Atlas is trying to reestablish the moon's orbit?"

Clio socked him in the arm and then smoothed a hand over the spot. "Not mortal anymore, remember? But to answer your question, Atlas is kind of the Navy SEAL of the gods. He can just do it all."

"Got it." Jax blew out an exasperated sounding breath. "Didn't exactly answer my question, but I'll let it pass."

"Best idea you've had today." A rosy blush spread across Clio's cheeks. "Well, second best."

Jax laughed and stroked his hand down her spine.

"For the goddess's sake!" Nia slapped down the clipboard she'd been holding, the crack echoing against the cavernous dome. "Just had to wipe out all memory of me from the mind of the man I love. Your lovey-dovey shit is not helping here. If you're going to be like that, take it home. I don't need the company."

A stricken look cooled the ardor in Jax's eyes. "I'm sorry, Nia. We weren't thinking."

"Not with your heads, anyway." Nia adjusted the display on one of the consoles. Satisfied with the settings, she faced her sister and sent her a tiny, mental nudge. "I'm fine here. You don't have to keep me company. I'd rather you go check on Zeus."

"Are you concerned, too?" Clio queried, her shoulders lifted toward her ears.

"Yeah. He hasn't looked completely healthy since Cratus held him in thrall at the Athenian." Nia worried that somehow Cratus had managed to steal some of Zeus's vitality while he'd been immobilized. If that had indeed happened, it could be disastrous for Zeus, and all the gods employed at Olympus.

As soon as Clio and Jax misted away into the void, Nia strolled to the coffee station in the corner. She'd made pot after pot since early afternoon, and was down to the dregs of the most recent batch. As she poured it into her mug, she found herself wishing for some amaretto to spice it up. But she needed to be vigilant tonight, so she settled for the Amaretto flavored creamer Bradley kept in the mini-fridge under the counter.

The atmospheric conditions in the observatory shifted, then solidified just as she settled in the reclining seat she'd moved to the base of the large scope. The space around her chest tightened as supernatural mist gathered at the foot of the stairs leading to the platform.

Polly and Mel hovered inches above the

ground. After staying cloaked for long enough to determine the coast was clear, the pair eased to the ground and banished the mist.

"What are you doing?" Nia asked, not bothering to rise from her comfortable spot under the refracting scope. Through the open dome, the heavens blinked and shimmered, a sight that typically managed to calm and inspire. Not so much tonight.

Mel climbed the grated metal stairs of the viewing platform. "Thought you might like a little company. Where is everyone?"

Polly dragged a chair, the legs bumping loudly across the metal deck. She positioned it next to Nia and plopped into it. While Mel made herself comfortable on the edge of the reclining bench, Polly consulted her cell phone.

"Darn, I forgot to shut off my GPS again." She closed her eyes, and blanked her face as she sent out a nudge. Nia was sure the jab was directed at a technician for the mobile carrier that could erase the data from her records. Mortals got a little flustered when immortals transported their cellphones with them through the Hollow. Which they did all the time. The Muses were as addicted to mobile technology as regular mortals.

"I gave everyone the night off since they'll all have to work tomorrow for the Founder's Day celebration." Nia took a sip of her coffee. Mel grabbed the mug from her hands and gulped it down.

Nia scowled at her sibling, but didn't bother to snatch the mug back. She'd had enough today.

"We're sending two crews from the station to cover it tomorrow. I'll be here as well."

"I'm glad. I want as many friendly faces in the crowd as possible. I'm a little worried. Thousands of people attend this event. There will be ample opportunity for Pierus and Mayhem to get up to no good."

Mel gasped and clutched her throat, not wasting the chance to be dramatic. "You think something will happen?"

"Can't take the attitude that it will be just any Saturday in the park," Nia retorted. "Mars promised extra undercover security, in addition to what the Institute has coordinated. Better to be over-prepared than caught with our guard down."

Polly finally looked up from the scrolling newsfeed that had held her attention. "There have been reports of violence erupting all over China. But the government quelled the uprisings before they got too out of hand."

"Any other reports of incidents brought about by Mayhem?"

"A riot in Athens, and a train bombing in Mumbai. Nia, these things might have normally happened given the economic state in Greece and the political insurrection in India. But what are the chances of them occurring on the same day? Not likely. No groups are stepping forward to claim responsibility. I believe it's part of Pierus's challenge."

Nia scrubbed a hand over her face, and shoved agitated fingers through her hair. "Too bloody many. I can't keep up," she muttered. "I can't win."

Mel patted Nia's leg. "You can. You will. We're all here to help."

The gentle smile on Mel's face warmed Nia. "Thanks, Mel. Just like we'll all be here for you when it's your turn."

"I wonder which stinking magpie I'll have to face." Mel wrung her hands like a Victorian debutant.

"Probably Doom." Polly shot Mel a look designed to tell the Muse of drama to reel the theatrics in a tad.

"Just my luck."

"If I fail, I wonder if the rest of you will have to face the challenge? Or if you'll just convert to magpies along with me?" Nia groused. But a thought blared like a klaxon in her brain. "We never attempted to negotiate the terms with Pierus. I wonder if we could petition Dice to adjudicate the dispute."

"It would be smart to ask the Goddess of Justice to help. That way, if any of us fail, we might have a second chance." Polly moved to the edge of her chair. "That's brilliant, Nia. Why didn't we think of it before?"

"Don't know. But why don't you two go check into that."

"Oh, sister. We don't want to leave you alone. We came to help." Mel's voice rose. Apparently Polly's nudge didn't work.

Nia sent a tiny nudge of her own toward Mel before replying. "I'm okay. Really. I'm just going to survey the heavens and clean up what I can from here. There's a scientist in Japan I need to poke a little. He's on the verge of developing a new lens capable of surveying and plotting out a universe he has yet to discover. I want to be sure he is set to move forward before…" She couldn't finish the thought.

Polly huffed out a breath and stood. Grabbing Mel's arm, she dragged their sister to her feet as well. She jabbed her finger in Nia's face. "Never say die."

More like never squawk die. Nia kept the thought to herself. "Let me know what Dice says. It's an angle worth pursuing."

Pressure built in the air around Nia as Mel and Polly began to mist.

"We'll see you tomorrow." Polly's voice floated on the cloud vapor as they blinked out of the room.

Before I become a magpie for all eternity, Nia finished her last sentence mentally. But Polly was right. Giving up before the challenge was over wouldn't accomplish anything. Some solution would present itself.

It had to, for all their sakes.

CHAPTER 22

The arrival of the weekend techs for the morning shift roused Nia from the restless slumber into which she'd fallen a short while ago. She'd worked all night, putting her affairs in order and had sat at the master console just to write one final email to her new contact at NASA. After she hit send, she'd shoved the keyboard away and laid her head down, intending to simply rest a moment, and had nodded off.

Yawning broadly, and with not quite an hour before the festivities began, she raced home to change. On her return trip down the broad, tree-lined avenue leading to the planetarium, she counted three magpies sitting among the branches, and one half-bird, half human form on the roadside. As she pulled alongside Mayhem's grotesque form, she braked, and rolled down the window.

Mayhem's fully human eyes looked obscene in her tiny, half-bald bird head. Nia curled her lips and let out a shrill whistle, hoping to frighten the creature away. When it didn't take to the sky, Nia whispered a nudge to it. "Don't get too comfortable. You haven't won yet."

As it waddled away, it emitted a loud squawk, a bird's cackle with human undertones. She no longer seemed capable of flight, a fact which sent shivers coursing down Nia's spine. Brazen bitch.

By the time she pulled into the Institute's employee lot, most of the spaces were occupied. She circled the drive seeking a place to park, finally finding one as far from the door as it could be. She locked the car and then headed to the palatial building along with the rest of the crowd. Families with children surged around her as she dropped her keys into her bag and searched for her phone to call Atlas for a report. Worry had taken up permanent residence under her solar plexus; the resulting ache made it hard to catch her breath.

"Ms. Nia!" An excited child's voice hailed her.

When she spun around, she discovered Hailey racing toward her, with Thomas trailing behind. Blood rushed to her face at the sight of him, strong, confident, sexy as hell in a T-shirt that clung to his broad shoulders and fell loosely around his trim waist. Dark shorts skimmed the tops of his knees and running shoes completed his casual athlete look. Goddess, his tousled sandy hair begged for her fingers to run through it.

His expression held a slight smile and his gorgeous green eyes were filled with curiosity, but no recognition. The fact sliced across Nia's heart like a rusty paring knife.

"Ms. Nia, you're here! I told him we'd find you." The girl barreled into Nia, who staggered back a step before recovering.

Holy Hades! Mnemosyne had scrubbed Thomas's memories free of Nia, but they'd forgotten about Hailey. They'd spent time together, like a family. The child would certainly recall the personal tour she'd given them and the breakfast they'd shared and remind Thomas. What else might he remember? Damn, damn, and damn. How could she have been so stupid?

She cast a frantic glance around. There were too many people nearby to attempt to freeze Thomas and Hailey into a state of stasis and call the goddess of memory back to finish the job. And with Hailey's arms wrapped around Nia's waist, pretending she didn't know the girl wasn't an option. Nudging a child typically had no effect on them. Nia's only option was to try to cast a thrall on the child. But carefully. It would destroy her if she harmed the kid in the slightest.

She laid her hands on Hailey's shoulders and

urged the child away. Concentrating on her task, she prodded Hailey's mind, sending her a command. *You don't remember me at all. We've only met here.*

Hailey frowned then shuddered, confusion blatant on her face. She tucked her hands behind her back as she stepped away. "I'm sorry. I thought...I thought..." The girl's hesitant voice trailed away.

A bird squawked raucously overhead and several festival attendees stopped to stare into the trees, as though searching for the source of the noise. Pressure built in Nia's chest, similar to what she experienced as she stepped into the Hollow, but different. Around them, people turned to train their gazes on Hailey. Nia squeezed her eyes shut and mumbled softly *go about your business.* Life returned to normal and the people closest to them resumed chattering as they moved away.

"What did you say?" Thomas asked with a deep frown creasing harsh lines into his forehead. He laid a protective hand on Hailey's shoulder.

"I didn't say anything." Hesitancy caused her voice to rise, her tone coming across as defensive. Erasing his memories hadn't affected his clairaudient ability.

He tipped his head to the side and jammed his fist into his pocket. "That's so weird. I swear I heard you tell Hailey she didn't remember you.

Not out loud, but in my head." He shook his head, as though trying to disperse a fog.

"You're right, that is weird." Nia clutched the strap of her purse, pulling it tight across her body.

"But why would you? We haven't met, have we?"

"I don't believe we have, although I've met your niece here." The lie was bitter on her tongue and hard to swallow past the lump lodged in her throat.

"Huh. Most people think Hailey is my daughter. How did you know she's my niece? You're so familiar. Are you sure we haven't met?"

Panic surged in her gut as the fight or flight instinct kicked in. She had to get away before he remembered too much. Or she burst into tears. "Of course I'm sure. I need to get to work." She pasted on a bright smile and swept her arm wide, spreading a prodding thought toward the Wildes. She voiced the nudge aloud though. "You should go enjoy the festival. Plenty to see and do."

"Right. By the way, I'm Thomas." He thrust his arm out, his gaze interested, warm and expectant.

"And she's Nia," Hailey said, pointing at her.

Nia stared at his hand a moment before taking it. The heat of his palm seared her, rousing memories of how perfectly his hands fit her body, how his fingers inside her made her shatter with bliss. The pulse that had been throbbing at the base of her throat burst into piston-speed, stopping her breath.

Thomas's eyes flared wide with the contact. His body jerked. Recognition flickered in his gaze then was replaced with heat, which faded to bewilderment. Confusion danced on his features and his ready smile melted away as Nia tugged her hand from his. He remembered for an instant. Somehow, Mnemosyne's memory wipe hadn't been strong enough. The speed with which his memory then faded matched the velocity of the spike of hurt hurtling from her gut to her heart.

Eyes watering, throat aching, Nia forced mental inspiration into her words. "Well, you should go enjoy yourselves. Forget you've ever met me and just have fun here today."

Hailey slipped her hand into Thomas's and tugged his arm. "Come on, Uncle Thomas. We have to go to the Campfire Scouts' booth. I want to see my friends."

Eyes curiously flat, Thomas offered her a nod, before trudging away with Hailey.

Following after them would have been an impossibility. Even immortals couldn't move when the last pieces of their hearts shattered. Cold loneliness washed over Nia, raising goose bumps on her arms despite the warm summer breeze flowing over her skin. About twenty paces away, Thomas pulled Hailey to a halt and turned to stare back at her. Confusion and something warmer lurked in his features. Even at a distance, the longing in his gaze pierced her soul.

Jostled from behind, she jolted from a trance of pain, need and love. With a hasty glance to her surroundings, she mumbled an apology to no one in particular and the crowd moved past her. A single tear she'd tried to keep at bay trickled down her cheek.

Above her, the damned magpie screeched an inhuman laugh and several black and white feathers floated to the ground at her feet. She brushed the tear impatiently away and imagined an arrow plunging into the bird's breast, then let it fly. The bird squawked once again then went silent. Reaching into her handbag, her fingers curled around her phone.

Hands shaking, she dialed and waited for her call to connect. "Zeus, we have a problem."

CHAPTER 23

The red-headed woman intrigued him. Something had stirred deep in his chest when he'd heard her voice. At first sight, his dick had jumped to attention. It was easy to imagine her whispering into his ear as he thrust into her. When she'd taken his hand, he'd gotten an image of her fingers digging into his butt, encouraging him to a faster rhythm. The snug fit of his shorts tightened as he'd held her hand for an instant. He wanted, no, craved, her lips under his.

Jesus Christ! When was the last time he'd had such a visceral reaction to a complete stranger? But...she didn't seem so much a stranger. Some part of him knew her. Magically and irrevocably knew her, and knew they were destined to be together.

If he believed in magic. Which he did not.

Around them, couples laughed together, and families raced and shrieked. Just a typical Saturday at a fair. But the sounds didn't ring true for him. It was as if he heard the noises through a closed door. Beside him, Hailey remained silent as they strolled down the path to the vendor booths.

He tightened his grip on her hand. "You okay, munchkin?"

She answered in a petulant tone. "I told you we knew her. But she didn't know us. Why, Uncle Thomas?"

Thomas glanced over his shoulder. His heart weighed heavier as he discovered the beautiful woman had moved away. He tugged Hailey to the side, off the path. Crouching in front of her, he ran his hands down her thin arms. "I'm sure she meets a lot of people. She works here, right? Maybe she meets too many people to remember all of them."

"But she should remember us."

Should she? Thomas couldn't shake the feeling that they had met, and spent time together. Quality, intimate time. "What do you say we just forget about all of this and just have fun?"

Hailey's nod launched the smile he loved to see on her small features.

"Okay?"

She nodded more vigorously.

"Let's go." He stood and offered her his hand.

The gravel path crunched under their sneakers

as they resumed walking toward the festival. An elusive memory tickled his consciousness. Someone had entreated him to keep Hailey safe. "Stay close, munchkin. There are a lot of people here. I wouldn't want to lose you."

As they wandered among the attractions and booths, Thomas couldn't shake the disquiet that had gripped him when they moved away from Nia. As they passed other patrons, many stopped to stare. Typically, it wouldn't bother him. He was accustomed to being recognized. Oftentimes, people approached him, asked for an autograph, and either wanted to discuss their favorite episode or offer him suggestions for a myth to bust.

Today was different. People stared and pointed, but not at him. Their attention seemed focused on Hailey. He gripped her small hand tighter, a cold sweat breaking out on his torso.

"Ow!" Hailey exclaimed and tugged her hand from him. "You were squeezing too hard, Uncle Thomas."

"Sorry." A couple passed them, silent and staring. They stopped just beyond Thomas's reach and turned to stare. "Hailey, I think we should go home now. It's getting late."

"Not yet. We need to look through the telescopes to say hello to Daddy and Mommy."

"We can do that from our backyard."

"Please? They'll be closer here. Not as close as

with the big telescope, but better." Hailey gestured toward the rust red observatory dome. She drew her brows together and pursed her lips. "Please can we stay a little longer?"

The other couple had moved on, lessening the odd sense of menace tripping up his spine. Thomas nodded, reclaimed Hailey's hand and led her toward the observation deck. Dusk was falling and the evening stars would be visible from the bank of telescopes situated on the edge of the cliff.

Several other families occupied the deck, but Thomas located a free scope. He lifted Hailey onto the small concrete pad at the base, and helped her adjust the viewer until she claimed it was in focus.

Conversation around them died, leaving heavy silence in its wake. Thomas turned slowly and immediately tensed. A semicircle of people had formed around them—every face ominously blank. Two burly men moved toward him, their steps awkward, as though they had no control over their bodies.

"Stay back," Thomas ordered as he shoved Hailey behind him. Spying a break in the circle, he firmed his grip on her arm and dodged to his left. The men moved with him, lunging to grab him. They restrained him, separating him from Hailey. One of the mothers from the crowd leaped forward and snatched Hailey from behind him, covering the girl's mouth to stifle her sudden scream.

Mayhem (Goddesses of Delphi Book 2)

CHAPTER 24

Nia spied Pierus in the shadow of the performance stage. His business attire caused him to stand out like a sore thumb among the casually dressed crowds.

"You'd think he'd try to blend in," Ken scoffed as he stood next to her. "Cocky son of a bitch, ain't he?"

"He hasn't won yet," Mars growled, glaring daggers at said son of a bitch.

Terri, who'd hired the bands for the events, edged closer to Nia and whispered, "He's up to something."

"Ya think?" Nia asked dryly. She lifted her chin toward the stage and pinned her stare on Pierus. Reaching out to him mentally, she taunted *I have my eyes on you.*

Pierus shrugged, his face a mask of arrogance

as he brushed at a speck of lint on his black jacket. His smartass voice filled her head. *I'm not who you should be watching.*

Nia crossed her arms over her waist, trying to quell the nerves fluttering in her belly.

"This crowd is quieter than is warranted." Ken twisted at the waist, surveying the area around them. "I don't like it."

Nia didn't like it either. Across from her, Pierus lifted the corners of his mouth in a smirk as he leaned a shoulder against the bandstand.

A scream rent the air. It sounded panicked and terrified.

"Let's go." Ken grabbed her hand and dragged her in the direction of the noise. Mars and Terri followed closely behind. Heart pounding heavily against her ribcage, Nia and the rest raced up the path to the observation deck. The screams grew louder and were joined by yelling. Her blood iced as they crested the hill and took in the tableau by the decorative concrete fence bordering the steep cliff.

In the midst of a silent mob, Thomas fought to free himself from the grip of two men while a third held a screaming Hailey over the precipice.

Oh, dear goddess. Hailey *was* the innocent foretold by Pierus. And the mob had her in their unaware clutches. Only Thomas seemed immune to the influence that had spread over the crowd.

The horror and determination etched into his face mobilized Nia.

Concentrating her energy, she covered the twenty feet to the observation deck in the blink of an eye, too short a span for her aura or sparkling lights to appear. She swept in next to the man holding Hailey and seized the girl around the waist. Ken was right behind her and knocked the man to the side. Then he turned the force of his gaze on the semicircle and spread his hands wide, holding them at bay.

Hailey flung her arms around Nia's neck, screaming in fear. Running her hand along the child's spine, Nia infused her fingers with calming vibes, and urged them into Hailey's chest. Her fingers sparked gently as she sent her influence through Hailey. The girl's screams dissipated, and Hailey buried her face against Nia's neck, sobbing quietly.

"Nia, we need your influence here." Ken nodded to the hillside above them. More people moved toward their position, everyone walking stiffly, as though in a trance. "This has Pierus all over it. How the fuck is he doing this with Cratus in custody?"

"Hailey!" Thomas yelled, still tussling with the brutes holding him.

Mars materialized behind the two men and crashed their heads together. Zeus, Gaia and all of

Nia's sisters blinked through the Hollow. Without a word, all the immortals formed a protective flank around Nia and Hailey. Mars grasped Thomas's arm and jerked him toward the center.

"Gaia, take her," Nia commanded, without turning to face her mother.

Gaia stepped forward and removed Hailey from Nia's arms. She nestled the child close to her chest, stepping backward. Mel, Terri, Thalia, and Polly formed a protective ring around their mother and the child. Thomas surged toward them, but stopped short as he encountered the energy field surrounding the small group.

"Leave them," Mars commanded as he gripped Thomas's shoulder. "They'll protect her."

"She's okay," Gaia shouted. "We've got her.

Thomas reeled toward Nia. "What's going on?"

Busy gathering energy from the heavens, Nia couldn't spare him any attention. She jabbed a fast thought into his brain. *"I'm sorry."*

Power palpated in her chest, pulsing heavily, like a second life form inside her skin trying to escape. The crowd edged forward, murmuring loudly. Menace and determination replaced the blank stares. The mob wanted Hailey and they weren't going to give up.

"Nia, up on the hill." Zeus's voice was strained as he indicated the crest.

Pierus and his half-formed offspring crowned the top of the rise. Mayhem had sprouted human legs, but hadn't lost her wings or beak. Raven black hair streamed from her head, snarled and tangled but wafting in a supernatural breeze. Nia repressed a shudder and refocused her attention on the task.

Picturing a lasso in her mind, Nia flung the imaginary rope heavenward, wrapping it around the descending sun. Hot electrical current spiraled downward along the invisible tether. Nia arched involuntarily as blazing heat surged into her. Her skin glowed as the power took possession of her body. The top of her head burned as though ready to burst into flames.

The crowd continued to approach, urged on as Pierus raised his arms, palms out. His fingertips glowed as he twisted his wrists and brought his hands together. Energy, red tinged and angry, gathered between his palms. He slammed his hands toward the ground and the mob surged forward in response.

Nia closed her eyes and corralled the power she'd harnessed. Picturing an ocean wave, she unleashed the influence and pushed the crowd away. As she forced the energy outward, Aerie, Corie, and Clio laid their hands on Nia's body, funneling additional power into her reserves. Callie slapped her hand on one shoulder blade, while Ken held the other. Zeus gripped Nia's neck, the sting of his superior power tweaking Nia's force.

"Make them slumber, daughter." A malaise Nia couldn't identify undercut Zeus's commanding voice.

But she followed the direction.

"Time to sleep," she commanded the mob. The echoing guttural pitch of her tone surprised her.

Imagining sweet Morpheus riding the wave she pushed over the crush of people surrounding them, she thrust the picture from the center of her chest, bowing back with the effort. Half the crowd dropped in their tracks as the wave breached them. The remaining group continued to advance.

Zeus punched additional power through his grip on her neck, and searing flame roared down her arms. Sparks detonated from her fingertips as she lifted her hands. Curling one hand into a fist, Zeus manifested a glowing kernel of light. The glare intensified, growing to softball size.

With a mighty heave, Zeus hurled the energy ball to the hilltop. When the force caught him square in the chest, Pierus's expensive suit burst into flames. Mayhem swatted the flames with her wings. The stench of burned feathers overpowered the bite of ozone left in the wake of the energy force Zeus had thrown.

Before Nia could raise her hands, Thomas barged in front of her. Recognition and trust filled his gaze. "What can I do?"

"You need to move, Thomas."

"Let me help."

"I don't see how." She tore her gaze from his to find the remaining mob almost on them.

Ken pulled him to the side, but Thomas fought to remain next to Nia. When she lifted her arm, sparks glowed under her skin as her power built. She aimed toward one side of the observation deck, and sucked in a deep breath, trying to center the force growing in her.

Thomas laid his hand on her arm, the blistering heat of his palm overriding the energy within her. She gasped as the voltage in her chest narrowed and focused. Some force within Thomas was actually aiding her quest. Beneath all the energy flowing through her, love swelled for the man helping her.

Laying her free hand over his, a bright blue glow flourished. He was mortal and this joint effort could permanently harm him. Or kill him. Summoning whatever strength he willingly shared, she cautiously siphoned off only what she dared. From the points of contact with Zeus, her sisters, and Ken, she channeled all the burn they offered to her.

Friction scraped along her nerves. Sweeping her arm from right to left, she projected slumber onto the entire crowd. One by one, they dropped in their tracks, succumbing to the power she harnessed from the sun, from the immortals, and from Thomas. The last one collapsed within two feet of her position.

On the hill, Pierus crashed to his knees, tearing the burned fabric from his body. His moans were audible in Nia's head, and she slammed the virtual door on the noise, refusing to be moved by the maniac's pain. He deserved it for trying to drive a mob to kill an innocent for the sake of the challenge. She spared a glance over her shoulder. Thank the goddess, Hailey was safe.

"She's safe, Thomas." Nia squeezed his hand and looked into his eyes, projected a thought filled with love.

His sandy hair stood on end, but the energy drain didn't appear to have affected him greatly. He stood tall and strong next to her, tossing a glance toward Gaia and Hailey, before turning back to her. He cupped her cheek, then threaded his fingers through her hair, a moment of peace after the storm they'd weathered together.

Zeus lifted his hand from Nia's neck and collapsed to one knee behind her. As her sisters jerked their hands away from her, a tearing sensation ripped at her soul. Ken and Thomas kept their hands on her as the Muses rushed to aid their father.

Nia dropped her head forward and remained standing only by the force of her will. Gentle healing pulsed into her through Ken's hand, restoring some of her energy. Callie stepped in front of her and jostled Thomas to the side. He didn't release her grip as Callie cupped Nia's cheeks. Warmth and subtle power thrummed from the tips of Callie's fingers, threading through Nia's brain, repairing the psychic damage.

And still, Thomas did not remove his hand from her arm. In fact, he slid it down and laced his fingers through hers, the heat in his palm bleeding into hers. When Nia gently pushed Callie's hands away, she nudged a silent thank you into her sister. A smile tugged the woman's lips up, and Callie nodded curtly before stepping away.

Nia turned to face Thomas, slipping her other hand into his. Behind her, Hailey's crying wound down as Gaia crooned an ancient Grecian lullaby to the child.

"Do you remember?" Nia questioned, her voice whispery soft.

His face was somber. "That you love me?"

"We can start there."

"Was it true?" He released one hand and raised it to wrap gently around the nape of her neck. His fingers were cool against the residual burn from Zeus's energy.

Heart leaping into her throat, she nodded.

Rapid footsteps pounded on the pavement behind them. Hailey squirmed between them, lifting her arms to Thomas.

He picked her up and hugged her close. "Munchkin, I thought I'd lost you."

"But you didn't. Ms. Nia saved us. I told you she was magic."

"She most certainly is." Thomas held Nia's gaze, his crowded with gratitude, love and wonderment. "I do believe in magic."

Air swirled in wild abandon, a sudden gust of wind blowing both hot and cold from the canyon behind them. For an instant, everything felt lighter, almost as if Earth's gravity had eased and even the heaviest of objects could float away. Weightlessness surrounded her, shifting the world, then snapping it into place again.

Into the right place.

Thomas's admission had just sealed her success in the challenge.

Nia sagged against him, grateful for the strong arms he wrapped around her. Not only did he believe, it appeared he possessed some magic himself. The power of love was the strongest, most magical force on the planet. He believed in her love for him. She could only hope his demonstration and assistance was proof of his love for her. For now, it was enough she no longer faced eternity as a magpie.

Wrapping her arms around the man she loved and the little girl who'd taken up residence in her heart, she held them close. Hailey tangled her fingers in Nia's hair, stroking soothing circles on her scalp. Nia turned her face on Thomas's chest, seeking Pierus. She sent him a nudge to get lost and take his hideous bitch of a daughter with him.

Laughter rumbled under Thomas's ribs. "I heard that."

"I'm glad." Nia joined his chuckle.

Pierus looked like he wanted to resist her nudge, but she increased the magnitude of her prod. He grimaced under the pain of her jolt. Ominous, black mist gathered at his feet and climbed his legs. Beside him, Mayhem screamed, her voice reverting back to strictly a bird, not a hint of humanity left in it. By the time Pierus was completely consumed by the mist and had vanished from the mortal world, Mayhem had changed back to a simple magpie. She fluttered up to the branches of the nearest tree.

Mars jammed his hands together then flung them in the direction of the bird, encasing it in a gilded cage. He levitated the cage and dragged it above the sleeping mob until he held it secure in his grasp.

"Sorry to break you guys apart," Ken spoke loudly as he joined them. "But maybe some damage control might be in order. We've summoned Mnemosyne and she'll be here shortly. Not sure if anyone on the other side of that hill noticed, but just in case someone decided to use their smartphone, we should take care of it."

Nia moved from the circle of Thomas's arms. She rubbed her knuckles over her chest, taking stock of her depleted energy stores. Not quite enough to achieve the kind of miracle they needed.

"Callie, Polly. A little help, please," she called. When the women approached, she explained. "I'm going to have a go at the sun to burn out a little memory on any cellphones in the area. I need some extra energy."

Ken drew Thomas and Hailey to the side. Thomas kept his gaze trained on Nia's face, love giving his visage a glow that warmed her to her core. She sent him a smile and nod before turning to her task.

Flanking her on either side, her sisters lifted their hands to her shoulders. She centered their power in her chest and then balanced the charge building from her center. She directed a bolt of energy toward the sinking sun. In her mind's eye, she saw the jagged shard slam into the surface of the sun, then explode backward, climbing toward the atmosphere. Just enough to create an electro-magnetic surge that would empty phone memories of the last few minutes but not enough to do any other damage.

Her shoulders slumped as she completed the task. The air pressurized around her as the pulse reach the earth.

Lime-colored mist swelled to the left of her as Mnemosyne materialized. She clucked her tongue against her teeth and scolded, "Another mess for me to clean up, I see." She looked at Thomas. "You again. I should have known. The power of love overcame the strength of my spell with you. Are all your memories intact?"

He nodded. "I believe so. I'm also ready to make some new ones with Nia, so I'm going to ask you nicely not to take them away from me again."

Nia's diminutive aunt emitted an infectious laugh. "I'd promise, but this isn't up to me. Zeus will decide when you get back to Olympus."

She turned and focused on the stirring crowd. Lifting her hand and shutting her eyes, she began to chant.

"Daughter." Gaia scurried toward them. "We will meet you in the boardroom. I'm taking Hailey with me."

Nia's heart sank. Likely Zeus would erase the memories from both Thomas and his niece. And where would that leave her? "Is that necessary?"

"Zeus believes so. We risk detection." She turned toward Hailey and laid a hand on the child's shoulder. "Did you do any of the rides today, sweetheart? I have one last treat to take you on. Brace yourself. I do believe you will enjoy this."

A look of wonderment and delight lit Hailey's

face as Gaia levitated them. Graceful purple mist swirled surrounded them. In the blink of an eye, they, the rest of the Muses and Zeus vanished from sight.

Thomas ran his warm fingers along the inside of her elbow, turning her to face him. "So Zeus really is your dad?"

"Uh-huh. Are you ready to take another trip through the Hollow? Our presence at the corporate headquarters is required."

In response, Thomas wrapped his arms around her waist, and braced his feet apart. "I'll go anywhere as long as it's with you."

Blinking away happy tears, Nia moved them into the Hollow after her mother.

CHAPTER 25

Pressure built in Thomas's head as the sky blue mist consumed them. He squeezed his lips tightly together and pinched his nose to pop his ears. Bright spots of light dotted Nia's void form and pale rose glowed in the center of her body, pulsing calmly. He glanced down his body, glowing with a simple silver with a spot of cobalt light pulsing weakly where his heart would be."

Hailey's charming giggle reached his ears, and he looked around for her. His sense of direction was wonky. A small burst of anxiety jiggled his heart and tensed his shoulders when he couldn't automatically track his niece.

She's just there. Turn your head to your left. See that small silver form in the midst of the large purple one? That's Hailey.

"How do you know for sure?" he asked, his

voice curiously muted, as if talking into pillow. He located Hailey, suspended in the midst of a purple haze with a golden center.

Her answer reverberated pleasantly in his head. *All mortals glow silver in the Hollow.*

The tension left his body as her calm voice soothed him. Nia's mist blanketed him, brushing against his body. Even though, at the moment, her form was basically a cloud, the sensation aroused him. His cock hardened and lengthened. Nia's soft voice chuckled through his head.

"You can feel that?"

Yes, and it feels wonderful." Warm, salty mist caressed his lips. *"But you'd better tame that reaction. We're almost there and my dad won't want to see you with a hard-on, you know?"*

He no longer heard Hailey's giggle and assumed it meant Gaia had arrived at their destination. The air surrounding Thomas intensified, crystalizing into shapes and forms. In the blink of his eyes, Nia's body transformed, solidifying in his arms. Her lovely face filled his vision, her blue eyes aglow, but pinched with nervousness.

"You okay?" she asked, her voice low.

He tightened his grip around her waist and pressed his mouth to hers. The soft satin of her plump lips under his was a heaven he wanted every day. He lifted his head and met her gaze, hoping she'd see the love in his. "I am now."

Behind him, a throat was loudly cleared. Pink flashed into her cheeks as she closed her eyes, and drew a deep breath. Thomas craned his head around and spied Zeus slouched in a plush, high backed chair, drumming his fingers on the padded arm.

Backing away from him, Nia laid her hands on his wrists and stepped out of the circle of his arms. Her red hair bounced on her shoulders when she turned to face her father. A wave of surrealism washed over Thomas. He'd fallen in love with the daughter of the king of gods. That he accepted gods existed as a truth might be the most amazing thing.

Thomas took his first look at the room they'd landed in. Eight women, every one a red-head, he'd seen at the festival sat around a spectacular conference table with a black granite top. Seven of them sent warm smiles at Nia, the eighth scowled at him. He tipped his head toward the angry woman and offered a smile. She rolled her eyes and flipped open the notebook in front of her.

"Ignore Callie." Nia lifted her chin, indicating the glowering woman. "She's the oldest and has always been crabby. It's her fault resting bitch face is a thing."

Thomas couldn't help but feel Callie had judged him and found him not quite good enough.

Didn't matter. He wasn't here for her. Nia and Hailey were his priorities.

His ears concussed as Gaia popped into the room. Without Hailey.

Panic arrowed up his torso and speared into his brain. He moved toward Gaia. "Where's my niece? What have you done with her?" After seeing the crowd at the Institute descend on them and hold Hailey's tiny body over the edge of the cliff, he wanted her tucked safely against his side.

Gaia laid her hand on his chest, right over his heart. A warm glow invaded his soul, easing his worry. She patted the spot as she spoke. "Hailey is safe. She's with Artemis in the childcare center. We didn't think she should be present for this meeting."

"Artemis?" Thomas searched his brain for who that was. Had he met her but didn't remember? The way he hadn't remembered Nia?

"The goddess protector of the vulnerable." Nia ran her hand over his face, stroking her thumb over his cheekbone. "All the kids love the childcare center Artemis runs for the company. There's a waiting list to get in."

With her hand between his shoulder blades, she urged him into one of the comfortable chairs surrounding the massive table. She took the seat next to his, claimed his hand out of sight, and laced their fingers together.

A door opened in the paneled wall and a man raced into the room, a helmet stashed under his arm. "Sorry I'm late. I was collecting the latest reports." He made his way around the table. Extending his hand to Thomas, he grinned. "I'm Hermes. I'm in charge of communications for Olympus. I've seen the video feeds of the incident. What you did was astounding, but we have a public relations mess on our hands."

Oh lord. Did that helmet have wings on it? This was the messenger god. Thomas did a covert check of the guy's leg, looking for a matching set of wings. What he saw was expensive Italian loafers and cuffed trousers.

Hermes smirked at him then twitched his pant leg up, revealing a wing-free ankle. "That part is made up."

"Hermes, please take a seat. We do have an agenda to follow. We'll get to your part shortly." Zeus's stentorian tone demanded attention. He turned his stark blue gaze on Thomas. "We must decide what to do about this mortal."

* * *

Despair flooded her system at Zeus's words. Nia had already lost Thomas once. The thought of the gods stealing his memories from him again chipped a chink of her heart away. It dropped like a rock into her stomach and settled hard and cold.

She tightened her grip on Thomas's warm

hand and pleaded with her father. "Zeus, please don't erase his memory. At least not of me. I'm begging you."

"Urania, you must not interfere. Remember, this is a mortal who denied helping."

Thomas fidgeted next to her, his cheeks flushed with ruddy color.

Zeus turned his gaze toward Nia, but frowned as Gaia lowered gracefully to the seat next to hers. Narrowing his eyes, he pointed to Gaia. "Woman, I do not need your prodding. Of course I'm going to do what is right."

"Be sure you do, or you will be sleeping in one of the guest cottages for the foreseeable future," Gaia replied, cold steel underlying her pleasant tone.

"Daughter," Zeus addressed Nia. "Did you do something to restore your mortal's memory?"

Hearing him refer to Thomas as her mortal sounded like heaven. Maybe Zeus would ignore his initial refusal and accept her love for the brave man at her side. "I did not. But know this…if I could have, I would. Today was the first time I've seen him since that night at the Athenian."

Thomas stirred beside her. "You took my memories away, but nobody thought about my niece, Hailey. She remembered Nia and reminded me frequently of her." He faced her, his expression relaxed and wondrous. "I smelled your perfume on my pillow. And found your hair in my brush. You were never completely out of my thoughts. Even though I didn't recognize you, I knew you. That by itself is magic."

Tears welled in her eyes. She blinked furiously to keep them from falling. She'd managed to make him believe in the power of magic, but at what cost? The public relations snafu Hermes referred to bloomed in her mind. Thomas had a wide platform of social acceptance thanks to the popularity of his television show. And now, he knew the reality of deities. For thousands of years their true purpose, to watch over and inspire mortals, had remained a closely guarded corporate secret. Thomas could expose them all.

Better that his memories were erased. His and Hailey's.

Desolation bulldozed her spirit. She slumped against the padded back of her chair. "You're going to have to remove the knowledge of gods and Olympus from his mind." She covered her face with a trembling hand. "That first good-bye at the Athenian nearly destroyed me. Having to go through it again surely will."

"Quit being such a drama queen," Mel scoffed, her laughter filling the air.

"That's rich, coming from the Muse of Theatrics," Clio retorted. She narrowed her eyes and glared at Mel, who fidgeted in her seat in response.

Zeus slapped a thunderous hand on the granite tabletop. "Daughters! You are not so old that I can't punish your misbehavior." He stared at each woman in turn, even pinning a quelling look on Gaia. "Where the Hades is Atlas?"

The door swept open again, admitting Atlas with Ken on his heels. "I'm here. Sorry, we had to double-check our calculations. Without Nia's help we got stuck with the gravity aspect." Atlas hustled across the slate floor toward Nia. After handing a sheaf of papers to her, he delivered another set to Zeus.

The paper whispered softly as Nia flipped through the report Atlas and Ken had pulled together in record time. While she studied it, Mars materialized from the Hollow. He went directly to Zeus's side, bent low and spoke quietly into his ear.

"What's going on?" Thomas asked, his voice low and meant for her ears only.

Nia set the papers on the table and laid her hand on them. "Remember I explained that the coronal burst a few weeks ago had misaligned the moon?"

"That was real?"

"Thomas, none of this has been made up."

"Sorry, it just seemed like, well, not possible."

"It was most definitely possible." Eyeing the whispered conference between Mars and her father, she tapped the report in front of her. "It appears in the instant you believed in magic, gravity released its grip on the world. Did you feel it?"

"Like a floating feeling? I thought that was because I'd held your arm while you were doing whatever it was that you did to put the crowd to sleep."

There was that. It was a memory she could hold dear while she spent the rest of this lifetime alone. And missed him desperately in the next ten or hundred. She crushed the thoughts before they made her cry. "I'm not sure why it worked that you were able to help me. But the instant you locked your hand on my arm, all my energy focused on the task."

"The power of love, baby." He pecked her cheek. "But what happened when we were all sort of floating?"

Desire bloomed through her at the touch of his lips. She fought to remember his question. "Without gravity to restrain his effort, Atlas shrugged the moon back into the correct orbit. That eliminated all but the most basic mayhem. The stuff you'd generally see during a full moon." She dropped her chin and peeked up at him through her eyelashes. "Do you remember the challenge?"

"You said you had to lead a man...me, to believe in magic or all of the Muses would become magpies. It's a good sign you aren't a bird, right?"

"Very good. We won this round. But Pierus isn't done. He'll be back to challenge another one of us."

"Can't something be done about him?"

"Zeus has a meeting with Dice next week. She's the Goddess of Justice. We are going to seek legal respite from Pierus's take-over attempt." She sat up straighter as Zeus waved Mars away.

Her father was pale and haggard looking, like the stress from the battle had rooted in him. Concern trumpeted through Nia as she tossed her mother a look. Worry had etched into Gaia's face, bracketing her mouth with pained lines.

"Father, are you well?" Nia questioned, her voice soft.

"I'm fine." Smiling weakly, Zeus surged upright in his chair. "Mars reports that as of a short while ago, most of the lunacy among mortals has ceased. Order has been restored, no one recorded any of the occurrences on their cellphones, thanks to Nia's quick action." He beamed at her.

Polly slapped her phone on the table. "The station just uploaded video to our cloud. I've reviewed the footage and it shows only typical festival activities. No film was captured at the observation deck."

"Mayhem has been released into the aviary with Tyranny," Mars reported. "When I left them, they were pecking each other. Typical sibling rivalry."

"It appears we've won this challenge," Zeus intoned, his deep voice reverberating in the room. He turned his gaze on Thomas. "Now we must decide how to proceed with Mr. Wilde."

Nia tensed. "Do we need to rob him of his memories?"

"Daughter, he is a public figure. He has a wide platform that exposes and debunks myths and legends. Like us."

"I won't expose your secrets." Leaning forward, Thomas looked at Nia with assurance and confidence in his eyes. He turned his attention to Zeus. "I want to spend the rest of my life protecting your daughter, all of your daughters, from scrutiny."

Zeus shook his head. "You have no idea what that entails."

"It doesn't matter. I'd do anything for Nia." Thomas slid his fingers through hers. "I want to marry her. If she'll have me after I refused to help at first."

Happiness charged up from her belly and wrapped around her heart. She smiled through the tears gathering in the corner of her eyes. "She'll have you." But would he still want her after they wiped his memories clean?

"Probably should have asked your dad first,

though." Thomas shrugged and glanced at Zeus, one brow raised. "I want to marry your daughter, sir. With your permission."

Zeus held his peace while Gaia hugged her from the side.

Gaia projected a quiet thought into Nia's head. *He'll agree. I'll see to it.*

"It is not just you we must worry about." Zeus studied his hands. "Your niece is aware of our existence as immortals as well. She's travelled through the Hollow. Without the benefit of slumber."

"Things were a bit crazy at the observation deck. You can't expect me to remember everything." Gaia's tone was sharp as she defended her neglect to put Hailey to sleep on the trip.

Zeus lifted his hand, palm out, and then resumed drumming his fingers on the armrest. He studied Thomas through narrowed eyes.

He hadn't denied Thomas's request, nor hers to leave Thomas's memories alone. Nia crossed her fingers under the table and prayed for a miracle.

Tucking one of her hands through his elbow, Thomas folded his arms on the table. "Has this been done on a child before?"

"This is one answer I do not have. But know this—we have never intentionally hurt a child before. We would take great care to avoid harming Hailey, son."

There it was. Son. A sure sign Zeus had accepted Thomas. Giddy lightness stole through her system.

"You understand that her well-being is my immediate concern. She's already suffered great loss in her life at the hands of terrorists. I will do what it takes to protect her."

Zeus bristled. "Are you comparing me to a terrorist?"

Nia bit back the groan in the back of her throat. One step forward seemed destined for a giant stumble back.

"Not at all. I simply want to ensure my child remains happy and healthy as part of this family." He stroked his thumb over the back of Nia's knuckles. "If we can selectively remove memories, I'm all for it. I distinctly remember Nia telling me that Hailey was in danger and to keep her safe. That memory stuck with me at crunch time. Can we do that?"

"We must wait until Mnemosyne arrives," Gaia chimed in. "To attempt to answer now would be futile."

"Is there other business to attend to?" If not, Nia was ready to head for home. Well, Thomas's house anyway. She'd induce slumber in Hailey to move her through the Hollow again. One less memory they'd have to deal with down the road.

"One final thing. I granted Jax an immortal

lifetime in sync with Clio's. I would gift this to Thomas as well. If he wishes." A smile jumped in Zeus's eyes, but he kept it off his lips.

Happiness fizzed sparkler-bright within her. Tears gathered behind her eyes and she blinked hard as a smile blossomed on her face.

Thomas turned toward her as all the Muses began to talk excitedly. Quietly, he asked, "What does that mean?"

"It means he accepts you as a son-in-law." She studied his face, her gaze lingering on his lips. "Muses mimic a mortal existence. We're born, we live a normal lifetime and then we die. But we come back in the next lifetime with all our memories intact. With that lifecycle Zeus is offering you eternity. With me."

"So I'll come back with my memories of you, find you again and fall in love with you over and over forever?"

"Pretty much."

He held her eye as he kissed the back of her hand, love shining for the entire world to see. "Sign me up."

CHAPTER 26

"How soon can we get married? And where would you like to have the wedding?" Thomas snugged Nia close to his side as they walked from the boardroom to the childcare center to retrieve Hailey.

"Um...have you ever been to a Greek wedding?" Nia asked. They were massive productions that could last days. "I'm sure Mother is already talking to Dionysus. Gaia will most certainly want us to get married here on the Mount."

Thomas drew to a halt. "Mt. Olympus?"

His look wasn't exactly skeptical, but Nia hurried to add, "But we could have a smaller ceremony in Delphi. In the Achilleion, or Helios Park, would be nice. Although Gaia will surely want us at the Athenian."

"Is there a way to get to Olympus other than through the...what did you call it?"

"The Hollow. And no, unless you are immortal there isn't. There is a portal to the Mount on the seventh floor for employees who prefer to live there." Which meant their mortal friends couldn't attend. Neither could Hailey. And Nia didn't want to get married without the little girl there. She'd come to mean so much to Nia. She was almost a daughter. A child she'd never meant to have. But she'd fallen in love with the child when she'd fallen for Thomas. They were going to be a family. And for the first time in any of her lives, she'd welcome a baby. If Thomas wanted one. "We won't have a wedding without Hailey. Gaia will just need to deal with that."

"Wouldn't most moms want to hold two weddings for their daughters?" They resumed walking, their footsteps clicking on the marble floor. "We'll be going on a honeymoon, which would kind of be the perfect cover."

"What are you talking about?"

"Hear me out," he said, lacing their fingers. His tone was pensive, matching the look on his face. "We have a wedding in Delphi, a mortal wedding. We keep it smallish, just close friends, family, that sort of thing. This one Hailey can be involved in. Then we leave on a honeymoon, but our first stop is Olympus, for the immortal ceremony. That would solve the dilemma, right?"

"That's brilliant." Heart nearly bursting with love for the man, she pulled him into a vacant office. She swung the door shut, easing it before it could whack home. Wrapping her arms around his neck, and leaning into him, she pressed him against the paneled wall. "I love you."

She rose on her tiptoes and slanted her mouth across his. Pressing his hands to the small of her back he drew her against his hips. He chased her tongue back to her mouth, devouring her with his greedy response. The hard ridge of his erection pressed heavy into her belly. Gentling his lips, his kiss evolved to tiny sips, lingering touches followed by lazy laps of his tongue. He trailed his mouth down the column of her neck to nibble on her collarbone, laving his tongue into the hollow between bone and sinew.

His touch was electric, igniting a flame hot enough to burn away the tethers holding her in place. The floating sensation she'd experienced when he'd laid his hand on her arm in the heat of battle returned.

She eased her head away, staring up into his hypnotic eyes. "How do you do that, Thomas?"

"Do what?"

Resting her cheek on his chest, his heartbeat struck an undeniable cadence in her. "Negate gravity with your touch."

"Maybe there's something of an immortal in me already."

She lifted her head as the thought struck her. "Maybe. Most mortals appear as silver light. While we were in the Hollow, you were silver, but I could see your pulse beat and it was cobalt. Partisans like Ken are typically the only ones with auras that shade." She fingered the buttons on his shirt. "Maybe there is something of the god in you."

"When Zeus offered me immortality, what exactly does that entail? Is there a ceremony or do I get a decoder ring?" Thomas ran his hands along her spine.

She snorted a laugh. "You can have a ceremony if you wish, but Zeus isn't really big on displays. He probably already has Human Resources working on the paperwork to employ you. Once it's processed, you'll be set."

He slid a finger along her jaw and tipped her chin up. "So I'll be able to leap tall buildings, etc.?" His wide grin set her insides to quivering. Goddess, he was beautiful.

"I doubt you'll notice a difference. You will be able to travel in the Hollow without me, but I wouldn't advise it. Jax, Clio's fiancé, got lost in it on his first solo attempt. You have to visualize your destination." She stepped from his arms. "I'll show you the building lobby before we pick Hailey up. Can't have you bouncing into the boardroom while there's a meeting going on."

The trip to the lobby took only a few minutes. With the mayhem and lunacy on Earth averted, they took their time venturing toward the play area where children of the gods and goddesses of Olympus entrusted their kids while they worked. Nia used her board member's all-access keycard to gain entry. They encountered Artemis as the security door clicked shut behind them.

"There you are!" The protector of the young and vulnerable looked childish herself. Her white blond hair had streaks of purple and yellow, and someone had woven violets into the ponytail streaming down her back. She fidgeted with the bright maroon pansy tucked haphazardly behind her ear. "Hailey! Sweet pea, your uncle is here."

Hailey's bright blond curls bobbed around her cheeks as she jerked her head up. She cast aside the toy horse and chariot she'd been racing around a small track with several other children. Sprinting over, she surprised Nia by leaping into her arms. Little hands patted her back, squeezing her neck.

"Ms. Nia, I was afraid, but you made everything all better." Hailey wrapped her legs around Nia's waist and leaned back, framing Nia's cheeks between her hands. "Then Ms. Gaia—she's really nice and so pretty—brought me here to play. I was worried about Uncle Thomas, but your mommy told me he was fine and I shouldn't worry.

So I didn't. I knew you were with him."

Nia planted a kiss on the girl's forehead. "I'm glad to see you are fitting in here so well. Are you ready to go home?"

"Can't I stay longer?"

Thomas shook his head. "We need to get going, munchkin. It's been a long day."

Wriggling out of Nia's arms, Hailey danced on the floor in front of them. "I want you to meet my new friend, Perses. His daddy is who they named the comet show after. The Persnickety Shower."

"Perseid," Thomas corrected with a what-the-hell look at Nia.

She nodded.

He kept a straight face as Hailey introduced him to the dark-haired little boy with the somber face. While they talked, Artemis drew her aside.

"Hailey had a lot of questions when she arrived, but she didn't seem shaken by her trip through the Hollow. Mnemosyne has already been in to discuss the best approach to blocking the child's memories. She agrees with me that erasing them is too risky."

"I'm glad she's consulted you." Thomas sat on the floor next to Hailey and Perses, elbows propped on his thighs, examining the toy chariot. Nia's heart shifted with joy in her chest, filling with love for her new family. "I plan to put Hailey into a deep enough sleep to get her back to Delphi and have Mnemosyne take care of everything before she awakens."

"A sound strategy. You can use my office to induce the slumber if you wish. I'll override the security for you."

"Thanks." Nia smiled her gratitude at Artemis. "Thomas, we need to go."

Thomas stood and formally shook Perses's hand. He and Hailey joined Nia and the four of them headed to Artemis's office.

Nia sat on the comfy couch Artemis used with kids who didn't feel themselves, or needed a small time out from playing. Pulling Hailey down next to her, Nia held her hands. She glanced at Thomas, who watched them with raised eyebrows and curious eyes.

"Honey, we have to go home now. We're going to go the same way you came with Gaia."

"Through the dark place with shiny lights?"

Nia nodded. "We call it the Hollow, because sometimes it echoes in there like it's a vast empty space. I know you weren't afraid when you came through, but before we go back, I'm going to put you to sleep."

"But I'm not tired."

"I know, sweetheart. But it's what I must do. When you wake up, you won't remember being here, or the Hollow or anything bad that happened today." Nia pressed her hand to Hailey's forehead and nudged a suggestion of sleep through her palm. "But you will remember Uncle Thomas, and me, and how much we both love you. Okay?"

Hailey's eyes drooped, then fluttered as she fought the slumber moving through her. She yawned. "Okay."

The girl leaned into Nia's shoulder and nodded off. Wrapping her arms under the small body, Nia rose from the sofa.

Thomas reached for her, but Nia waved him off. "It's better if I carry her through the Hollow since you're a novice at this manner of transportation."

He shrugged. "If you say so. What should I do?"

"Stand next to me and put your arm around my shoulder. As my mist rises, you'll feel a change in the air pressure. The best way to handle that is like you would on a plane. Keep swallowing and if it's really bad, pinch your nose, close your mouth and force an exhalation through your sinuses. I promise, it will get easier with time."

He moved beside her, his hand descending on her back and curling up over her shoulder.

"You ready, Artemis?"

Nodding, the goddess waved her hands in a circular motion over her desk. Behind her, an alert beeped, signaling she'd engaged the override. "You have fifteen seconds. Good luck with Mnemosyne."

Nia called forth a mist as she prepared to move into the Hollow with Thomas and Hailey. As the mist enveloped them, Thomas's form turned to cobalt, the color of partisans. But instead of yellow his core pulsed with a strong dose of silver. Pinpricks of white light dotted him, just like her lights. Another sign their destinies were tied together.

She navigated back to Thomas's house, materializing out of the mist in his gourmet kitchen. He took Hailey from Nia's arms and carried her upstairs. Mnemosyne arrived shortly after he'd laid her in the bed.

"Haven't I already swept this mortal's memories once?" her auntie questioned.

"Yes, but he's no longer mortal. He's one of us. You're here to see to Hailey."

Mnemosyne glanced to the bed. "Ah, yes. I spoke to Artemis about her." She glided to the bed and lowered onto it, taking Hailey's limp hand in one of hers. Closing her eyes, she pressed her other hand to Hailey's forehead and began chanting in ancient Greek.

"What's she saying?" Thomas's whispered question tickled her ear with warmth.

"She's settling a permanent block on all things supernatural Hailey witnessed today. Her memory isn't gone, just buried very, very deeply." She took his hand, weaving their fingers together. "Hailey may experience flashbacks of sorts from today, but they'll seem like déjà vu. Nothing more."

Before Thomas could reply, Mnemosyne stood and dusted her hands together. "All done."

"That was fast." Thomas moved to Hailey's side. "She's smiling."

The girl did indeed have a smile tugging on the corners of her lips. She resembled a peacefully sleeping cherub, nestled among the pink pillows adorning her bed.

Mnemosyne turned toward Nia. "Must go. Have some last minute add-ons left from the debacle at Helios. Next time, you girls should try harder before it gets so far out of hand."

As if they had any control of it. Pierus would be back. Who knew which Muse would end up on the hot seat next time? If he followed the schedule he'd set this time, they'd have a brief respite while he licked his wounds and plotted the next strategy in his hostile take-over bid.

Struggling to stop the involuntary roll of her eyes, Nia leaned in and accepted a good-bye kiss from the woman. "We'll do our best, Auntie."

The air concussed around them as she blinked out without calling the gentling mist.

Thomas swallowed hard and pulled on his ear lobe. "Will Hailey be okay?"

"She's young. They bounce back quickly." Nia rested her hand on his shoulder and urged him toward the hallway. "She's going to sleep for a few more hours."

Thomas turned on the light on the bookshelf before they exited the room. The door closed with a quiet snick, and Thomas led her toward his bedroom. After easing his door shut, he gathered Nia in his arms and possessed her mouth with a hunger that matched hers. She opened under him, and he swept his tongue in, stroking hers. Where her body molded to his, heat ignited, stirring the flame in her torso and lower.

Breaking apart after the intensely passionate kiss, they both panted.

Thomas found his voice first. "I do love you. And I will for many lifetimes with you, my love." A chuckle built in his chest, a rumble she felt in her breasts. "As odd as that sounds."

"Sounds wonderful to me." Nia tipped her face up, eager for another kiss.

After he'd indulged her, he combed his fingers through her hair. Staring deep into her eyes, he sighed, his warm breath fanning her face. "A month ago, if you'd told me Doubting Thomas would ever say magic was real, I'd have laughed. Or called you certifiable. But you've made me believe. Your love has stilled my doubts."

Deep emotion brought tears to her eyes and one leaked out to trickle down her face. "Love is magic. And my love for you transcends the ages."

"I'm looking forward to spending eternity with you," he lowered his head and murmured against her lips, his mouth but a whisper away from her.

Her answer was in her kiss. Eternity might just not be long enough.

Coming Soon
GREED
(Goddesses of Delphi Book 3)

Financial reporter, Polly Thanos, Muse of Hymns, is certain the proposed merger between Delphi's two largest firms spells doom for mankind. Eos Corporation's long-time goal — to provide scientific and philanthropic solutions to the benefit of mortals — is lost in the quest for profits. Her challenge starts with an impossible task — inspire one mortal skeptic to believe in the magic of *what if.*

Scientist Ian Sommers is researching a healthier way of life for impoverished people. When his boss orders him to pursue a chemical, rather than organic solution, Ian suspects the pursuit of the almighty dollar will lead to delivering poison to the unsuspecting population.

In protest, Ian's prepared to quit his job. But he's shocked to discover the woman he's falling for is an immortal tasked with stopping corporate avarice. As their attraction grows, so does the risk to them and to all humans. Without Ian's help and his love, Polly's faces a world not safe from the by-products of greed—death and disease.

CHAPTER 1

"You're late."

Skidding to a stop in front of her older sister, Polly Thanos dropped the insulated cooler she carried to the ground. "Hey, when the mayor of Delphi holds a press conference to talk about economic growth and you're a financial reporter, you do not duck out on his speech." Polly glanced around the covered pavilion where her family had gathered. "Besides, Zeus isn't here yet, which technically makes me not late. Back off, Calliope. This is supposed to be a fun family gathering."

"I should be working," Calliope complained, pursing her dusky-rose lips together.

"Jeez, Callie. We all should be. But we just survived another major challenge. We deserve a little break before the next time Pierus rears his fugly head. Or one of his daughters does. That's why Gaia planned this Labor Day picnic."

"But as oldest, I have the most responsibility in this entire fiasco."

308

"Dramatic much lately?" Polly aimed a mental pinch at Callie's bicep. It was probably not the smartest thing to do, but when one had the gift of being able to move things with their mind, it would be a shame to waste it on simply inspiring mortals. "You should leave the theatrics to Mel."

Callie scowled as she rubbed the spot on her arm. Taking satisfaction in knowing she'd successfully nudged her older sister, Polly was more pleased when Callie didn't retaliate.

"Besides," Polly continued. "You're only older by two years. And when you've lived six-thousand years, that's kind of like a twenty-year-old saying she's twenty-and-a-half. I'd say we're all equal in this century."

Polly and her sisters were honest-to-goddess Muses, deities focused on inspiring mortals to excellence. Their roles were to lead humankind to new discoveries, and new heights in arts and sciences. However, there was no denying it was getting harder to crack human insistence that gods didn't exist.

Being a god implied immortality. But the Muses' life spans deviated from the standard. Unlike their parents and other extended family, Muse life spans mirrored the typical cycle of man. They were born, they lived an average of sixty years, and then they died. When they were reborn in the next lifetime, they came back with a complete set of memories. About the time they turned eighteen, their supernatural powers began to resurface. Until they were at complete strength, the world experienced a lull in creativity and inventiveness. The entire Great Depression had occurred while Polly and her sisters were in a dormant cycle.

"I hate waiting to find out who's next. What if it's me?" Was that anxiety she heard in Callie's voice?

Polly laid a hand on Callie's arm and urged calming vibes through the point of contact. "We all hate waiting. But we must while Pierus regroups. It gives us a chance to lay the groundwork for the legal challenge. Zeus told me he'd set a meeting with Dice and the other justice gods. But he's having trouble getting on their schedule."

Recently, an ancient demi-god, Pierus, had re-emerged…bent on revenge. In the early days of their existence, Pierus had bragged that his nine daughters were superior to Zeus's children. That had pissed Zeus off, and as punishment the god of gods had transformed Pierus's brats into filthy magpies. The transformation had been meant to last for all eternity. But Pierus had found loopholes and every few thousand years, exploited them in a quest to restore his daughters. Which was why

Zeus and Dice were meeting.

The greedy megalomaniac was staging a hostile take-over of the family firm, Olympus Industries. The Thanos women's lives depended on winning. If one sister lost, all of them would lose...condemned to live in magpie form for all eternity.

Each Muse had to face one of Pierus's nine daughters, defeat the bitch, and save the world in the process.

"If I were reading this story I'd probably throw the book at the wall by now. It's like a really bad B movie." At least Callie smirked when she said it, proving that Polly's cool-your-jets vibes had worked.

"Unfortunately, the villains in this story are not made up, and not so easily vanquished." Polly adopted a teasing, surfer-dude tone. "But hey! We're freaking Muses. Those bitches had better watch out."

Their younger sisters, Clio and Urania, had conquered their challengers. But in both cases, defeat had loomed before they managed to overcome the odds.

For the challenge, each sister had to partner with a man who'd lost his belief in magic. It had worked for Clio and Nia. Jax and Thomas had each come through in a pinch to save the woman they'd

311

fallen in love with. Although, it had been close with Thomas. He'd almost resisted too long.

Polly dreaded the time when it was her turn to take on one of the magpies. Pierus had been underhanded and devious so far. She doubted he'd change his tune going forward. Although, Nia had injured the bastard in the process of winning, leading all of them to believe they'd have a brief respite before the monster unleashed his next dirty trick.

"I hate feeling like I'm just waiting for the other blasted shoe to drop." Callie's tone took on a distinct whine, something Polly had never heard before. Callie crossed one arm over her chest and dug her fingers into the opposite shoulder. "I am struggling for every single word I'm adding to my manuscript."

"Sounds like we need to call a whambulance." Thalia, Lia for short, or for funny as she said, scoffed as she joined them. Aiming a water pistol, she shot a stream of liquid at Callie's face.

Callie swiped her hand over her cheeks and sputtered. "Dammit, Thalia. That was unnecessary."

Lia jammed her free hand on her hip. "No work talk! No discussion of the challenge. Those topics are off limits and anyone breaking the rules is subject to a whipped cream pie to the face."

Thalia embraced Polly and whispered in her ear. "Actually it was necessary. Bitch has been raining on the parade since she got here." Her low chuckle was meant for Polly's ears only. Lia spun, crouched down, and fired the toy gun at Callie's legs. "The look on your face was hilarious."

"Ha ha," Callie deadpanned. She stomped away, awkwardly trying to brush away the excess water on her legs.

"Polly, Ian Sommers is here with Jax and Clio. He's been scanning the group like a searchlight for the past thirty minutes. I think he's looking for someone." Lia bent and retrieved the cooler Polly had dropped.

The mention of the man's name snagged Polly's attention. "Well, he can't be looking for me. I've reached out to him three times in the last few days and he has yet to return my calls."

"He's probably been pretty busy. I hear changes are coming for his company."

Precisely why Polly had been trying to contact him. Ian was a scientist for Eos Corporation, a research and development entity studying methods to aid the most destitute countries. They specialized in clean water techniques, vaccine delivery systems and the like.

The announcement, delivered by the president of Eos and the mayor of Delphi, was the reason

Polly had been running late. They'd announced a contract that would result in an additional thousand employees for the corporation. Which meant new economic growth for Delphi. The largest percentage of the new workers would be employed in the factory, but higher paying administrative positions were being added as well.

"I was just at a press conference along with Zeus." Polly laced her arm with Lia's and together they strolled after Callie to the food table Gaia had arranged. Polly's cooler contained the baklava she'd bought from the Greek deli on Hyperion Street.

Lia grinned, popping a dimple on her right cheek. That dimple was about the only way to distinguish Lia from her twin, Mel, whose dimple was on the left cheek. One lifetime they'd been reborn with the dimple on the same cheek. That had been confusing during their entire existence in that century.

Soft laughter escaped Lia's mouth. "Don't know squat about that. Ian's been talking baseball with Jax and Thomas this whole time. Zeke's been reciting statistics for every comment. A real ticket to yawns-ville if you ask me."

"I'd rather have them talking baseball than listen to another second of Callie's bitching."

"Damn straight, sister." Lia, the Muse of

comedy, had the best laugh. It started in her belly and rose like bubbles in champagne.

The tinkling sound made Polly smile. She continued grinning as Ian lifted his hand and waved her over. She drew Lia to a halt. "Can you arrange the dessert on the table for me? Do not let Gaia or Callie see that it came from Pandora's. I'll never hear the end of it."

"Why not? It isn't as if they don't know you're domestically challenged."

"Remember the last time I showed up with store-bought souvlaki? I thought Mother was going to go ape-shit on me."

"Yeah, Gaia did ding you on that." Lia laughed again. "Okay, I'll cover for you. Why don't you grab a beer and join Mr. Studly there." She tipped her chin in Ian's direction.

"Mr. Studly?"

"Sister, do not pretend you don't find him handsome."

"I'll concede that point, but studly?"

She'd be lying to herself if she continued to deny it. With his shaggy golden hair and mysterious brown eyes he truly did qualify for Polly's personal hottie hall of fame. Her guilty secret was that she'd been a fan of long-haired men since she'd met Alexander the Great in Babylonia. He'd had amazing, thick honey blond waves. Just like Ian's.

Add in Ian's lean runner's build and the long, ropey muscles in his arms, and the way his jeans rode low on his hips, and he'd be any woman's ideal date.

She left Lia at the food table and moved to one of the beverage coolers in the shade of the pavilion, conscious of Ian's gaze on her the whole time. Heat climbed her cheeks at his continued perusal when she bent to grab a soft drink from the icy water. Nodding at one of Clio's co-workers from the Delphi University Library, Polly sauntered toward where Ian and Jax sat laughing with Zeke, Clio's brawny partisan, or immortal bodyguard.

Ian stood as she approached. "Sorry I haven't gotten back to you. I knew I'd see you here and figured we could talk in person." He hugged her.

Polly was pretty certain his lips brushed her hair, which sent a small thrill up her spine. She squelched the shiver. Ian was a family friend. Hot as hell, but nonetheless, still squarely in the friend-zone. A fact she wouldn't mind changing.

"Except Lia told me no business today." Polly settled in the seat Ian had vacated.

Clio joined them, sliding onto Jax's lap. "Thank the goddess you're here. These jokers would have talked baseball or video games all afternoon." She slipped her arm around Jax's shoulders and mussed his dark hair.

"We'd have changed the subject the second you stopped arguing strategy on *Call of Duty*."

Polly sipped her drink then put it in the cup holder on the arm of the lawn chair. "But that's Clio's favorite game."

"Not anymore." Jax splayed his hand on Clio's belly and shot her a grin. "We found one she likes better."

"Not even going to ask." Polly debated sending a knock-it-off nudge to Clio, but decided against it. The woman was young and in love with her newly-minted immortal.

"Did you go to the press conference?" Ian asked, distracting her from the cuddling couple in front of her.

"Uh-huh." She nodded. "Hey, have you noticed anything weird about Scott Peltier lately?"

"Eos's president? Not really. But he's a whole lotta rungs higher on the corporate ladder than me. I don't interact much with him unless it's for a specific project. Why do you ask?"

"Can't put my finger on it. I've interviewed him before, on the desalinization project. Today, he just seemed…different." She shook off the feeling of oddness that had blanketed her since the press conference. "What do you think about the expansion plans?"

Ian furrowed his dark blond brows and scratched his chin. "It doesn't make much sense, if you ask me."

"Really? Why not?"

"Off the record?"

She nodded, eager to hear his take on the proposed merger.

"The changes will lead us in a different direction than what has been mandated by our Board of Directors. Our focus has been on helping third world countries achieve the necessities to development. It's written into our mission statement. But the new direction seems to be focused more on corporate profits than the altruistic nature prescribed by our ongoing R and D."

"Hey!" Lia interrupted as she plopped down to the grass next to Polly's chair. She swilled her orange soda. "No shop talk." The small bag of chips she held crinkled as she ripped it open.

Aerie drifted to the ground next to Lia. "She's right, you two should be talking about something else."

Like how fast you can get this man's clothes off. He's hot. Aerie projected her voice directly into Polly's head, the thought tickling her brain. Aerie always chose non-verbal communication when she played matchmaker for her sisters. Always had.

Polly spared a glance at Ian, judging Aerie's words as truth.

"We're not talking about work," Ian protested. He winked at Polly. "We're discussing the difference between altruism and corporate greed."

Lia screwed up her face, squinting at Ian. "Sounds suspiciously like work to me."

"Come on, Lia. The announcement from Eos will impact the Greek Chorus as well." Polly mentioned her sister's comedy club. "More employees for Ian's company equals more people living in town. More citizens…more business for you. More business, more money in your pocket."

"Maybe. But if the move isn't right for Delphi then I'm not greedy enough to want them to take that step. I love our little town just the size it is." Lia drew her knee up and rested her arm on it. She glanced from Polly to Ian and back. "If you have to discuss work, why don't you and Ian take out one of the paddle boats and keep all the gruesome business talk away from the rest of us whose only aim is to have fun."

"Great idea, Lia." Ian jumped up and extended his hand to Polly. "Once I get you isolated on the water, I can bore you with all the crazy baseball stats I know."

"You know that isn't really an enticement to get in a boat with you, right?" Polly laughed and accepted his hand.

Aerie pursed her lips at Ian, as if blowing him a kiss. Polly knew her sister, the Muse of Love, had nudged the man. Polly held her breath, waiting for his response.

"Would it work better if I agree to talk dirty to you?" He laughed, but Polly caught a gleam in his eye, as if he was sincere about the offer. She bit her lip and raised an eyebrow in Aerie's direction.

But, damn…the idea sent squiggles of delight straight up her torso. Good goddess, they'd been friends for a couple of years. But she'd be lying if she claimed she'd never hoped he'd be interested in her that way.

She was saved from responding when he sauntered away toward the boat dock on the other side of the picnic pavilion. He stopped about ten feet away and twisted to look over his shoulder, one brow raised.

"You better catch up," Lia prompted. "You wouldn't want to miss any of his smutty talk. He probably has a Ph.D in that as well as science."

Polly shot a half-hearted fuck-you nudge at her younger sister, which just resulted in Lia nudging back. Her poke was more like a pinch on Polly's butt, causing her to jump and then hurry after Ian. Lia's musical laughter joined with Aerie's chuckle, and the sound danced after Polly.

It would be interesting to see if Ian really did talk dirty to her, or if their conversation would remain about business.

She mumbled to herself as she caught up to him. "Damned if I understand why I'm only half hoping for the sexy talk."

ABOUT THE AUTHOR

Gemma's favorite desk accessories for many years were a circular wooden token, better known as a 'round tuit,' and a slip of paper from a fortune cookie proclaiming her a lover of words; some day she'd write a book. All it took was a transfer to the United Kingdom, the lovely English springtime, and a huge dose of homesickness to write her first novel. Once it was completed and sent off with a kiss, even the rejections addressed to 'Dear Author' were gratifying.

After returning to America, she spent a number of years as a copywriter, dedicating her skills to making insurance and the agents who sell them sound sexy. Eventually, her full-time job as a writer interfered with her desire to be a writer full-time and she left the world of financial products behind to pursue an avocation as a romance author.

To learn more about Gemma and her works visit:

Website and Blog

http://www.gemmabrocato.com

Facebook

https://www.facebook.com/gemma.brocato

Twitter:

https://twitter.com/GemmaBrocato

Goodreads

https://www.goodreads.com/author/show/7229886.Gemma_Brocato

Newsletter Sign Up

Sign up for Gemma's Newsletter for updates, exclusive content, new release information, cover reveals and more.

http://eepurl.com/54Kqj